A DEATH FORETOLD

"I tell you," the Kanik went on, his voice very low in the near-darkness, "if you do not kill me, and harm comes to the people of my village, I shall not rest until I have hunted you down like a rodent, like a slug, and slain you. *That is a vow, Alcheringian!* And we do not forget our vows. Never."

"Who are you, who talk so much?"

"My name is Garm."

"It is a sound," Asa said, "like a sickness in the gut."

"So it will be," the other snarled. *"Your gut!"*

The Memoirs of Alcheringia

Part One of **The Erthring Cycle**

Wayland Drew

A Del Rey Book

BALLANTINE BOOKS ● NEW YORK

A Del Rey Book
Published by Ballantine Books

Copyright © 1984 by Wayland Drew

Library of Congress Catalog Card Number: 83-91271

ISBN: 0-345-30887-5

Printed in Canada

First Edition: May 1984

Cover art by Darrell K. Sweet

Map by Shelly Shapiro

FOR SCOTT

"The sacred is what man decides unconsciously to repeat."
                                    JACQUES ELLUL

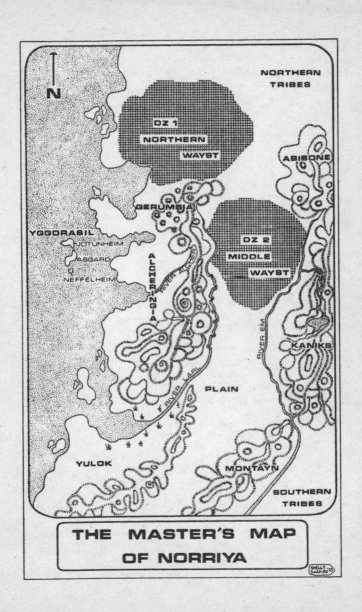

THE MASTER'S MAP
OF NORRIYA

PART ONE

THE
WAYST

ONE

WITHOUT WARNING, THE GOD SPRANG ABOVE THE FOREST and charged.

They could not help seeing him. He trailed streamers of sun. Eyes like small suns blazed from his belly and his arms. He howled like wolves.

Both knew they would die now, for they had seen and would remember. The god would drop and shred them and strew pieces of them across that hillside.

Both fell forward and covered their heads.

Rani screamed with his face buried and his whole body writhing as if such puny violence could deter the huge violence of the god. Asa was shaking too, but he had determined to die fighting. Perhaps he would take the god with him, for he knew that gods also died; he had seen their ocher corpses.

He twisted away from Rani and scrambled crablike across the clearing screaming his war cry. He was pummeled by blasts from the god's wings, deafened by the shrieks and thunder of the god's voices. He fell, rolled, and rose on one knee with his lance ready, looking up through grasses lashed by the buffeting wings and through dust spuming so high it screened and distorted the hurtling god himself.

He saw the glare of the fierce eyes, and the claws curled and extended like fists, and the green scales peeling from the body. In that maelstrom he saw a face staring through a hole in the god's body, a huge-eyed face tangled in the guts and organs of the god. And he saw too—there was no mistaking it—his grandfather's tree-mark on the god's flank.

Then the god was gone as suddenly as he had come. He passed over them and dropped behind the trees to the east. Wind cleared his dust and the acrid stench of him. His clamor faded.

Rani's arms wrapped his head and he was still screaming into the moss for his mother, thrashing as if he would shrink and disappear lizardlike into some crevasse. When Asa touched his elbow, the boy shrieked for mercy.

"Its only me, Rani! It's Asa!"

"I saw! He came right at us. All at once. We had to look!"

"Come on. Over here."

A copse of conifers stood to the right, and Asa dragged the whimpering boy under the boughs that drooped down like protective arms. Rani had stopped shrieking, but he was still making enough noise to draw Kaniks if any were passing near. Asa knew he should not have brought him; a war party was no place for a child. Rani had even wet himself. Still blubbering, he was pulling up clumps of moss to dry his legs.

"He'll come back!" Rani said.

"I don't think so. Not now."

"Then another will come and kill us. We *saw*!"

"Listen to me." Asa crouched and forced Rani's head up. The boy's face was a pale, pathetic oval in the shadows, smeared and beardless. "That wasn't the first time you've seen a god, was it? Tell the truth."

Sniveling, Rani shook his head.

"Of course not. You've seen lots of them—air gods, earth gods, sea..."

"Never like that! Never *close*!"

"Listen." Asa shook him gently. "It doesn't matter how close. The point is you've broken the law before and you haven't died."

The boy pulled a hand across his nose.

"And you won't die this time, either. Not now. If he was going to kill us he would have done it then. Or he would have come back by now." They listened. There was only the silence, and the wind moving through the trees, and the call of a fretting hawk. "See?"

The thong that held Asa's black hair off his face was black with sweat, and sweat streamed over the red hand painted on his face, its fingers pointing at his eyes. *Here is one*, the hand said, *who watches, then acts*.

"Awful! Big fangs! Enormous red claws..."

"Nonsense."

"Eyes flashing. Maybe a hundred eyes!"

"You looked, Rani, but you didn't *see*. You were trying to crawl into the earth. *See* next time! There was dust and a lot of noise, but it was just an old god with scales falling off and some of his eyes out. Now, if you want to talk about this, talk to Romoke when we get back, or to Jared. Not now. I'm going on, now. Do you want to come or not?"

Again Rani rubbed his nose and nodded. Asa cuffed him. "All right. Come on."

Movement was vital. Movement stilled fears, scattered problems. Movement, his grandfather had taught him, separated the courageous from the cowardly, the living from the dead. When in doubt, his grandfather had said, move and keep moving!

They moved.

Asa crouched briefly at the edge of the copse, checking the ridges and clearings that sloped northward toward the Wayst. He saw no gods, no Kaniks on the arid land. Still crouched, he moved out into the open and began to trot in the smooth, loping pace he could maintain all day. His moccasins were new and thick. Deerskin leggings wrapped his legs. A deerskin breechclout and jerkin covered the rest of him. Inside his jacket, his ivory crane totem swung on new rawhide against his chest. A small pack hung against his back, together with his quiver and his water pouch. His lance and his bow he carried in his left hand.

He glanced back once to make sure that Rani was following. At the top of the rise, beginning the long zigzag descent to the Kanik plain, he increased the pace. He angled southeast, away from the Wayst, although he peered back into its hazes as he ran. Ahead, through the low mists of the plain, lay the Kanik Mountains. The sun played such tricks that they seemed almost close enough to reach by nightfall. Asa knew better; Romoke's map, folded carefully in his pack, told him that they were at least a day off. Maybe two.

They ran effortlessly across the plain, pausing occasionally to leave signs for those behind. Asa ceased to think about the gods—their ominous appearances, and their rankling laws. There would be time for them later. He ceased also to worry about the child jogging behind him.

He thought only about the coming battle with the Kaniks. It would be his first combat.

TWO

—Yggdrasil Radar, this is Hugin Two Nine. Over Larl at one five. Altitude nine hundred. Estimate Yggdrasil fifty-two. Over.

—Hugin Two Nine, this is Yggdrasil Radar. Fog and visibility zero. Surface wind one one zero at ten. Normal ADF approach. Over.

—Request vectors, Yggdrasil.

—Maintain altitude, Hugin Two Nine. Course two six zero. Call entering Neffelheim hold. Expect approach clearance at five two. Over.

—Roger, Yggdrasil. Out.

THREE

It was bitterly cold on the plain that night.

This was not the chill that slid seaward from the mountains, nor the coolness that lay in the hollows of the marshes, nor the damp that the first of the autumn breezes rolled inland off the sea. This was the clear, piercing cold that would come if the heavens cracked and all heat deserted earth. Limitless cold. Cold that notifies a man that all hope, all triumph, all the comforts of belief are illusory, and that the only realities are astral indifference and fleeting moments of precarious human warmth.

North, along the edges of the Wayst, wolves howled.

Asa dared not light a fire. On such a clear night, even a small fire might be seen for miles, drawing Kanik warriors to investigate, and what chance would runners have against horses on such a plain?

They huddled close together. They chewed their dried meat. They shared the last of their water. They wrapped their clothing tight.

Gods passed occasionally under the stars, some silently, some with long whines like cords stretched to hold the night together. They watched these gods, but they did not speak of them. Asa laughed once when one came lower than usual, a quiet, bitter laugh.

Rani trembled.

"You don't have to go," Asa said.

Rani shook his head.

"You could wait here. Or go back to the Larl. There'd be no shame. Everyone knows you came as a favor, to make up the Nine. If you went back..."

"No," Rani said, still shaking. "I want to go."

"People will get hurt."

"I want to go anyway."

Asa shrugged and patted Rani on the back. Somehow—he was not yet sure how—he would make sure that Rani missed this battle when the time came. "Better sleep."

"Asa?"

"Hm?"

"Are you afraid?"

"Of course. Only a fool would not be afraid."

"That god today—"

"Don't talk about that, Rani! Not now. Wait until we get home. Go to sleep now."

Falling asleep himself, however, Asa could not get rid of the image of the god. Shrouded in wild dust, the scabrous green-brown body drifted on the fringes of his dreams. It was identical to others, crumpled and eaten with rot, that he had stumbled upon in the remote places where his hunting had taken him, the charred and grotesque corpses that told him beyond any doubt that gods died.

Others possessed this knowledge also, although no one had ever challenged Romoke, the shaman, when he declared solemnly that the gods lived forever. Men glanced at each other, but no one spoke. Nor had Asa, nor Rusl, nor Kenet challenged Jared the Wanderer, who had been like a father to all three, when he told them—watching closely—that indeed gods were immortal. "And unknowing is eternal," Jared would always add, smiling gnomically and raising a warning finger to Asa.

Asa hated gods.

Even now, sleeping fitfully, he hated the god that hung in his dreams—hated his noise, and his stench, and the humanoid face peering from his belly. He hated the god's power to strike terror through him even for an instant, and to make him grovel with his face on the ground. Most of all he hated the gods for their enigmas, for the questions which could not be answered.

Why, for example, had the god that afternoon borne the tree-sign on his flank? It was a broad tree with three thick, distinct roots, and Asa had come to know the symbol well through his childhood. It was unlike anything that he had ever seen scratched in the beach at Alcheringia, or in the packed earth of a path, or blazed on a tree, or painted by any of the families of his clan on lodges or ceremonial objects. Only his grandfather had drawn such a sign. Only his grandfather, sitting puzzled in the sun beside his lodge, brooding upon the sea and the mists of the great beach, had summoned the boy Asa and scratched that sign in the dirt or on a scrap of bark, and then stared at him intently through old and rheumy eyes, through eyes clouded by cataracts, hunting in vain for some glimmer of recognition.

Asa's grandfather had always been old. No specific infirmity had prevented him from hunting, or from gathering the vegetable food that grew within half a day's walk from the lodge, or from walking at evening on the beach, perhaps to laugh with old friends there, to watch the surf. He had suffered no physical disease. Rather, he had been surprised by a general malaise that had turned him inward to his memories, a man stricken by uncertainties.

Years earlier he had vanished for several weeks, and when

he returned his talk was so garbled that people shook their heads and turned away. He had had a vision, he said. Many visions. He claimed to have been with the gods. Many others, over the years, had made the same claim. They were ministered to by the shaman, and sometimes they recovered from their madness and returned to live among the clan; but sometimes they did not.

Asa's grandfather had never recovered. Again and again he told the same strange tale, adding details as time passed. Old friends avoided him out of both boredom and fear, and at last even Romoke turned away.

Only Asa was left to sit beside the old man in the sun on the south side of the lodge and to wait for the tales to begin. Sometimes he waited half a day, watching. Always the tree symbol came first, and while the old man spoke he would contemplate this drawing with surprise, as if a separate being— and not himself—had sketched it.

Why was the symbol on the god?

Asa slept restively.

He was awakened by a thin scream. His hand closed on his lance and his bow before he opened his eyes. Dawn. Clouds with pink bellies hung over the Kanik mountains. Rani slept. Again the scream came, drawn and mournful and dying into a cold morning, the call of a soul lost in all eternity.

A hawk. Asa looked up and saw the bird circling. He nudged Rani with his foot and stood up, slapping warmth back into his stiff limbs.

In a few minutes they had eaten and were moving again, loping toward the mountains. They left their signs as they went—the arrow with the swaying fishtail: fish out of water; Alcheringians coming from the coast; fish on the attack!

The day was clear and cool. Their pace quickened as their muscles warmed and stretched. The clouds above the mountains shredded away in the lightest of west winds, and no others moved in to take their place.

Asa had never felt more alive. He picked up the pace.

By midmorning they had crossed the River Em at a shallow ford, and for several hours after that they passed through only the arid scrub of the plain. Then, late in the afternoon, they drew close to the mountains and the stream. They had seen the water since noon, a glittering upright thread of silver against the green flank of the nearest hills. Meltwater from snows high in the mountains, it would be ice-cold, so cold that it would hurt one's teeth to drink it, and it would be as sweet as mint and wild roses, fragrant with the mosses and mushrooms along its banks. All afternoon the spray drifting from its falls had scented the air around them.

But they could also smell the Kanik camp. They could smell smoke on the wind and the pungency of horses—the corral blend of hot flesh and dust and manure. Neither of them had encountered this smell before, but they knew immediately what it was. Asa held his nose and turned down the corners of his mouth. Rani mimicked a man gagging with both hands on his throat, and they both snorted in laughter.

Then Asa signaled to the right, and they ran low that way, slipping behind whatever cover the forest provided, circling so that they could approach the stream from the south and keep it between themselves and the Kaniks. From the lazy spirals of smoke they could tell that the Kanik encampment lay at the mouth of the little river, exactly where Romoke's map said it would be. It stretched along the bank of a lake that the map showed draining north into an unnamed river that emptied eventually into the south-flowing Em.

Safe in the heavier cover of the foothills, Asa paused. They were in a spot where they could see anyone approaching without being seen. Asa took both water skins. "Stay here," he said, "and keep out of sight. If Kaniks come, be a raven. If I'm not back by the time the others get here, come up and get me. But not before, Rani." He punched the boy's shoulder gently. "Do you understand that? *Not before*. Don't come up by yourself. Promise."

Rani nodded. Asa turned away and slipped silently up the slope toward the waterfall. He felt a path under his moccasins, an old path overgrown with low brush. The main path to the Kanik encampment lay on the other side of the falls, to the north.

The forest was darkening rapidly, and he approached the glade at the foot of the waterfall through a twilit tunnel. He lingered in the cover for several minutes, watching. There was no movement except for the slender ribbon of the falls, and no sound except for the rumble of water foaming into the little pool. From the pool, the river dropped in a further series of cascades through the forest toward the Kanik camp.

Asa waited twice as long as he thought safe, searching the

glade and its forest perimeter. He was sweating heavily, and was parched from the long run, and had he been arriving home at the pools of Alcheringia he would unhesitatingly have flung himself into them, clothes and all. Now, however, he watched warily, muscles quivering with tension, ready to leap aside at the twang of a bowstring, ready to dodge back into the cover of the forest.

But there was no movement. He slipped into the open, keeping low. The empty water skins scrubbed against his leg. When he reached the pool, he tugged out the wooden plugs and plunged the skins into the frigid stream. In his left hand he held his bow with a war arrow notched and ready. He kept his gaze fixed on the path from the Kanik camp. Beside him the water roared. Around him the twilight thickened.

When the skins were full, he hesitated. He wanted to drench himself. He wanted to immerse his face and drink long and leisurely. Eying the path, the bow readied, he scooped water cautiously over his head and shoulders. Rivulets ran over his chest and belly, darkening even more the sweat stains on his loincloth. The red hand on his cheek did not run. It would not. He had mixed the paint himself from the fresh grease of an antelope, and he would not scrub it off until he returned home and could do so with Alcheringian sand.

The water felt so good that he bent impulsively and plunged his head and upper body into it. Underwater he pulled off his headband. He rubbed his scalp and beard, scrubbing away the sweat and the caked dirt of the trail, and when his head came out of the water his hair hung like a curtain in front of his face, the water coursing off it.

Through a break in this curtain he saw two Kaniks enter the glade.

FOUR

——Yggdrasil Control, this is Hugin Two Nine. Entering Neffelheim hold. Altitude nine hundred. Maintaining eight five knots. Course two six zero.

——Hugin Two Nine, this is Yggdrasil Tower. Turn right now. Steer two seven zero. Begin descent to five hundred. Over.

——Course two seven zero. Altitude five hundred.

——You are one and one quarter miles from touchdown, Hugin Two Nine. Maintain two seven zero. Descend to three hundred.

——Roger, Yggdrasil . . . Altitude three hundred.

——Two seven zero is closing you slightly from the right, Hugin Two Nine . . . You are on glide path for final approach. Descend to two hundred . . . Three quarters of a mile from touchdown . . . You are ten feet below glide path . . . Steer two six eight . . . Slow to one five . . . one zero . . . zero five . . . Steer two six five . . . Approach complete, Two Nine. You are over pad. Touchdown. Debrief in Room Two Six B. Out.

FIVE

Speed and twilight saved him.

The same instant the Kaniks saw him he rolled sideways, rose on one knee, and drew the bow taut. Trimmed merganser feathers trembled against his cheek. The point was aimed halfway between the two figures on the far side of the clearing.

One of them was a woman.

She was about seventeen. Asa's age. Dark hair framed her face and curled on her bare shoulders. A deerskin skirt hung loosely around her hips. Asa saw that she had been gathering morels in the basket that dangled in her right hand, and the elf-cap mushrooms gleamed with deathly pallor, like rotted pieces of bone, in the last of the light. When she saw Asa she made no sign of submission nor of fear, but simply took the basket in both hands, so that it covered the lower part of her body. She raised her chin.

Her companion was a step behind, in deeper shadow, and he had begun to reach back over his shoulder for an arrow that hung in the quiver there. Asa half rose and drew the bow so taut that the back edge of the point nicked his finger. His biceps and shoulder muscles trembled under the pressure, but his aim on the man did not waver. He had noted that his enemy was left-handed, and he guessed that the Kanik would move left, away from the girl, if he decided to fight.

But the man did not move. His left hand came away from the quiver and slowly, very slowly, inched out from the shoulder, palm toward Asa. His right hand moved outward also, but it still held the bow.

His movements were smooth and feline. He, too, was the

13

same age as Asa. His hair was so blond that it was almost
white, and his eyes were the slatey luminescence of the sky
before the dawn. They were a wolf's eyes. He watched Asa,
but he also watched the edge of the trail to his left, calculating.
His smile was no smile, but the fixed grimace of a threatened
animal that sees freedom only a bound away.

"Kanik," Asa said, "if you do not want to die now, leave
your bow." He saw the bow drop and heard its clatter on the
stones. "Leave your shafts." He saw the quiver shrugged off
and also dropped. "And your knife." The knife glimmered as
the Kanik slipped it from his legging and laid it gently beside
the other weapons. *I will be back for this*, the gesture said.
"Now, come forward ten paces and sit. You too," Asa said to
the girl.

They drew together as they advanced, but Asa's arrow jerked
so violently that droplets flung off his hair. They separated.
Only when his two prisoners were sitting in the grass four paces
apart did he allow the grim tension of the bowstring to relax
a little. Prisoners! What good were prisoners *before* the raid?

The young Kanik sat motionless. He held his head high,
like the woman beside him. His gray gaze fixed Asa fearlessly,
and when he spoke there was no tremor in his voice. "Alcheringian fool, what are you doing here?"

"I am breathing poisoned air," Asa said. "It is full of the
stink of Kanik horses."

The other warrior laughed abruptly, showing white teeth.
"I smell only the stench of Alcheringian fish rotting in the sun."
He sniffed and made a face. "You are too far from your water."

"And a long way from death, with only Kaniks around me."

"Fool! If I were the captor now, and you were the captive
sitting here, I would kill you without a thought. I would kill
you as a man rubs a mess off his moccasin. I would not *think*,
Alcheringian. That is the difference between us. I am a warrior
and see what must be done. *You are thinking!*"

Indeed, Asa was thinking. Very rapidly. It would be dark
in minutes, and one or the other of these two might escape in
the darkness and warn the camp below before Rani and the
rest of the party came up.

"I tell you," the Kanik went on, his voice very low in the
near-darkness, "if you do not kill me, and harm comes to the
people of my village, I shall not rest until I have hunted you
down like a rodent, like a slug, and slain you. *That is a vow,*

Alcheringian! And we do not forget our vows. Ever."

"Who are you, who talk so much?"

"My name is Garm."

"It is a sound," Asa said, "like a sickness in the gut."

"So it will be," the other hissed. *"Your gut!"*

Night fell.

Asa decided to kill them. He would shoot Garm first, through the throat; and then, as she started up in shock at her lover's dying, he would shoot the woman.

Garm saw what he had decided, and his gray wolf's eyes narrowed, settled, searched out a place beyond Asa's head, and did not waver. The girl also saw. Asa heard then—barely heard, it was so soft—the death chant of her people:

> "From darkness we are born to light:
> In light we bear joy and sorrow;
> In light we bear memories.
> Be kind to my memories, O gods,
> For they are orphans.
> Be kind to me, O gods,
> For I am an infant again,
> New-born into darkness."

As a warrior, Asa had permission to kill, but he loathed the thought of doing it. He had never killed anyone, although he had seen many die in violence. He had seen Rittor stand up from a hunters' campfire where the boasting had suddenly turned ugly, and walk away almost negligently with a knife in his belly, almost as if he were merely going to the edge of darkness to relieve himself, and then jerk convulsively, and fall, and make a keening wail like a ruined cat until he died. And he had seen Jenta pinned to the ground with a Kanik lance, begging for someone to kill her in the tone that women use to complain of little things—a skin rash or a broken needle; and he had seen Goj, her man, fall on the Kanik raider who had done that to her and so rend the man in his rage and grief that Asa—eight then—vomited when he looked at what was left. He had seen men die under the hoofs of beasts, and on their horns, and fixed in their claws, and sometimes in the grip of loathsome plagues that pocked them or turned them pustulant and yellow.

Asa had never killed a person, but he had killed animals more times than he could count. He had taken them from snare or deadfall and killed them with a merciful quick twist of the neck. He had killed with spear and arrow. He had killed gut-shot deer with a slash across the throat. He had killed seals with a blow behind the head. He had even killed weir-caught pollack with a club while the others laughed at him and tossed their catches to flop desperately on the bank until they died.

He loathed killing. Something hard formed in his stomach when he killed, something blind and stubborn that refused to believe that it was he, Asa, killing spirit, beauty, strangeness, otherness.

He took no joy in killing, as Rege did, laughing his manic laugh, eyes bright, cutting living flesh; or as Thorel did, berserk with battle. For Asa, killing was simply another job, a dirty job, and when he had to kill even the smallest thing he did that job swiftly and efficiently. But all the time in the center of him there was something that screamed in protest, screamed in sympathy with the dying.

Garm waited for the arrow. He had even loosened his tunic to expose his breast. His gray eyes were hooded and calm, fixed on Asa, and his lips curled with disdain. He asked, "Shall I come closer? I do not want you to miss."

The girl had finished her death chant. She too was waiting, and she too seemed calmer than Asa. She had seen his hesitation, and her eyes had widened slightly in surprise. They were black and luminous, those eyes, almond-shaped, and slanted slightly inward. In their fixity, they seemed almost to cross.

Asa knew that if he waited an instant longer he would not shoot.

He waited.

"What's your name?"

"Persis," she said.

"Lie on your belly, Persis."

She did not move. She said nothing.

"Down."

"No. I think I shall die better sitting." She embraced the basket of mushrooms like a child on her lap.

"You are not going to die," Asa said.

Garm laughed bitterly and called him a coward. He spat. He spoke so quickly to Persis in the Kanik dialect that Asa could not understand.

"Down!" This time she obeyed. "Now you," he said to

Garm, rummaging in his pack for thongs. "On your belly."
When Garm hesitated Asa strode forward and let him feel the
edge of the chert point, not gently, against his throat. The
Kanik obeyed slowly, cursing.

He bound Garm's wrists behind his back and tied them to
his ankles so tightly that the Kanik was arched backward, his
thighs and shoulders off the ground. "I guess," Asa said when
he had finished, "that you weren't anxious to die after all."

Only Garm's eyes replied, bright with implacable hatred.

Asa bound the woman in the same way, although not so
tightly, and when he had finished he sat and waited for the rest
of his Nine to arrive.

Rusl came first, gliding along the edge of the clearing and
halting when he came to the bound Kaniks. The others followed
close behind. Rani and Kenet arrived together, and with only
perfunctory glances at the captives, they went straight to Asa.
"You all right?"

He nodded.

"What are these?" Rusl asked, laughing. "Are these *Kaniks*?
Are all Kaniks *flat*? Have we come so far to fight *flat* men?"
He ignored the girl and dropped on one knee beside Garm,
twisting his head up to look into the man's face. He grunted
at what he saw. "Why is he alive, Asa, with these wolf's eyes?"

"Because I choose," Asa said.

Rusl stood and thrust a finger onto his friend's chest, above
the heart. "You will pay dearly if you let him live. He will not
forget this shame. Kaniks do not forget. One day he will kill
you."

Rege, Thorel, Noxor, and Sim came out of the forest then
in single file and raised their hands to Asa before flopping
down to slake their thirst at the side of the pool. Big Thorel
let the upper half of his body sink, arms spread, beneath the
surface and lay immobile a long moment in the current before
he suddenly snapped to his feet, like a snare springing, and
walked toward the captives, laughing in the darkness. Garm
strained against his bonds to see him. Thorel the Mad, his
friends called him, because he sometimes laughed like this
when there was nothing funny. Clowning at such moments
when they had all been younger, they sometimes overturned
stones or peered into trees or their own armpits to find what
was funny. Later they had stopped that foolish game, because
they had learned that when Thorel laughed like that, and walked

like that, his thick body rolling like a bear's, there was nothing funny. Nothing. Anywhere.

So now he came through the darkness and the grass already dew-wet, to where the woman Persis lay. He pushed the rest of them aside and pulled her deerhide wrap down around her legs, and with his foot under her hip he rolled her over.

"No!" Asa said.

"Later," Rusl said. "Thorel, later!"

"Brothers!" said Thorel, looking from one to the other in astonishment, spreading his hands.

"Yes," Rusl said. "But later. You have to fight first. How can you fight if you are woman-weakened?"

"Thorel," Asa said. "There will be others. There will be better. You must fight first." He was trembling.

The hulking man swung from one to the other, his head canted so low between his shoulders that he looked like one of those who had long since passed from earth, like one they had seen painted on the smoky walls of a cave they had found in childhood. "Well then," he said, "if we are to fight, let's fight!" And turning away he kicked Garm hard across the side of the head.

They squatted in a circle at the edge of the pool. Gorg, who had arrived last of all, had scouted the Kanik encampment, and he told them: "It is small. Not more than thirty lodges. Forty men, at most." He scratched an outline in the sand. "We should go in from the south, here, on the open side. There are lodges here, here, and here that we should strike first. Then these. The corral is in the center, here."

They studied the drawing. They took their time to ask questions. They planned their retreat. Then, when silence began to curl among them, Rusl said, "Now!" And they clasped hands across the circle and followed him at a dogtrot back down the path.

Asa went last, taking Persis with him. As he left the glade he looked back at Garm. The Kanik was just a vague, arched shape in the darkness, but Asa could feel the hatred in his gaze, and far down the trail he could still hear the guttural Kanik curses over the roar of the falls and the whine of the rising wind.

Rusl set a quick pace, fast enough to ensure that when their hearts raced they would believe it was from exertion and not from fear. Asa's fear, however, was like a lambent grassfire rippling through his veins to his very fingertips. Fear lengthened his strides, and when they came to that place on the plain where the Kanik fires glimmered at the end of a tunnel of darkness and Rusl paused, waiting for Asa to rebind the woman so that she could be picked up later, Asa tied the knots with trembling fingers.

"Why," she said, and there was the beginning of incredulous laughter in her throat, "you are more frightened than I am!"

Asa bound a gag across her mouth, trying as he did so not to look into her eyes.

"Rani!"

The boy came, dancing like an insect in the wind.

"Stay with this woman."

Rani stopped short, as if he had taken a blow in the stomach. "What? No!"

Asa grabbed him and shook him roughly. "No? *No?* Have you forgotten your oath?"

"No, but—"

"You promised to obey. That promise is the only reason you're here. Now, obey!"

The boy's eyes filled with tears, but his jaw stayed firm. "You shame me, Asa. You do. I came to fight, not to guard women."

"You came to do as you are told."

"Rani." Rusl had come silently back in the darkness. "We need you more here than there. Wait for us." He laid a firm hand on the boy's shoulder. "Wait for us."

And so they went silently toward the Kanik camp, leaving Rani to tear up clumps of grass in his frustration beside the bound woman.

Their objectives were horses and young women. Use of livestock was specifically forbidden to the Alcheringians by the Tabuly, their sacred laws, but years of raids and counter-raids with the Kaniks had led to compromises and exceptions. Now, if horses were captured, the raiders were tacitly permitted to ride them back as far as the River Larl, provided they freed them there and cleansed themselves thoroughly in the sacred river before reentering Alcheringia. For two years raiding parties had done just that, and a score of young warriors now remembered the manic joy of riding Kanik steeds.

As for the women, they were needed to replenish the Alcheringian breeding stock. "Marry enemies," the elders said.

SIX

IN THE DEBRIEFING ROOM, A MAN WITH A LUXURIANT RED beard leans forward in his desk chair and motions to the two crewmen to sit. "I realize," he says, "that a debriefing is unusual, but you've had an unusual flight. I understand that you had to terminate a clinician station. Is that correct?"

"Yes sir," the pilot says.

"I understand also that you had visual contact with aborrs."

"That's true, sir," the technician says. "It happened just outside—"

"The station first. Which one?"

"This one, sir." The pilot uses a large wall map. "G Sector, Yellow Zone, Number Sixteen."

"Usual reasons?"

"Yes, sir. Erratic behavior. Unit had broken cover apparently several days before our arrival, and had lost all contact with the monitor. We found it staggering half a mile away—"

"Staggering is the word," the technician says. "In human terms the thing was reeling drunk!"

"What's most disturbing is that when it saw us it advanced with sensors extended. There's no question in either of our minds what it intended. Right, Jim?"

"Right. Absolutely no question, sir."

"So you terminated it."

"Correct."

"And performed routine disassembly?"

"Yes sir. And found the usual signs of deterioration—metal fatigue, capacitor failure, silicon friability, unaccountable program lapses—"

20

"In other words, bad maintenance," says the man with the red beard.

"Well sir, it *was* seventy-five years old."

"A Mark Two?"

"Correct. And there are limits to what's possible in the field on those old things."

"Yes. I'm sorry."

"In fact, you could say, sir, that what we found was a general systems deterioration, rather than specific faults."

"Believe me," the technician says, running grimy fingers through his hair, "we tried. We did everything that could have been done."

"A *lot* of good work had gone into that thing. Some of the repairs we saw were brilliant, absolutely brilliant. You know, sir, it had a *steel chassis*! Can you believe that? No magnesium. No strontium. No ferro-alloy. *Steel*! And there was even some copper wire. And it was literally bolted together. You can imagine the condition it was in, and the problems of trying to integrate ceramic parts into that hulk, trying to tie silicon and carbon fibers to those old circuits. Whew! Somebody had done that. But there comes a time when nothing more can be done, and you've got a FUF, a full-unit fatigue. That's what we had."

"Problem is, sir, it's going to be happening more and more often. This is the third clinician that we've had to neutralize this year. I know that missions in other sectors are finding exactly the same thing."

"What would you recommend?"

"Frankly, sir, we think the whole clinician system is close to collapse. From what we've seen, nothing short of a full replacement will be adequate."

"How long?"

"Five years? Ten years? Ten years maximum."

"Thank you. Now the aborrs."

"Well sir, it was hardly anything at all, but just as we were leaving the Wayst—"

"Your altitude?"

The technician flushes. "It's true we broke regulations. We were very low."

"Go on."

"We passed over two aborrs. One was flat, but one was up and running. With a lance."

"What tribe?"

"Alcheringian, I think."

"Go on. Describe him."

"Seventeen or eighteen. War paint—a red hand on his face. Looked as if he wanted to take on the chopper."

"He saw you?"

"No question."

"And you took no action?"

"What would you want us to do, sir? Kill them?"

The man with the beard suddenly looks very tired. "No," he says quietly. "Of course not." For a moment he is silent. Then he lifts his head. "That's all, gentlemen. Thank you. You're probably off to Val now, are you?"

"Absolutely, sir! You can count on that!"

"Well, enjoy."

SEVEN

THE KANIKS HAD NO WARNING.

More than a year had passed since the last Alcheringian raid, much farther north. This camp had not even bothered to post a guard.

Rusl, Asa, and the six others crept upwind to within fifty strides of the outer lodges and paused there, on their bellies behind a little ridge.

People were cooking, and scraping hides, and drawing water from the lake, and simply idling beside the fire. From the stream the wind brought the laughter of children. Asa counted only eleven warriors among the fires and the lodges, and only three of them bore weapons.

Thorel was making a sound like a large cat.

Rusl raised his right hand and swung it forward in a chopping gesture as if to split the encampment in half.

They moved together, and were past the outer lodges before the first of them loosed the high, ululating war cry of the Alcheringians, and before the first of the women screamed.

After that, Asa was unsure of the sequence of events. He was swept up in a whirling dance. He had almost reached the corral before he met any real resistance. He saw campfires kicked into showers of sparks and figures twisting away from the light, but he had passed one fire and lodge, then another and another, until the ludicrous notion struck him that he was invisible.

At that moment a spear brushed his shoulder and stuck in the ground three strides ahead of him. He felt pain and heard the spear thrower's shout of exasperation at the same instant. He snatched up the spear as he passed it, brushed his hand over the slippery cut in his shoulder, and twisted around to see his enemy coming low and fast twenty paces behind. Then he was at the gate of the corral and heaving it open. Rusl was there pulling with him, and Thorel, laughing, and two or three others were already over the fence and reaching for flying manes, and the horses had begun a panicky circling. The gate swung back, and at the same moment the Kanik spear thrower, knife low, hurled himself at Asa. He was older and heavier, less lithe, and when Asa dodged his thrust the man's momentum carried him past and into the hardwood railings. Nimble with horror and elation, Asa brought his ax down doublehanded on the man's head, smashing through gray hair, and the Kanik died against the railings with his feet pushing.

"Here! Here!" Rusl was shouting, as if offering a fantastic gift, and when Asa looked up from what he had done, a rivulet of horses with their manes adrift was flowing toward him in the moonlight. He seized the mane of the first and flung himself across its back, struggling to mount properly. Rusl grabbed the second, and the others grasped and hurled themselves clumsily on the horses as they trotted past, all shouting amid the dust and pandemonium of arcing arrows, hurled lances, and swinging axes.

Asa gripped hard with his heels. He found that what the others had told him was correct: The Kanik horses responded to touches on the sides of the neck.

Over the head of his mount he saw women running, scattering among the lodges, and with a hunter's instinct he singled out one of them, wrapped his feet around the horse's ribs, and leaned down as they passed to seize the woman under the armpit and across the breast. He dragged her up, snarling, and flung her across the beast's shoulders, and when she twisted back catlike to sink her teeth into his thigh, he cuffed her across the back of the head. Then the horse broke into a gallop, and he felt the woman turn all her energy to holding on. One hand clutched his ankle, the other reached up and seized the tangle of the horse's mane.

The others followed close. Whooping wildly, Rusl rode a piebald with a dark splash like a mask across its eye. Thorel had somehow seized two women, losing his war ax in the process; his immense fist descended like a mallet on the neck of a hapless Kanik clinging to his leg. Ten or twelve riderless horses swept past them, fanning out into the dusty freedom and the moonlight of the plain. They had emptied the corral; horseless, the Kaniks would be unable to pursue.

Laughing, Asa gave the horse its head, and the plain unrolled beneath him.

He was still laughing when they reached the place where they had left Rani and Persis, but his laughter faded as the others rode up. There were only seven. Sim was gone, and Noxor had been hurt so badly that his eyes had already begun to search a country deep inside himself. Rege had a shattered arm; bones pushed like gleaming sticks through the skin. He kept hissing.

Real pain came to Asa, too, as his shock wore off and the sliced shoulder stiffened. The shaft of his war ax still held the hard-soft vibrations of the blow with which he had killed the Kanik elder. He was cold.

The women whimpered in a forlorn little group.

Suddenly Asa did not feel brave and daring. He felt very small and vulnerable in that cold night, with indifferent gods above. He wished he had a mother.

Ahead, the moonlight glinted on the bends of the River Em like the slitted eyes of a hunting wolf: *I will kill you*, Garm had said. His voice echoed down a tunnel of time; Asa had been here before, had lived all this before. *I will find you and kill you!*

"Come on!" he said. "Let's *move!*"

EIGHT

THE PNEUMATIC DOOR HISSES OPEN, BRIEFLY PERMITTING THE rustle of distant activities to invade the room. There is the muted breaking of surf on rocks, and a helicopter lifting into the fog, and the insect whisper of a speaker monitoring a far-off conversation. Then the door bumps shut and the room is silent once again.

For several minutes the red-bearded man remains at the desk, massaging his temples and his eyes. Then he rises and walks with a heavy limp to the map that covers one wall. He is a tall man, not fat but big. His left foot is a shapeless mass.

The map shows a stretch of coastline, perhaps three hundred miles. North of center, an archipelago of three small islands, shaped like a question mark, lies twenty miles offshore: *Yggdrasil*. Surrounding the mouth of a river in a bay to the south is an indefinite area marked *Alcheringia*. Inland, other areas bear other names; some stretch to the coast. Two coastal mountain ranges angle from northeast to southwest, and two rivers, the Em and the Larl, meander through their valleys. Between them stretches a plain forty miles across. One large area of this plain is crosshatched in gray, as are other areas on the map.

The map is backlit with a fluorescent glow. A panel of buttons at its right edge permits certain features to be highlighted. The man touches one of these. Instantly, blue dots cover the screen, and a blue sign reads CLINICIAN NETWORK. At the touch of another button, sector lines drop across the map. Peering close, he locates one of the blue dots, near the crosshatched area, and speaks its number and a code into a microphone beside the buttons. A moment later the blue light winks out.

The man studies the map a moment longer, and then speaks another order into the microphone.

"Yes sir?"

"I want an A-level technical briefing, please."

"Yes sir."

"On the Clinician Network. Tomorrow morning at seven hundred hours. My office."

"I'll try to arrange that with Neffelheim, sir. If there's any problem—"

"Tell Neffelheim top priority."

"Very good, sir."

"If I'm needed later, I'll be in Val."

"Yes sir."

He leaves the briefing room. A short, halting walk takes him to the elevator. The elevator slides him silently down to the GEM platform, and a small light hovercraft whisks him, one of four passengers, up the coast to Val. He could have traveled underground, in the sea-bed tubes that link the islands, but he prefers this ride across the sea, beside the dark coast. He prefers to sit by himself in a window seat, smelling the tart seaspray and hearing the exuberance of the young men ahead of him. He prefers to leave the craft unrecognized and to stand briefly in line waiting to touch the dermascope, knowing that when he does so, Heidrum, the computer, will flash his name and rank instantly on its monitor—SHEM/DREAM MASTER/WEST NORRIYA—and the attendant will free the gate for him to pass. Then he will follow the four ordinary Yggdrasilians (are they flyers, technicians, statisticians? He can't be sure) into the fantasies that make life bearable.

For Val is the Yggdrasilian dreaming place. Here it is that one may dream with no risk, and awaken purged and utterly refreshed.

Val delights Shem. He spends little time in the outer regions, where people sing, dance, and drink wine and liquor, for these activities are nothing more than the diversionary pleasures of the Old Ones, and part of their great failure. They had been kept only as expedients, preliminaries. Under the skilled guidance of the attendants, visitors to Val soon pass through them and beyond—as Shem now does—into the heart of Val and the delights made possible only by the infinite patience of scholars and the technicians' skill.

Here robots hum in silent halls, responding both to remote

commands and to sensed needs. From the quiet green rooms, technicians nod as he passes among walls of glass, and he acknowledges their greetings and sometimes pauses to watch what they are doing.

Beds electronically contoured to subjects' bodies move through their areas, hesitating only briefly between one zone and the next, and when the technicians have completed preliminary tests on the comatose forms carried on these beds, they are rolled beneath the scanners and analyzers. In moments the first stage of the work is done. Two things are known now: what the patient wants, and what he needs. Sometimes these are identical, sometimes different. With this knowledge, the computers select options, compose personalized scenarios.

The beds move forward.

Above the entrance to the next section of Val is an inscription: *Nec deus intersit, nisi dignus vindice nodus inciderit.* Years before, one of the scholars told Shem this means that a god should not interfere unless some difficulty arises that warrants his intervention. He said that it was the motto that the machines themselves had produced, after much consultation, in answer to someone's playful inquiry.

Calmly and efficiently the machines now work. Their computers whir and click with cybernetic exactitude, talking to each other, drawing upon layered banks of memory and knowledge. They are so efficient that it is tedious to watch them, and Shem prefers to enter one of the viewing rooms and give his attention to the various screens where monitored dreams appear. He watches them first just as they are recorded, just as they are being dreamed, and tries to discern some order in their chaos. Then he sees them slowed, played in minutes instead of milliseconds. Sometimes, anticipating the analyzers, he is correct in his diagnoses, and had he ordered a course of treatment the patient would have been precisely enclosed in a web of his own desires as comfortable as the bed on which he lies. But sometimes he is wrong; then, human and fallible, if he had been in control instead of the computers, he would subject the patient to torture unspeakably refined. For so subtle are the tiny impulses activating synapses, so delicate the chemistry, so complex the chromosomal skein of necessities on which all action depends, that no human mind can comprehend their synergism, much less design the catharsis that is the reason for Val's existence.

For that, only the machines are competent.

Shem watches with mixed feelings. He fears such relentless precision, and yet he loves to watch the repressions of troubled souls transformed to satisfactions. "'From the table of my memory,'" he murmurs to himself, "'I'll wipe away all trivial fond records . . .'"

He is about to leave, then pauses.

One of the screens before him has filled with horror. Curved walls teeter out. Windows stare like emptied sockets. Doorways gape over rubble like broken teeth. Men taut with terror creep through shadows cast by a sterile sun.

He knows what he is seeing: the dreads of a forager in a city of the Old Ones, sent to scavenge parts made safe by time, substances kept fresh in airless jars. Shem inhales deeply and holds his breath. His palms sweat, for he has gone on such excursions.

Out of another screen a ghastly insect dances gibbering toward him, all silver in the sun, and he knows that it is the dream memory of one of the technicians he has interviewed that evening. He sees the berserk thing snapped crazily apart by a hail of bullets. He sees glittering pieces spin away. He sees it collapse, writhing.

He sees other horrors on other screens, and one by one, gratefully, he sees them assuaged by gentle monitors and replaced by the healing visions of human peace and yearning. Among these, often, he sees the green hills, the crystalline waters, the shading groves, and the cool savannahs of the youth of man.

Later, he sits in the outer garden of Val with people content in every fiber, people transported far past happiness, and joy, and even ecstasy; people incapable of imagining not cooperating on the Project in any way required, and working until they die.

Much later that night, in his own rooms, Shem touches other keys on a console, and other monitors flicker into life. One shows nothing but fog over the sea. Another gives a view of distant mountains across a plain; another, a hundred yards of dark beach. For a little while he watches the waves roll out of the fog and wash across that beach. Then he sighs heavily and presses the key that darkens all screens together.

He rises, turns toward the waiting bed, and suddenly stiffens in a paroxysm of pain. "Stop...it!" he says through gritted teeth. *"Stop...it!"* He is speaking to the vise of agony that is his foot, but his gaze is fixed on the desk clock whose digits whirl time away in milliseconds, so fast that they vanish before they properly exist.

NINE

THEY FLED FROM THEIR SHADOWS. THEY WERE A LINE OF wavering spears, these shadows, pursuing them across the plain and into the new day.

The eight horses had spread out as they galloped through the dawn, the stronger ones gradually drawing ahead, the weaker ones—or those with heavier burdens—lagging. Four riderless animals kept pace for a time, but at sunrise two of them angled off to the north and vanished.

They did not pause until they reached the Em. Froth covered the muzzles and withers of the mounts, and sweat gleamed through the dust on the bodies of men and women. The horses waded immediately into the river, snorting with pleasure, and the people followed.

Asa's shoulder hurt badly. Blood from it had caked his chest and legs. He could use the arm, but it was stiff. He washed the wound carefully, and found to his surprise that he was hurt in other places, too. Kanik arrows had nicked him in the right side and across the right thigh.

All the others were stiff with similar hurts, and two were wounded much more seriously. The bone ends sticking out of Rege's arm looked ghastly in the new sun; blood covered his mouth, for he had bitten through his lips to keep from screaming against the jarring of the horse. Noxor had slumped forward and lay unconscious on the horse's neck. The captive woman riding with him had wrapped her arms about him to hold him on. When they lifted him down he screamed once, and when they bathed his face he looked at them but did not see them.

Sim was gone. Rusl said that he hoped he was dead, for he had seen him fall under three or four Kanik warriors, and if he was not dead then he would be given over to the relatives of the dead, and he would curse that day, and all the gods, and every breath that kept life in him.

Thigh-deep in water, grinning, Thorel held up fingers to count his slain Kaniks. Four. At least four. Maybe six. He roared in laughter and reached out his huge hand as if to seize the sun from the sky and hurl it back again.

The four captive women gathered in a little group, murmuring and clutching their garments to them. Thorel had already ravished one of them quickly and brutally, and the others tried to comfort her. Only Persis had protested, and Thorel had slapped her hard and told her, with a leveled finger, that she would be next. Eyes watering from the sting of the slap, she spat at him. He struck her again, and was lifting his hand for a third blow when Asa waded out into the shallows and pulled her away.

"Scum!" she shouted at Thorel. "Alcheringian dung!"

"Stop," Asa said. "It will be easier for you."

Thorel was pointing at her, laughing and nodding, saying, "Next. Next."

"He is sick sometimes," Asa said. "He likes to hurt."

She did not resist Asa, but went with him to one of the riderless horses. Hurt though she was, her gaze was dark and defiant. Her nostrils flared, and the muscles at the sides of her jaw clenched and relaxed. Angered, there was an equine quality about her; she even had a way of tossing her hair off her face, like a horse throwing its mane.

"And *you*," she said to Asa when they had mounted and Rusl led them single-file across the ford and through the scattered aspens on the west bank of the Em, "you will die too. When Garm comes to take me back, he will kill you."

"Perhaps." Asa could see through the trees the beginning of the great plain that stretched between the two rivers, the plain where the old god had appeared to him and Rani.

"Be sure of it," Persis said. "He swore."

"It is a long journey. Hurts heal. Oaths get forgotten."

She laughed mockingly. "You do not know Garm. He does what he has promised. Always. Besides," she added after a moment, "I am his woman."

"There are many women."

"You are a *fool*! You are an Alcheringian! He will come for me and you will die."

Asa made the cut-off sign for her to be silent.

They had emerged onto the plain, and the horses, refreshed, had broken into a trot. Like the others, Asa was looking warily toward the north, toward the Wayst. For the moment he was less worried about a horseless Kanik behind him than he was interested in that region ahead, to the right. He glanced at Rusl, and Rusl winked and nodded.

Furtively, Asa touched Romoke's map like a talisman. It lay folded within his shirt, a creased and sweaty piece of deerskin. Romoke had made three such maps at the last council fire before their raid. Rusl had one, Kenet had one, and Asa had the third. Drawing them, Romoke had squatted in a circle of clean sand beside the fire and used a sharp stick to trace fine vermilion lines on the parchment. His white hair had hung like a tent about his face, so no one could tell what he was thinking. Occasionally he chanted to himself. Sometimes he murmured unintelligibly, and once, when his stick traced the region close to the Wayst, he moaned and could not continue drawing for a time, and the sand beneath the downcast cowl of hair was dotted with tears.

Romoke: shaman who moved on the borders of reason, passing in and out. It was said of him that many years earlier, in his youth, he had been a leader, and had taken raids not only against the Kaniks but against the Yuloks to the south and the Abibones to the northeast. It was said that he was a splendid hunter in those days, and an even more successful fisherman and porpoise-taker, who knew his way in even the thickest fogs. But then, when he was about nineteen, he had given all that up. No one knew why. There had been no act of renunciation; he had simply drifted away from leadership, drifted into lonely sojourns in the wilderness, drifted into restlessness. Even when he returned among his people his eyes never held theirs but were settled always on the horizon, searching.

When he had finished the maps, Romoke said, "Follow these safely to the land of the Kaniks and back again. But beware." His dried pen circled over the Wayst. His voice was like a starving bird's. "Beware! Here is the place cursed by the Old Ones, and cursed by their descendants. Forever!"

"Forever!" echoed the elders of the inner circle. They squatted, smoking, their rheumy eyes flickering from the fire to the young warriors of the new Nine.

"When you go near," Romoke went on, "you must look for the boundary markers here. Here. And here. They point to a cairn on the horizon, here. If the day is cloudy and you cannot see the cairn, do not proceed. If the markers have been shifted by animals or by design, do not proceed. The line from the cairn to markers is the boundary of the Wayst. Never overstep it."

"Never!" said the old men, and their voices turned the word into the scuttling of dried leaves.

"You know the names of those who have vanished there, and those who have come back full of idiocy, and those who caught the poisons there and vomited out their lives. Say them!"

Obediently, they launched into the droning chant they had memorized from the time they could barely speak.

"Where are the Old Ones?" Rusl asked, beginning, his voice dutifully raised a singsong half-octave. "Where are the fathers of all fathers?"

"They are nowhere," the others answered. "Their dust is in the Wayst. There are no bones."

"Where is Manfird? Where is he that would know their fate?"

"Nowhere. His dust is in the Wayst. There are no bones."

"Where are the wondering Nine? Where are the Nine who would *know*?"

"Nowhere. Their dust . . ."

And so the chant proceeded through the nine names—Elihu, Strem, and Uz; Marul, Dozer, and Tram; Mefst, Xene, and Alaber—the names of the legendary Nine who in a time older than time had broken the Tabuly and the faith and gone in search of knowledge in that Wayst. None had returned.

Thorel grunted throughout. He could never memorize the list, but he swayed his big body and cast his eyes piously upward, and the elders forgave him because he was the most childlike of them all.

"It will be beautiful," Romoke said when they had finished, and for the first time he raised his head and the gray locks touched his shoulders. They could see his eyes now, and his eyes were full of a remorse so profound that even were they to enter his knowledge and plumb it to their limits, they would not come near the bottom of what he knew. His sorrow was a still, deep pool under sunlit cliffs, and when he talked it was as if he himself sank deep in it, searching for something irretrievably lost.

"Beautiful," he said again. "It will seem lusher, far richer, far more plentiful with game than any land through which you have traveled in all your life. You will see lakes and strange tall trees. It will be like a dream which you can enter at will and leave at will. With your own . . ." Romoke searched for a word, circling deep, deep in the currents of that private pool and uttering a jubilant cry when he found it, shaking his locks like a wet dog. ". . . *curiosity*, for you will scoff at the injunction that prevents you from entering, and you will wonder what is hidden there." His voice dropped to a whisper. *"Do not go!"* Then he lowered his gray head and said nothing more.

After a moment, Rusl made the lifted-palm gesture, and the chief, Kurc, nodded to him, and the speaker's staff was passed. "It is said that the Wayst may no longer be a place accursed. It is said that . . . that some have entered it and left unharmed." Rusl spoke diffidently, his gaze respectfully lowered in the presence of the elders; yet his words raised a murmur of consternation.

Kurc's eyes narrowed. "Cursed," he said. "Do not go! Do not *think* of going!"

Romoke looked up slowly, and he regarded the young leader so intently, for so long, that it seemed to the others that the two of them were enveloped in a single question. His voice was not even a whisper; perhaps he did not even speak. Only Rusl heard him. "It may be that you *must* go. It may be that you will have no choice when the time comes."

Quickly then he distributed the three maps, one to Rusl, one to Kenet, one to Asa, and he strode out of the circle of firelight. It was left for old Jared, the Wanderer whom they had known since childhood, to proclaim the special dispensations that permitted them for the duration of the raid to mount horses and to kill if necessary.

So they had gone. They had gone single-file and silently. The first night they had camped on the Alcheringian side of the Larl, glancing across their firelight into the mists and shadows gathering on the bank beyond, and listening through the night to the distant calls of steppewolves and great cats.

The next day they had entered new country. At high noon they reached the boundary markers of the Wayst, aligned as Romoke had said they would be, and they went at a dogtrot across the arid plain toward the cairn that rose like a blunt dowel on the horizon, joining earth and sky. They kept outside the border, but none could resist gazing north into the Wayst and seeing that it was indeed as alluring as Romoke had predicted—purple, and dark green, and shimmering streams of silver wind-brushed beneath strange trees. Rusl had gazed longest of all. No one had spoken.

That night they lit no fire. In mudflats they had seen hoofprints left by Kanik horses less than a day earlier. They had eaten cold pemmican from their packs, and afterward they had drawn straws to see who would scout ahead, and Asa and Rani had drawn the two long sticks from Rusl's cupped hands...

Now, with women and horses, they were going home to Alcheringia. Off to their right, the Wayst lay cool and purple and even more seductive than it had been two days earlier; but a bit farther on, perhaps because they were hungry and had begun to hunt, they began to see odd details in the landscape that they had not noticed going out. Rani was the first to comment. "Aspens," he said, pointing. "Aspen saplings. But they're *bushes*. Like mushrooms!" And indeed there was a copse of these curiously deformed trees beyond the meadow. Rani galloped over to look at them and came back shaking his head. "They no longer reach for the sun," he said, "but curve back toward the earth."

Later, Thorel saw spruce that crept along the ground as they did on the crests of sea cliffs, flattened by gales; but there was no wind at all in the sheltered canyon where Thorel saw them. And later still Asa laughed at a field where each of the swaying daisies bore two heads. Rani glanced reprovingly at him. "It is sorcery," he said. "It is the changing of the elements of things before they even come into being. You ought not to laugh." He was right, Asa thought. There was indeed nothing funny in that place of jumbled destinies, where things were both what they were determined to be and what nothing like them had ever been.

Farther on, during a halt, two of the women gathered groundnuts, and one dug the tubers of sweet potatoes. When they brought their finds to the others they were seen to be grotesque, the nuts misshapen by swollen buboes, and the tubers crusted with pox. Rusl looked at them thoughtfully, and then gestured to the women to throw them away. Afterward, they scrubbed their hands in the sand.

A little farther and the lead horses shied violently, side-stepping a gang of hares that exploded out of the gorse ahead of them. And when Thorel, whooping like a happy child, had galloped after them and bludgeoned two, they were found to have the ears of foxes and lank rats' tails with only a tuft on their ends. These anomalies did not bother the hungry Thorel, who had shucked the skins even before Rusl shouted at him to throw the things away. "They're *morphs*, Thorel. Leave them. There'll be more. Better."

For a little time after that, Asa and Rusl rode side by side. Rusl rode with his eyes shaded, saying nothing, looking deep into the Wayst. He was a big man, the largest of them all except Thorel, but he had a kindness Thorel lacked, and he was more troubled by possibilities. Perhaps it was this which made him a good leader—that he saw alternatives others overlooked. When they were very small, it was Rusl who would watch the soaring of seabirds on updrafts from the cliffs, or who would whisper at night that he had seen the passages of gods in the distance and he did not know why mortals, too, should not fly like birds. It was Rusl who once confided to Asa that he thought much of the Tabuly was foolish, and that if he were one of the gods he would have given more sensible laws or none at all. It was Rusl who had led them on all their boyhood expeditions, and on their hunting trips as they grew older. And it was Rusl, naturally, who had proposed the raid on the Kaniks.

No one doubted that Rusl, someday, would be chief.

"And so," Rusl asked, turning from the Wayst to his friend, "what is it to be a man?"

Asa smiled. "It is to want to know," he said. "Still."

"Do we go or not?"

"Of course we go. What do you mean, 'or not'?"

"Forbidden! Forbidden!" Rusl mimicked the stringy voices of the chanting elders. "Forbidden by the gods."

"All the more reason," Asa said. "But we need an excuse."

"We have it," Rusl said, pointing.

Ahead and to the right a fine buck had broken cover and headed northeast, toward the Wayst. They saw now its rack, now its flag, as it bounded among the low bushes. Instantly Rusl swung his horse and gave chase.

They had fallen behind the main party, and Asa waited only

long enough to call cheerfully that they were going after supper. Kenet waved acknowledgment.

Asa wheeled his horse and galloped after Rusl. A moment later the Wayst opened before them, cool and purple, and they crossed the boundary laughing.

Only Rani saw them go.

TEN

THE SQUEAKING OF THE CART'S TIRES IS LOUDER THAN THE purr of its electric motor. It travels swiftly, smoothly, through the bright tunnel, deep in the seabed, that connects Neffelheim, the southernmost island of the Yggdrasilian archipelago, to Asgard, the central one.

The more agreeable way of making the short trip is by hovercraft, but it is a tempestuous morning and the young man riding alone in the cart has no romantic attachment to nature. He is a rational man. He is an engineer. He prefers order and predictability. He knows precisely now where he is going, whom he will meet, and what he will say. He has thoroughly briefed himself.

He sits erect. Black hair close-cropped; premature touches of gray; chiseled face impassive. His gaze is fixed on the tunnel ahead and on the ramp where it begins to rise toward the Asgardian station. He wears the blue and yellow uniform of a captain in the Biological Unit, the elite of the Engineering Corps that controls, from Neffelheim, all the technical functions of Yggdrasil.

He is twenty-four years old and is Yggdrasilian bred and born. In fact, he can trace his lineage back to the first Yggdrasilians handpicked by the Old Ones before the Entropies.

He is pure Yggdrasilian, with no corrupting admixture of main-land stock. For this reason (among others) he is disdainful of the man whom he is going to meet, a man without a history, a man imperfectly formed.

The young engineer's name is Nidor.

Because of the weather, the Yggdrasilian station is busier than usual. Three other vehicles are already parked there, and a fourth, from the northern island of Jotunheim, arrives at the same time as his. He nods curtly to the two scholars riding in it, but moves quickly ahead of them to the elevators and takes one for himself. He prefers to be alone. He knows from ex-perience that he will be irritated by the incessant conversation of the scholars and by their foolish questioning. He prefers to be calm.

Those he passes in the corridors nod to him but do not smile or speak. He acknowledges them with the slightest movement of his eyes and head. He lets his uniform speak.

In a few minutes he has entered Shem's office and is sitting opposite the Dream Master of West Norriya. The two men do not shake hands.

"You ordered a full briefing on the status of the Clinician Network."

Shem nods. "I expected someone from the Cybernetics Unit."

"The responsibilities overlap," Nidor says, closing his eyes slowly and slowly opening them again. He is a little distracted by the whining of the wind, out of control just beyond the draped windows of Shem's office, and by the rain lashing the panes.

"Please go ahead."

Nidor summons Shem's VDT into life, selects a disc from his slim briefcase, and refers to various displays as he speaks. Charts, diagrams, and lists appear as required.

"Development of this network predates the Entropies by at least a decade, and is therefore simultaneous with the construc-tion of Yggdrasil itself.

"The basic 'clinician' unit is a radio-controlled vehicle with independent capacities—it will respond to local stimuli, for example, provided that its somatothesic sensors function prop-erly. Most units were pneumatic hexapods. Mark V and Mark VI models were equipped with CCDs that permitted refinement of edge detection.

"Originally they were conceived as multipurpose recording

units, and the early plans for them included radiac dosimeters and transmitters, of course, but also sensors for substances considered threats at that time—neutron radiation, PCBs, lead, mercury, dioxin, acidic precipitation, nerve gases. They also included a synergistic decoder and projector which was quite cunning for its time.

"The point is that they were designed initially to be passive, and it was only a late request by those who were called at that time *social scientists*"—Nidor speaks the words carefully, as if they were capsules containing a foul taste—"psychologists, anthropologists, sociologists, and so forth, that caused them to be equipped for any active role. That step seems to have coincided with the realization that the nuclear balance of terror the Old Ones had developed would, ironically, so overshadow less awesome threats that they would develop unimpeded, and the final debacle would not be a holocaust at all, but a synergistic entwining of horrors."

"The Krakon Syndrome."

"Precisely. Tactical nuclear weaponry played a relatively small part at the end, and pockets of humanity survived in ecological niches sufficiently complex and integrated to be homeostatic."

Nidor pauses and sips the water Shem has provided. "I find it distasteful to cover this ground. It is really the domain of scholars, but you did request a full briefing, and this is relevant material. Obviously I am treating it cursorily. If you require more depth, please indicate."

Shem shakes his head. He is listening closely, his chin in his fist.

"The 'clinician' mode was therefore developed as part of the Gaian Expedient—one further device for keeping surviving populations in various types of hunter-gatherer existence until the research task, the Project, could be completed. The clinicians were intended for use by those on the ground, the peregrini, when myth and taboo seemed in danger of losing their efficacy and when persuasion had been to no avail."

"I know the history," Shem says. "I need to understand the technical aspects—why they're malfunctioning."

Nidor nods. Images of the human brain, whole and in cross section, appear on the VDT.

"Terra incognita," Shem says.

"Not at all," Nidor replies. "Like anything else, it can be *measured*; consequently, it can be known. Even before the

Entropies the Old Ones knew quite a lot about protein synthesis, metabolic regulatory systems, membrane-bound oscillators, neurotransmitter interference, synaptic inhibition, and so forth."

"Layman's terms, please."

"Very well. By the Entropies, the Old Ones knew enough about the functioning of the brain to have developed several ways in which memories or impulses might be excised completely. Such procedures were obviously useful in selective control of populations. They were of two types.

"Class One procedures, the more sophisticated, involved the inhibition or neutralizing of neurotransmitters essential for memory function. For example, by inhibiting the production of acetylcholine it is possible to induce Alzheimer's disease, with irrevocable cell damage and the onslaught of premature senility. Or by blocking the production of the neurotransmitter serotonin, it is possible to prevent the neuron adaptations necessary for the retaining of information. Or by terminating production of norepinephrine, one can prevent the transformation of short-term memories into permanent memories by prohibiting implantation in the neocortex. These are only a few examples. They are all quite beautiful and simple procedures which we now perform routinely in the laboratory.

"Class Two procedures were cruder but equally effective. Surgery, of course, is crudest of all. Using surgery, it is possible to neutralize the hippocampus, thus eliminating short-term memory. Similarly, one can interfere with the processing of memories through the amygdala, or excise Broca's area, where short-term memories are stored. Or, chemically or surgically, we can amputate or alter the spines of the dendrites of the neuron, thus preventing the connecting of neurons and, consequently, the passing of information.

"We routinely use all these procedures, also, in the laboratory." Nidor looks placidly at Shem, and for a moment loses his train of thought. "Through a computer microscope neurons are quite beautiful. Use a silver Golgi stain and you can trace the whole branching structure of the dendrites. The resemblance to a tree..."

Shem nods slightly and moves his fingers. *Carry on.*

"Initially, clinicians were equipped with two methods, either of which could be selected by the operator. They were quite sophisticated; in fact, the Mark V and Mark VI models were too sophisticated for field conditions, and it is amazing that they've lasted this long.

"The first option, if the elapsed time is *very* short, is to use selective electrical shock to paralyze the dendrites in the amygdala and prevent the neuron compression that facilitates transmission. But this must be done in the twenty-to-thirty minute consolidation period before impressions are transferred to long-term memory.

"The second is to inject ribonuclease into the visual cortex.

"All clinicians were programed originally to perform either of these procedures, depending on which of their algorithms was activated.

"However, there was a third function which seems to have been programed almost as an afterthought, a fail-safe device: In emergencies, they can excise parts or all of the frontal and temporal lobes, thus either effectively preventing the subject from making plans, or producing in him the 'eternal now' of continuous retrograde amnesia."

Nidor sips his water and taps another command into the console. "Now we come to the crux of the present problem. As you know, the units are deteriorating. There have been a variety of failures—everything from solar-cell, stroboscope, and ribbon-switch fatigue to more fundamental problems such as a fusion of parallel processes, similar in its symptoms to human senility.

"However, although the machines are 'dying,' they have retained their most basic functions in their equivalent of our medulla. To complicate matters further, the technicians who have worked on them over the decades have not always had the materials or the expertise to maintain them properly, and sometimes they've even meddled with the firmware and destroyed the ROM.

"What's left seems to be what was last programed—the power simply to destroy massive regions of the brain. From all reports, when a clinician goes berserk, that's what it uses. The pattern is consistent. Pathologists' reports on aborrs recently exposed to clinicians note massive lesions of the frontal and temporal lobes."

"'The iniquity of oblivion,'" Shem says to himself, "'blindly scattereth her poppy ...'" And then, seeing Nidor's raised eyebrow, "What's your conclusion?"

Nidor smiles for the first time. "If I were not a scientist I would say that it looks like vengeance."

"And what do you advise?"

Nidor shrugs. "When something becomes unpredictable and uncontrollable," he says, his blue eyes staring innocently at Shem, "get rid of it."

ELEVEN

ASA RODE.

He imagined later that it was like going berserk in battle. He had no fear, passing the boundary. Only elation. He was conscious of no sensation except the hot wind on his face, and even that was distanced from him, as if it were an unearthly wind on someone else's face. He was conscious of no sounds except the manic snarls and whoops of some crazed animal.

He rode.

He could not have told how long he rode, or how far. Space and time lost meaning. There was only the flag of the buck, and the hunched back of Rusl in front of him, and the power of the beast beneath him.

Rusl gained steadily on his prey. Twice his racing mount actually drew alongside the deer, and twice Rusl leaned out with his lance raised to strike. But both times the buck veered away and widened the gap between them. Asa too had a chance to strike, but the buck avoided him as well.

After this third failure, the horses lost heart for the chase. The day was hot and they had been going at a full gallop. Sweat drenched their backs and necks, and wild froth blossomed on their muzzles. The men too were tired, and when the horses began to flag they did not press them. Rusl flung a wave at the buck—good-bye and good riddance!—and collapsed forward onto the neck of his mount. The horses slowed to a trot, then to a walk, then stopped; their tails whisked through clouds of flies.

The buck bounded away to the northwest.

Laughing, Rusl leaned over and prodded Asa with the butt of his lance. "You're alive!"

"Just barely." Asa's eyes were clogged with sweat and grime. He was choking, and when he spat he could taste the coppery tang of blood. The insides of his thighs were raw from chafing against the horse.

"Alive," Rusl repeated. "In the Wayst."

Asa looked around. They were alone. Asa had half expected Kenet to follow them. He realized with a flush of shame that Kenet had not done so not because he was afraid, but because he was more responsible than they. He was the third map-bearer. He would become the leader if they died.

The flies swarmed.

Asa turned his horse. "Let's go back."

"What? Go *back*? No. We've come to *know*, haven't we? Come on, let's look around."

The flies rose in clouds, whining and stinging. They were the only life. No warblers sang. No hawks swooped low over the sterile plain. No marmots rose up to look at them. No squirrels chattered in the copse of stunted trees off to their left. For miles there were only sedges and grasses bending in the wind that curled over the tops of the low hills. There was only the sound of the wind, and the buzzing of the insects, and the snorts of the stung horses.

"Rusl, let's get out of here. Let's go back!"

"No. I'm going to look. Up there. Come on."

Reluctantly Asa followed to the top of the nearby rise, and from this vantage point looked north, into the very center of the Wayst.

What he saw would haunt him forever. Far to the north (he could not tell how far in the strange, shimmering light) lay what seemed at first to be only another line of low hills. Peering closer through the haze, however, Asa saw that these hills were different, for they had been leveled and carved into symmetrical shapes—cubes and rectangles and flat-topped pillars—as if by some playful giant long ago. In their myriads, these cubes stretched as far as Asa could see, overlapping and mingling, a ghastly accretion on the face of earth. Spidery arms stretched out from this mass to vanish in the haze, and over it all the colors shifted constantly, now white, now pink, now the deep, strange purple that they had seen when they looked into the Wayst from far off.

"*What is it?*"

"The place of the Old Ones," Rusl whispered.

"So *big!*"

"'Their lodges squatted upon the ground so thick that a man could walk two days, passing among them...'" Rusl said, quoting one of the Fables of the Old Ones, "'and people lived higher than the tallest trees, and thicker than ants or hiving bees...'"

"'And at last,'" Asa finished, "'they were taken up into the clouds.'"

The wind rose. The dead city sighed.

The horses stamped and shivered, and Rusl's suddenly started to descend the slope.

"Don't go closer!" Asa shouted after him, and Rusl twisted around, gesturing with his lance for Asa to follow.

"I'm not," he called. "I'm going *there*." He pointed to a slab of what appeared to be granite protruding from behind a low ridge. But it was not granite. It was perfectly flat and squared at the edges, as unnatural an object as Asa had ever seen.

"Don't do it, Rusl! Come on back!"

But the wind scattered his words, and Rusl either did not hear or did not want to hear. By the time Asa had nudged his own horse into a cautious advance, Rusl had dismounted and was approaching the slab. He seemed to be following a path...

Events happened so quickly then that Asa would never be sure of their sequence. He saw that an oblong was etched in the top of the slab, and he was thinking that this might be a sign or message from the Old Ones when the whole coffin-shaped segment moved.

It moved very fast.

It vanished, dropping down into the body of the slab. For a moment there was only the black hole, and then out of the hole climbed a large silver insect.

It was like nothing else on earth. Long after, groping for words, Asa would say that it was like a huge spider or crab, large as a horse, the color of river rapids when low sun glints across them. On top flashed red eyes, brighter than brilliant autumn leaves. Its cry was the high-pitched whine of a wolf pup for its dam, unceasing and unwavering, driving like new knives into Asa's ears.

Most horrible was the speed with which it moved. In two mincing bounds it left the gray slab and seized Rusl.

One of its six feet toppled him and held him on his back. Another, tipped with square pads were fingers should have been, explored his entire body, feeling him as a blind man feels a face. Its sound altered, grew lower and less regular, like the noises of a child too young to speak, and the round eyes on its cylindrical top glowed with a deeper red. Rusl lay frozen as the creature's forepaws reached out with hideous tenderness and closed over his temples.

This was the last Asa could recall with certainty. A gulf opened inexorably and sucked him in. Everything he did in that gulf he knew for certain he had done before. He believed he slid off his horse and ran forward, raising his lance. He believed the spider thing turned its attention from Rusl to him. He believed he hurled his lance, and that the blow did not affect the creature in the slightest. It came on. On. Whirling. Eyes. One eye. A frenzy of flies. Hands like clamps on his body . . .

He was adrift in timelessness. The gods claimed him, wrapped him, bore him gently to their great tree and laid him underneath it. They whispered into his ear, "You will *know*. You will remember."

Even unconscious, Asa cursed them for what they had done to him, cursed them for the weakness they had given him. They held up placating hands. "But," they whispered again, "you will *remember*!"

TWELVE

IN SOME DREAMS HE RUNS THROUGH MEADOWS SWAYING UN-
der a green wind, and the land is full of life. In some dreams
he swims in a green sea, and friendly shapes swim with him,
beckoning toward a bright surface...

But in some dreams water rises in his captive room, and he
drowns. In some he cannot escape pursuing teeth. In some he
is crushed and smothered beneath myriad particles, each inef-
fably light, like snow.

He screams. He screams a frenzied, high-pitched *EEEP
EEEP EEEP* reptilian scream—

"*What! What is it?*"

"Clinician Network, sir. We have a monitor alert."

He gropes for a light in the smothering darkness.

"Sir? Sorry to disturb you, sir, but under standing orders—"

"Yes. Go ahead."

"A contact. G Sector, Number Twenty-four. Shall I put it
on your screen?"

"Yes."

A map fills the VDT, sprinkled with bright penlight dots.
"This one...here." A cursor angles down, pointing.

Shem says, "That's five kilometers inside the Wayst. It must
be a peregrinus contact. Do you mean that you disturbed me
to report a routine—"

"Negative, sir. Not routine. All peregrini have reported at
other stations. This is a random contact."

"An animal."

"No, sir. Definitely not. We have a visual transmission from
the unit."

"Run it, please."

Shapes whirl chaotically across Shem's screen. Something is being awakened, or being born. A sudden burst of sunlight, a swarming of flies, and then the rapid focusing and distinctive curvature of a wide-angle lens. An apron of concrete lies at the bottom of the screen; at the top, a row of hills along the skyline; in the center, a man on a horse and a man walking, closer, caught in midstep. The walking man carries a lance. He is dressed in skins. Sunlight glimmers on abundant hair. He is very young. He is staring out of the screen with mingled horror and wonder.

"We have no sound, sir. Apparently this unit—"

"All right. Let me watch, please."

It happens in seconds. There are vibrations and then a rhythmic rocking as the man's body slides beneath the camera. Pads reach gently from either side of the picture to grasp his temples. Fear and anger in the man's eyes give way to surprise, then to mild curiosity, to amusement, to bland trust.

"Damn! Dammit! That unit was just serviced. Why is it—"

"Unpredictable, sir. Typical aberrant behavior. This is the third this month. You have our report on the phenomenon, sir."

The man lies unconscious. Pads release his temples, his shoulders, his waist, his thighs. There is a brief, horizonless glimpse of pure sky, as if the owner of the silvery arms had flung back his head in exultant laughter.

Then the horizon reappears and settles, undulant and featureless. A horizon of desert. The second man advances, his lance poised. His horse thrashes, dances sideways, turns a wild eye until the man swings down and frees it. Then he stands alone with his lance, and the camera stalks intently toward him—

Shem suddenly moves close to the monitor. The image is unclear, dissolving into shimmering lines and dots, constantly blending and separating as the man moves, lifting his arm to hurl the lance; and yct, in that face . . . Shem draws back so he can see better, focus better. *"What's the elapsed time in this transmission?"*

"Sir, it's live."

Shem is transfixed by the face, by its opened mouth, by the high cheekbones and wide-spaced eyes, by a memory—

"Can you restrain that unit?"

"Possibly, sir. We can try transmitting—"

"Do it!"

The man hurls his lance. It arcs directly into the eye of the camera, but veers right before it strikes. The camera shudders, then settles and again moves forward.

"Sir, it's only an aborr. What difference can—"

"Do as I tell you!"

The man is not fleeing, but is crouched with his knife drawn. The spindly arms reach out for him. Shem is aware of a stream of faint and rapid signals, like the broken whine of a mosquito. The advance of the camera slows, stops.

"Responding?"

"Yes, sir."

The man has fallen forward and lies motionless. Dread is like a weight in Shem's stomach.

"Can you control that unit?"

"I think so, sir."

"If you receive the slightest aberrant impulse, I want you to terminate it. Destroy the unit. Is that clear?"

"Sir."

"All right. Order it forward double-slow. Physician mode— Is it receiving?"

"Yes, sir."

"Check vital signs." The insect commands go out. Delicate sensors move along the prostrate body.

"It's transmitting normally, sir. Pulse rate, seventy-five, blood pressure—"

"Any aggression?"

"None. It's a very obedient unit at the moment. Blood type A, RH positive— Say, here's something unusual!"

"What?"

"It claims the man's an epileptic. Let me double-check . . . Yes, that's the correct code: epileptic; classic grand mal."

"Can you get the unit back into its bunker?"

"I think so, sir."

"Good. And signal the closest GEM patrol to come in and remove those men from the area. And their horses. Get them outside the Wayst."

"Very good, sir."

THIRTEEN

Asa remembered his first seizure clearly.

He was five. He sat beside the fire listening to his grandfather tell a tale, watching the monotonous repetitions of his mother's stitching, hearing the wind moan along the hollow coast like the voice of earth itself.

Suddenly, all his surroundings had receded and begun to move over him like a giant bowl. Sounds stretched into gossamer threads. All was familiar. He knew with absolute certainty that he had been in this place and time before, and that he had laughed in just this way at the same absurdity.

Gods appeared. They too were laughing, and they raised him gently out of himself, leaving his body sitting calmly, like a waiting shell. With them he flew to a tearless place where no clawed creatures prowled on the edges of night, where there was no hurt, no death. With them he sat in the filtered sunshine under a great tree, and the gods and goddesses moved close to touch him and ask his name. When he told them they laughed and said, "But you belong with us. You belong here. It is only your shade that moves in the other place."

When he returned, his whole body shuddered, unwilling to accept him.

His mother was holding him. His grandfather watched.

After that there were many similar journeys, many similar meetings. All began the same way, with the certainty that time was not what it appeared; that he had lived this incident before, in the same manner, in the same place.

He could recall, too, the first time he had left a group of friends to make such a journey. They were seven or eight, and

48

they had been playing on the edge of a tidal meadow, a wind-swept stretch of tall grass bordering a broad beach where walrus sometimes bred, and calved, and took the sun. All of them were at that sad stage where games begin to lose their innocent wantonness, and acquire intent.

So, on this occasion they were not merely frolicking any-more, although they had been moments earlier, but they had seen suddenly two great geese drop from a passing flock and land on the beach nearby. Creeping closer through the weeds, they saw the reason why. One of them was hurt. A tired wing drooped down to lie on the beach, and its owner, the female, had turned to look at it as one regards a child that has just refused to do what it is told. The male waddled close, making guttural sounds.

Rusl had seized command. With his lance he split them into two groups and signaled what each was to do. One group was to frighten the male and hold him at a distance; Asa's group was to kill the wounded female.

Good leader even then, Rusl made sure these instructions were clear. Then they moved. What happened occurred so rapidly that it was only a blur of images in Asa's memory—Sim's club catching the squawking female squarely on the back, then on the neck, then on the head; her great wings beating convulsively; the startled retreat of the male for a few steps down the beach, his turning, his screams of rage, and his attack, wings beating and great beak flailing at them all. Most absurd and most horrible, he recalled crazy Thorel's answering scream, and his rushing to seize the bird despite the battering wings and the beak striking at his eyes, and then his biting into its throat, through its vertebrae, through the last scrap of neck skin that held the head to the body, and then his turning to them a laughing face full of blood and feathers...

Asa had felt his body dropping away from him then, drop-ping away until the last image he could recall was that of himself sitting placidly on the beach near the bodies of the two great birds, which seemed, even in the contortions of death, to be drawing ever closer together.

He had seen it before. He had seen it all before...

"It is unfortunate that you must go back," said the gods, after a time. "You will be ashamed," they said, under their great tree, "and that will be a new thing for you, the first of many new things. You must remember that it is happening only to your shade. It is moving there as these shadows move here, and it has, at last, no substance."

Indeed, the shame was new for him. He grew aware of his friends surrounding him, laughing. Their faces were all blurred in the radiance of the sun which splashed through their hair and over their necks and shoulders. He could not have been gone long; when they helped him to his feet the last of the blood was still pulsing from the gander's neck.

"You were *frightened*, Asa," Sim said.

"You couldn't kill her," said Rege. "You couldn't strike a *bird*!" That was true, also. He could never deny that he had been smitten by the beauty and the futile courage of her.

Grotesque Thorel danced amid their mockery, thrusting close his blood-spattered face, and one of the others flung himself into the sand flopping his arms, jerking and gagging first on his stomach and then on his back in a bitter parody of the death of the geese. The rest doubled over in their laughter; Sim had to lean against the rocks for support.

Asa stood and walked into the sea.

Their laughter ceased. Shellfish sliced like tiny knives through his moccasins and into his feet, and the water clamped on him so coldly that he gasped. Yet he reveled in the pain. He washed himself, and when he was clean he stood for so long in the sea with his arms across his chest that his lower body was numb when he at last turned and strode out. "You will need poles," he said to Rusl, gesturing toward the huge dead birds. "Otherwise we cannot carry them."

So they had cut the poles and slung the geese from them for the two-mile journey to Alcheringia. On the way the banter gradually revived, but no one made any further reference to his spell. There were no more jokes; not even from Thorel.

After that, when the void opening in Asa's center warned him that a spell was near, he would simply go quietly into his lodge, and on the hunt he would drop to one side of the trail, perhaps with Rusl, perhaps alone, and wait quietly for the coming of the gods who had afflicted this sickness on him.

Now, after the encounter with the silver spider, he came back slowly to his body. He lay with his eyes closed. He was aware of his feet, his fingertips, the irksome pressure of a stone in the small of his back. He was aware of a breeze, and of the gentle rustling of leaves close above him.

He remembered flies, but there were no flies now. He re-

membered the terrible sounds of the creature in the Wayst—
the buzzes and clicks and metallic creakings as it moved; but
now there were no such sounds. He remembered Rusl unconscious on the ground with the creature's padded hands moving
over him, but when finally he opened his eyes and looked into
the thick foliage of the tree under which he lay, someone said,
"At last!" And there was Rusl, sitting calmly beside him with
his legs crossed.

Asa lifted his head. "Where is it?"

"Where's what?"

"The creature. The silver thing."

Rusl laughed. "In your dreams, my friend."

Indeed, the thing was nowhere to be seen. Beyond the edge
of the forest stretched the green plain with the shadows of
clouds moving like soft hands across it, caressing the grasses.
Beyond the plain lay the Wayst, a seductive purple haze. Two
horses browsed in the shade nearby.

Asa sat up. "How did we get here?"

"Rode here," Rusl said.

"From the Wayst? How did we get out?"

"What?" Rusl grunted, a kind of laugh. "What?" He was
smiling, and his gaze was steady and bright.

"Rusl, there was a *stag*. We chased it into the Wayst, you
and I. We saw the lodges of the Old Ones far in the distance.
There was a thing like a spider. It held you down."

Rusl's eyes widened incredulously and he shook his head.
He shrugged. "You had a spell, I guess. You told me, and we
came here, into the shade. The others went ahead. It's been
half a day." He tossed aside the stick with which he had been
doodling in the sand and brushed his hands together. "Ready
to go now?"

They both stood. Asa seized his friend by the arm. "Rusl!
Rusl, you *have* to remember! Don't joke! It was that tall, and
it came out of—"

But Rusl twisted free, and neither his voice nor his expression changed. "We should hurry. The others are a long way
ahead."

"Rusl. Tell the truth. It's no good unless you tell the truth!
Nothing is any good!"

"Truth? Truth?" Rusl's eyes were blank. Then he grinned
slyly and wagged a finger. "*I* know what the truth is. You've
told me. When you have a spell you see gods. You fly with

them. You swim beneath the sea with them. You see such things as never were on earth."

Asa's mind tipped. Was it possible that he had indeed imagined it all? He was certain of one thing only, and the knowledge filled him with smoldering rage: Gods in the winds, and waters, and in the blossoms of the clouds conspired for some incomprehensible reason to trick him. Their laughter sang at him like the laughter of adults years before when he had done foolish things; he listened to it like a child, mystified, helpless, utterly alone.

Rusl was on his horse and the animal was prancing sideways, shaking its head, anxious to be off.

Asa moved unsteadily to his own mount, and as he did so he saw that he was stepping over Rusl's idle drawing in the sand. It was partly scuffed away, but enough remained for Asa to see clearly what it had been: the silver creature, charging, scrawny arms reaching and a single wild eye protruding from the center of what, in an animal, would have been its face . . .

Through the rest of that warm afternoon they traveled at a brisk trot. Normally they would have talked; now, they did not. Asa rode wrapped in his thoughts, trying to recall every detail of the morning's events. Rusl rode serenely, gazing straight ahead, his face lit with a childlike smile.

In the evening they came to the ford on the Larl.

The Larl rose far to the north, in that nebulous region where the Alcheringian Mountains mingled with the tufted hills of the Gerumbians. Its sources were many—small unnamed rivers and streams that meandered down from late-melting snows, and springs that bubbled out of rocky hillsides. Flowing southward, the Larl skirted the western edge of the Wayst and marked the boundary between the mountains and the Kanik plain. Legend said that in the days of the Old Ones the river had been befouled and poisonous, noxious, emptied of all life, and that those who bathed in it sickened and died. But now the river was fresh again. The fish had returned, and among the marshes of the upper reaches of its meanderings, choruses of bullfrogs sang in the still nights, and beaver swam homeward in the last of the afterglow, their snouts spreading silent vees across the calm surface. Moose browsed in the marshes below the headwaters, water lilies and roots dangling from their chops, their antlers streaming, and downstream, deer stepped through open meadows and came to the river to drink. Whatever it may once have been, the Larl along its length was now a source of burgeoning life, all the way to the south of the Alcheringian Mountains where, meandering through salt marshes, it came at last to the sea in the land of the Yuloks.

Perhaps because the Larl had miraculously restored itself, the river was held in special respect by the Alcheringians. Sometimes the desperately ill were carried across the mountains to be bathed in its waters, and sometimes the very old asked that they be taken to die beside it. To the north of the ford, the sandstone cliffs were pocked with their graves. It was said that the original Tabuly had been buried near the banks of the Larl, although no one knew for certain.

It was the river of beginnings as well as endings, for here the Nines of boys on the verge of manhood held their last ceremonies before venturing on westward raids across the plain, and here they bathed on their return. Here too, at a place two miles downstream where a broad waterfall cascaded into a hundred pools, Alcheringian girls were brought and kept in seclusion by watchful matrons until the first evidence of puberty had passed.

It was a sacred river, the Larl. It enclosed Alcheringia both physically and imaginatively, and kept it safe.

At the ford, it was a long stone's-throw across, boiling across a shallow bed of stones.

The others had arrived well ahead of them and had built a large driftwood fire on the gravel bank. Rusl and Asa had seen this fire, like a beacon, for the last three miles of their journey, and their pace had quickened, for they were tired, and stiff, and yearning for the caress of the river's currents.

But there was death in the camp. Asa sensed death even before the horses had slowed to a walk, even before he saw the covered body beside the fire with the two warriors keeping a vigil over it.

Kenet came forward to meet them.

"Noxor?"

Kenet nodded. "He vomited blood. He could not stop vomiting blood."

Asa glanced at his companion, but the serene smile never left Rusl's face. "Too bad," Rusl said, shrugging. "Poor Noxor."

Asa dismounted and walked stiffly across the cobblestones to his friend's body. Gently he drew back the covering from the face. In death, Noxor looked mildly surprised and puzzled, as if this new experience was not quite what he had expected. Congealed blood lay across his cheek and jaw. Asa touched his hair; he remembered many things, for they had been children together, and had survived the same winters. "Go carefully," he whispered.

Behind him Rusl was asking, "Is there any food here? Anything to eat?"

"We'll bury him at the place of the dead," Kenet said, laying a hand on Asa's shoulder. "Later. When you've rested."

"Yes."

"Where's the food?" Rusl was grinning genially, as if he had arrived late at a party. Someone handed him meat, and he immediately sat down and began to chew with gusto, smacking his lips and belching. Thorel sat beside him, and soon they were both chuckling hoarsely, gesturing toward the women, who were gathered together in a small group at the edge of the firelight. Asa saw Persis among them. She was holding her side. Ugly bruises shone on her throat, and her face was swollen. One eye was almost shut. She was glaring at Thorel with a steady and implacable hatred.

"What happened out there?" Kenet whispered to Asa.

"I—I'm not sure."

"You went into the Wayst, didn't you? How far?"

"I don't know, Kenet. Honestly. I can't talk about it now. Maybe later. Maybe when we get home."

In the darkness they buried Noxor. They carried him on a makeshift litter along the bank to the sandstone bluffs where countless other cave-graves had been hollowed out over the years. They buried him on his side in the womb of earth, curled as he had been before he entered life. With him they buried his weapons and sufficient food for the long journey westward to the Islands of the Gods. They sprinkled red ocher on his corpse and his belongings.

Kenet spoke for them all, for Rusl was unable to do so; Rusl had fallen asleep like a contented child beside the fire, oblivious to all around him.

Later that night, those who had not already done so freed their horses, sending them with a swat across the rump galloping back eastward into the night on the Kanik plain. They burned all clothes and equipment from which the scent of horse could not be washed away. They bathed in the deep pools above the ford, methodically scrubbing with fine sand until all horse scent and all traces of war paint had been washed away. Rani and Asa woke Rusl and took him to the river, and he sat on the beach with his legs in the water, whimpering like a child while they cleaned him. At sunrise, men newborn, they would cross the ford of the sacred river and follow the paths homeward through the low mountains to Alcheringia.

Still later that night, a few of the Nine turned their attention to the Kanik women. Asa was not among them. In fact, he did not even know what was happening. By the time Rani crept back through the night to sit beside him, shocked and sickened by what he had seen and frightened by the morphs of his imagination, Asa was sleeping deeply.

FOURTEEN

THE HELICOPTER WITH THE TREE INSIGNIA EMBLAZONED ON its fuselage descends as it approaches the Alcheringian Mountains, banks steeply to port into a narrow pass, and intercepts a radio beam that leads it to a remote clearing.

It hovers, gently settles. An old man hobbles out of the night and is assisted up into the dimly lit cabin. Sliding doors click shut. Turbines whine. The craft lifts, sideslips across the cliffs and the gently frying surf beneath them, and skims seaward, gaining altitude. The pilot murmurs into the night ahead, and out of that night a confident voice responds, giving numbers and staccato guidance. Radar sweeps across an offshore landmass—three islands shaped like a question mark.

Soon the islands themselves are visible in the clear night. On the center one, a light blinks. The aircraft swoops down toward this beacon and settles gently on a concrete pad. Again the cabin door slides back. The old man steps down with some difficulty, crouches, and hobbles through the buffeting of the still-whirling rotors. Another figure, erect and red-bearded, detaches itself from the shadows where dim figures move in green light and comes forward with outstretched arms. "Jared. Jared. It was good of you to come."

"You know how much I like this wretched place."

"I know. We'll have you back tomorrow. I promise."

The men embrace. Shem keeps his arm around the stooped shoulders of his friend. "It's a warm night," he says. "Let's not go inside quite yet. We can walk along the bluffs. You'll feel right at home."

They leave the concrete, walk a short distance on gravel, and soon reach a meadow as wild as the one Jared has just left on the mainland. To their right is a thick, sea-blown tangle of vegetation stretching as far as they can see. To their left is the shimmering phosphorescence of a calm sea. "At least," the old man says, "you didn't send one of those submarines for me."

Shem chuckles. "So. Do you hate the sea so much?"

"Ha! I love the sea. You know I do. How many times in the old days when we were both peregrini did I plead to be sent back south, to the Yulok, my own people? And how many times, my dream master, have I pleaded with *you* in the last few years to send me? I love the sea. I want to be buried overlooking it. But I want to stay on *top* of it, where men belong."

They walk a little way in silence, looking into the still night. All is silver and purple. Patches of black breeze scamper on the surface.

"We never do that," Shem says. "Peregrini never go home. The Old Ones would have called it the curse of Cain. Anyway, you haven't asked for a transfer for years—four or five at least."

Jared laughs abruptly. "You're right, come to think of it. I guess I've given up."

"And grown fond of Alcheringians?"

The old man glances at his friend. Under the white eyebrows the black eyes are still penetrating, like agate points. "Perhaps. I admit it. Is that a sin?"

"Of course not. You've been with them many years. They trust you. And they are an attractive people, a comely people."

"Then why do you ask me about them?"

Shem shifts his weight to his sound right foot and slowly lowers himself onto a stone bench placed for the best view of the northern sea. His brow is furrowed, perhaps with pain. "Something is wrong, Jared."

The old man cackles with incredulous laughter, sinks to the bench beside his friend, and leans forward with his elbows on his knees. "Something is wrong," he says, opening his hands to the sea. "The man says something is wrong."

"Are you losing faith, old friend?"

"In the Project? Of course not. It was always an act of faith. After all, there were no alternatives *except* to have faith, were there?"

"In that case"—there is a cool edge in Shem's voice— "spare me your sarcasm, plase. I know the problems better than you. I deal with them every day. Equipment breakdowns. Inadequate supplies. Human errors. Cantankerous and quarrelsome scholars. Arrogant technicians . . ."

"I am sorry. That was rude of me. But you don't want to talk about the Project, only that small part of it conducted, according to his lights, by this aged peregrinus. Yours truly. Correct?"

Shem nods.

"Go ahead. I'm listening. What have I done wrong?"

"I don't know. Perhaps you can tell me. I know only that Alcheringia is breaking."

Jared sighs. "It was always a difficult assignment. They're a proud people. They think. They prefer freedoms."

"Of course. I'm not criticizing you. No one is. In fact, I've said nothing to anyone else, and the matter has never been discussed in the Arborea, so far as I know. But tell me the truth, Jared. You feel it too, don't you? Alcheringia is in great danger."

"Yes," the old man says softly, looking at the sea. He strikes his fist into his palm. "Yes. In spite of everything. It's true. Alcheringia is less stable than it was when I went there." He sighs heavily. "Probably it's time I . . . Probably you need a younger—"

"No. We need you. If you can't hold it together, no one can."

"I'd rather not, you know."

"I know."

"But you're going to hold me to my oath."

"Yes. I am."

The old man stands slowly and retrieves his stick from the corner of the bench. "Cold," he says to the sky above Shem's head. "Very cold. Let's go inside. Since I'm here I may as well sit in your overheated Yggdrasilian rooms and eat your wretched overcooked Yggdrasilian food. Besides, I think you have things to show me and questions to ask. Correct?"

"Correct."

They move among the shadows of the room with green lights, back through the crisp whispers of controllers and the muted whining of helicopters arriving and departing. They move down carpeted corridors, sometimes exchanging greetings with others that they pass. They are lowered gently to deeper regions by an elevator that makes no sound, and they end at last in Shem's large office.

"Horses," Jared says. "We made a mistake about the horses, I think."

"Perhaps." Shem is pressing buttons, causing a VDT to glide out on silent arms, ordering programs to be delivered.

"We should have kept their Tabuly intact. Start compromising and making special dispensations and look where you end up."

Shem shrugs. "The change was happening anyway, and for good reason. Either we had to legitimize it or end the raids and risk inbreeding. That was a decision of the Arborea and fully discussed. You have a raiding party out at this moment, don't you?"

"Yes."

"A Nine?"

"Yes."

"And you prepared them and know them all?"

"Yes."

"Tell me, then. Who is this?"

Dust clouds billow up on the screen, and in their midst Jared sees a man face-down and another scrambling sideways, then standing upright with lance raised and eyes staring directly into the camera. A painted hand crosses half his face, fingers stretching toward broad-spaced eyes.

"Where . . ."

"To the south of DZ Two. The day before yesterday. Two mechanics in a chopper had a radar failure and returned early. He saw them."

"I don't recognize him," Jared lies, trembling. "He's too far away."

"Alcheringian?"

"By the markings, yes."

"And this?"

A young warrior moves forward with a spear, toward what seems to be the apron of a platform, or a stage. There is no mistaking him.

"His name is Rusl. He is the leader of that Nine."

"And . . . this?"

A young man dismounts and jumps away from his lunging horse. He braces himself, hurls his spear, and then in slow motion falls forward to his knees, to his stomach.

"Jared, who *is* that?"

"His name is Asa."

"The markings are the same as on the other, the man photographed from the helicopter."

"So it seems."

Shem switches off the VDT and they sit in silence. Then he says, "Such bold young men worry me."

"Leaders."

"Exactly. Leaders who break rules worry me. They become agitators. Malcontents."

"Shem, they were on a *raid*. There has to be latitude—"

"Shall I tell you where this happened, this second occurrence?"

"Where?"

"Five miles inside the Designated Zone. *Five miles!*"

"Fi!— What happened?"

Shem shrugs. "They were curious, I suppose. In they went." He runs back the tape and holds Rusl in freeze-frame. "They activated an obsolete clinician unit. The technicians' log shows that it had been checked the day before, but frankly I doubt it. I doubt that anyone has looked at the thing for years. Technicians don't like to go that deep into the Waysts, for obvious reasons. As far as I can see, the thing malfunctioned. It apparently thought it detected some deviation in the boy—"

Jared's hand covers his eyes. "Rusl," he says.

"—and took action. We don't know exactly what it did. You'll know, of course, when you return."

"And Asa? The same thing?"

Shem switches off the screen. "No. We stopped the unit before it reached him."

"So. Then he'll remember."

"Perhaps. He was unconscious, or in a trance. The unit diagnosed epilepsy, but it can't be trusted, of course. I sent a GEM in to take them out."

"He has spells, true, but if he saw the unit he'll remember it." Jared leans forward and looks hard at the younger man. "I hate those clinicians. You know that. They're part of what's wrong with us. If I had my way I'd destroy the lot of them. I've never used one and never shall. But why did you stop that one?"

Shem looks at his palm. He does not answer.

"Why?" Jared persists. "Why would you do that, if you're worried about Alcheringia? He has courage, Asa. And intelligence. He will ask questions. He will test laws."

"I could see that. He charged the unit."

"Then why?"

Shem stands up suddenly. He laughs curtly, mirthlessly, like a man who has lost a gamble. "Odd that you of all people should ask that."

"Oh. The dilemma."

"Of course."

"The famous Yggdrasilian dilemma. I wasn't thinking of it. You must control such people and yet—"

"And yet we need them." Shem points a finger. "Intact. Otherwise we shall be left with only our own definitions of humanity; and inevitably, in defining, we shall simplify."

Jared is on the verge of asking another question, but refrains from doing so. Discreet waiters bring food and ready a table. At the console, Shem has caused the strains of a flute concerto to fill the room. Serene, amused, delicate, melancholy, but never bitter, the instrument soars within the prison of the form, deepening its themes with embellishments that leave order intact but profoundly enriched. Ever playful, it insists on joy in the face of the incomprehensible, in the infinity of the universe, in the ineluctable mystery of the simplest human soul.

Both men listen. Their dinner cools. Jared massages an arthritic wrist. "Your atavism," he says, smiling. "Tell me, do you think it was worth it, after all? Those seventeen hundred years? To have produced one Mozart?"

Shem sits with difficulty, lifting his lumpish foot. He sighs. "Unless it was worth it, you and I are wasting our time, aren't we?"

FIFTEEN

AT DAWN THEY CROSSED THE FORD OF THE LARL. THE WOMEN followed sullenly. The hills of Alcheringia lay ahead with their tips light green in the new sun, their flanks deep purple. The trail led upward into the mists of their valleys.

They traveled silently all morning, and at noon crossed the narrow pass from which the path led down westward through scattered forest and broad meadows to the sea. The encampment of Alcheringia nestled two miles away, around the mouth of the River Alcher.

Far beyond, on such clear days as this, travelers could sometimes see the Islands of the Gods, and when he looked at them Rusl used to say laughing that he would someday go out to them. He would take his canoe and go, and when he returned he would show that the old myths were foolish, empty superstitions. The islands floated now like three proud chieftains brooding in council, and although he looked at them Rusl said nothing, and his expression did not change from the vacuous smile he had worn since the incident in the Wayst.

Kenet led now.

In single file they wound down the last of the trail, glimpsing the sea, and the beach, and the camp at the river's mouth. Asa rejoiced in the sea, this endless sheet of silver in the sun. He could not have lived apart from it as the Kaniks did, or the Abibones, or the benighted Gerumbians. The mere sight of it now was a salve like sanity itself on all the dreads and mysteries raised by this troubling raid. He inhaled life with the scent of it.

The path broadened as it descended, and for the last mile or so it ran beside the Alcher, the river that drained the network of springs and freshets from the plateaus and slopes above. Fed by these tributaries, the river rushed seaward, springing off ledges in exuberant waterfalls until at last it made its final descent, tumbling two hundred feet into a foaming pool behind the beach.

Talk and laughter began as they drew close to home. Asa was at the rear of the party, just behind the four women captives, when Rani dropped back to join him.

"Noxor and Sim . . ." Rani began.

"Are dead. Too newly dead to speak of, Rani."

Rani glanced at him and nodded. "But otherwise, except for their deaths, it was a good raid." He had intended to make a manly statement, and he nodded vigorously as he spoke; but he was so small, so vulnerable and uncomprehending, and his boy's voice tipped the comment so ludicrously into a question, that Asa almost laughed.

"*Good?*"

"Of course. We have the captives—the women—and . . . and we are men." Rani flushed.

Asa looked at him hard, and then ahead at the pathetic and bedraggled women. "There are many ways to be a man," he said.

"I *wanted* to go!" Rani's flush of shame turned to anger. "I wanted to go with you. Into the camp. You wouldn't let me. You made me stay with the woman!"

"We needed you there."

"You didn't! You could have tied her! You could have hobbled her!"

The boy's vehemence surprised Asa. "You won't forget that, will you?"

"No. Never!" Rani's weasel face was white, his lips pressed tight together. Yet, underneath the anger there was something else: a worry. He hopped along a few paces in silence, favoring a hurt foot. "Asa, you won't . . . you won't *tell*, will you?"

"Tell what?"

"You know. About the god. About how I . . . I screamed and couldn't look at him."

"You didn't scream. You shouted to frighten him away.

And you were right not to look. You know what the Tabuly says."

Rani's glance was filled with gratitude. "I hate it when they laugh at me."

"That will stop," Asa said. "You will grow, and the laughter will cease."

They had crossed the last plateau. On their right, the Alcher sprang toward the sea and tumbled through the arms of rainbows to the pool below. There were women and children playing in the pool, but no one challenged them until they were very close. *There should be a guard*, Asa thought.

The camp embraced both banks of the river. On the north bank, the Cranes had raised thirty lodges that summer, and on the south bank the Ravens had twenty-four. Although separated this way by tradition, the clans intermingled freely in all the activities of Alcheringia.

They were simple and elegant structures, these lodges, conical swirls of skin or bark on a framework of thin poles. Smoke bloomed from the tops of some. They would last for only one season, and then those that their owners had not dismantled would be scattered back to their elements by the winds and sleets of winter. Never was there any talk of building more substantial structures, for that was specifically forbidden by the Tabuly. All lodges stood with their backs to the winds and the sea, the arms of their smoke flaps raised toward the east. In the space among them, women called to each other and laughed as they worked. Children scampered about. The breezes carried the mingled scents of smoke and drying fish into the hills.

Fish had brought them to this place for generations. Each spring the Alcheringians gathered here for the easy summer, and each spring salmon were split and smoked on trestles built over smoldering fires. Sometimes porpoise flesh and other meat was smoked as well. Over the summer, food was packed into bundles for carrying back into the interior when the days began to cool and the birds gathered. Then families spread out inland, returning to ancestral winter hunting grounds. The next spring the two clans would gather again, at the mouth of the Alcher.

The river enfolded both halves of the encampment in its bends before emptying itself into the ocean across and through a great beach. Its mouth was protected from the full ferocity of storms by a sandbar built by offshore currents. On the outside of this bar, driftwood lay as deep as a tall man, enough for the fires of many generations. On the inside was a gentle slope, rimmed by strands of froth left by falling tides, where the sea canoes could be hauled up onto high, dry sand.

Children playing saw the returning raiders first, and raised a shout which alerted the whole encampment. Children came running toward them.

Rani touched Asa's arm. His eyes were bright with conspiratorial cunning. "I won't tell, either," he said.

"Tell what?"

"*About the Wayst*," Rani whispered. "About what happened to Rusl!"

"How did—"

But Rani suddenly jogged ahead like a spindly grasshopper, and the next minute they were surrounded by laughing children, and by older youths clapping them on the back, congratulating them.

Squealing with delight, the children scampered ahead down the trail, and by the time they had wound down past the falls and crossed the ancient tidal flats to the encampment, the entire village was coming to greet them.

They passed in single file through the throng to the watering place on the river. Amid all the jubilation, Asa saw Kurc and the other elders pointing first to Kenet and then to Rusl, noting the extraordinary change in positions, for it was the first time in memory, unless the original leader had been slain, that a party had returned with a new leader.

For the moment, however, this fact was lost in the general flood of excitement. Children and young men frolicked into the water, and the raiders were touched and kissed one by one as they arrived. Rege had fallen into unconsciousness from the pain of his smashed arm, and he was gently lifted into a litter and carried away for Romoke to attend to him. His mother wept. Sim's mother came to Asa when she could not find her son, and gripped him hard by the arm until she saw in his eyes that her son was dead. Then she sank slowly to her knees, and Asa sank to one knee also and held her until she began the high-pitched keening of the bereft, and until other women came and took her. Sometime that evening, or perhaps in the night, she would cut off the first joint of the second finger of her left hand. The end of her index finger she had cut off years earlier, when Sim was an infant, when her husband had taken his canoe to sea for the porpoise and never returned.

The Kanik women were tired, and hot, and filthy dirty, and they too waded directly into the river and sank down into the cold water, drinking. The Alcheringian women lined the banks with their hands on their hips, jeering as custom demanded, and asking what strange frogs these were. A few tossed token clods of earth. There was more ritual than malice in these performances, for the Alcheringian women were known for their kindness and their sympathy.

Gradually, as they revived, the Kaniks tossed insults back, for they knew that if they did not show spirit in the face of adversity they would be regarded as lifeless and worthless. So one by one they stood, and flung their wet hair back, and stared defiantly at their tormentors. Asa watched Persis, but she did not look at him.

Then young men pushed forward through the women to pry open the Kaniks' mouths and inspect their teeth, and feel the strength of their thighs and buttocks. One of these, a stout fellow named Rigurd, two or three years older than Asa, seized Persis' garment and ripped it open to the waist, exposing her breasts. Without thinking, Asa strode through the shallows and the confusion and laid a warning hand on Rigurd's wrist.

It was a foolish gesture. He had acted impulsively. Out of pity? He could not have said. He caught Persis' glance of surprise and gratitude as she covered herself again.

Rigurd pointed at Asa as if he were a small child who had just embarrassed himself, and laughed raucously. A few of the Alcheringian women shrieked in derision. For a month the Kaniks would be common property, and any display of favoritism toward a captive was seen as a lamentable weakness.

Asa shrugged and turned away. The laughter followed him. He walked up the left bank of the river without looking back at Persis or any of the other women. He wanted only to reach his lodge, and to eat, and then to roll himself into his sleeping robe for a long, long sleep.

He was exhausted. His mind ached. Parts of him were numb. Too much had happened, too much that he did not understand. Some of it, later, might make sense, but for now he cared about nothing but his hunger and his deep need for sleep.

Asa brushed past Kenet, who touched his arm and asked some question. He was aware that Thorel called something to him, his voice booming out of the throng, but Asa did not hear what he said and he did not respond. He kept walking toward his lodge.

The village opened before him.

Through his fatigue he saw Persis' eyes. He blinked and shook his head.

He still saw Persis' eyes.

SIXTEEN

THROUGH THE OPEN WINDOW OF THE MEETING ROOM, SHEM watches the sun lift out of the sea. It is a copper plate behind the mists. Breezes skitter away from it and twist through the window, bearing a whiff of freedom, tugging at Shem's tunic. It will be a warm day. Perhaps later in the afternoon there will be time at least to walk in the southern meadows. Perhaps, if there is a journey to the mainland to be made in the last of the dusk, he might—

"No time for that now. No time..." The voice penetrates with complete clarity through the outer offices, through the reception room, through the open door of the conference room. Shem imagines the swift approach of his superior, surrounded by assistants who veer off one by one, dispatched on the errands of the day.

He turns, squaring his shoulders. He waits. The room waits, its carpeted silences trembling under the rush of time. Time falls in slices from the second hand of the big wall clock; time shatters in tiny shards from the digital counters on the table. Across the fingers folded behind his back, Shem feels the last of the seductive breeze.

"Good morning," Horvath says, entering. His body is sleek. His gray hair is close-cropped. His neck rises stiffly out of the high collar. There is something reptilian in his movements and in his gaze, a saurian vigilance. Shem is certain that Horvath blinks less than ordinary men, and then so quickly that the movement seems like the diaphanous flicker of a nictitating membrane. Shem respects this man, but there is apprehension mixed in his respect. In the old world, where ascent in a hierarchy was linked inevitably to self-interest, Horvath would be a dangerous man, perhaps a business baron, an anarchist of the worst sort. Even now, committed though they all are to the Project, the great danger in him is the clarity of his intellect, essentially a drastic readiness to narrow choices. Shem believes that when Horvath dies he will do so as he has lived, so coolly distancing all emotion and all pain that they become simply options he will not choose.

"Good morning," Shem says. "Beautiful day."

"Yes." Horvath looks at the wall clock, then out the window. He sits, places his hands flat on the table. "Moran's late?"

"He's on his way," Shem says, also sitting. He positions himself so that he can gaze through the window at the sea. Above the distant flutter of helicopters comes the song of warblers. "Emergency at the last minute."

Horvath regards him mildly, incredulously. His glance says that in a world where punctuality is all, such emergencies simply do not occur. He touches a series of buttons on the console ready at his hand, and they watch the list of names and figures that appears on the large screen at one end of the room. It is the raw, up-to-the-minute report of all events in Yggdrasil—conceptions, births, deaths; statistics from departments estimating remaining resources; arrivals and departures of all patrols and missions; and the morning report on the crucially important labors of the scholars.

Both men note the deaths particularly, as well as the names of peregrini who are ovedue in reporting and might have met with misfortune in the country. Both men will be responsible, soon, for making new appointments.

With another command Horvath calls up upon the screen a large map with pinpricks of light indicating the last positions of various peregrini, as well as other information. Horvath muses on this map while they wait. He is making decisions.

The map shows the same section of ragged coast as the one that Shem has frequently consulted—two hundred miles of shoreline with Alcheringia and the Yggdrasilian Archipelago at the center. To the north, beyond the curved range of coastal mountains, is a larger area with uncertain boundaries marked *Gerumbia*, and north of that is a heavily crosshatched area, fading into space, marked *DZ 1 (Northern Wayst)*. To the south, as the mountains dwindle into hills, the River Larl angles to meet the sea off the southeast shore of a large island; the area around its mouth is labeled *Yulok*. Across the Larl, directly eastward from Alcheringia, between the coastal mountains and the Kanik Range, is the plain which Asa and his party have just crossed, and immediately to the north of this plain is *DZ 2 (Middle Wayst)*. Far to the northeast of the Middle Wayst is a region labeled *Abibone*. East of Yulok, at the bottom of the map and at the southern end of the Kanik Range where the River Em straightens and broadens, is the region of Montayn.

This map is crucial to these men, for they are responsible for Norriya, the region it depicts. Horvath is the Master of all Norriya. Shem is his lieutenant, responsible for the western half of the region; all the coast is Shem's—Gerumbia, Alcheringia, and Yulok. The man they are waiting for, Moran, is in charge of the east—Abibone, the Kanik Range, and Montayn.

Moran arrives suddenly and apologetically. "Sorry. Sorry." The door of the conference room hisses shut behind him. He is a large, soft bear. Stout little legs carry the rotund torso resolutely forward into the chair that awaits it, but the upper half of the body behaves as if it had passed beyond its owner's control. Shoulders hunch spasmodically, hands and arms jerk out suddenly in bizarre directions, and Moran utters a stream of little grunts and exclamations, as if he were surprised to see parts of himself where he had not expected them. "Couldn't be helped. Last-minute call from Montayner *peregrinus*." His moon face is wreathed in smiles that work it into constantly shifting networks of creases, and his fringe of mustache bobs incessantly. From behind thick glasses childlike eyes gaze out upon a fearsome world. With every step, every gesture, every fractured sentence, the man says *Don't hit me! Don't hit me!* At first meeting he seems a disheveled fool, a genial baboon.

And yet, Shem knows from long experience with Moran that he is not a fool, that in the middle of the most banal and disjointed conversations he can grip the heart of an issue. "Ah!" Moran had said once when Shem admired his ability. "Not everyone who snores is sleeping, eh?"

Horvath observes Moran's arrival with flat eyes, and when the chuckling, the spasms, and the welter of odd sounds have all subsided he says quietly, "Moran, we have half an hour for this meeting which you requested. We are nine minutes late in starting. Perhaps you would tell us what is on your mind."

"Well, right . . . of course . . . it's a matter of ah, oh . . . arh . . . how shall I, ah . . ."

Shem notes food stains on the tunic that bulges around Moran's girth; a button has popped where the garment has tried heroically to close across his breast. *Good heavens*, Shem thinks. *Is it possible that one-fifth of the known world is in our hands—Horvath's, Moran's, and mine?*

"Horses," Moran says suddenly. His glasses glitter.

"Horses," Horvath repeats, his eyes flat.

"The crux of my problem. What can I say . . . hm? I mean, fact is, uh, horses are for Kaniks. No? Hm? Otherwise, balance upset. Um-hm. No certainty." His pudgy hands spread, freeing chaos.

"What's happened?" Horvath asks.

"I think I know," Shem says. "Some of my Alcheringians—"

"*Your* Alcheringians? Yours?" The lizard stare fixes him. "What are you, Shem, a dream master or a slave owner?"

"I'm sorry, sir. Inevitably one grows attached."

"That of course is a danger. Against which you are always vigilant. Correct?"

"Yes, sir."

"Continue."

"In a recent Alcheringian raid, horses were stolen from the Kaniks. You recall the debate in the Arborea four—five years ago, and the decision—"

"Of course I recall."

"So you will also recall the special dispensation for Alcheringian Nines, on their first raid, to deviate from their code, the Tabuly, within strict regulations. They must free the horses on the east bank of the Larl. They must bathe—"

"Yes, yes."

"That decision was sent to my peregrinus among the Alcheringians, Jared, who insinuated it as usual into the mythos of the tribe. Everything was in order."

"And so?"

"A raid has occurred. Alcheringians have stolen horses."

"And violated regulations?"

"No. I don't believe so." Shem looks inquiringly at Moran.

"Oh no oh dear oh heavens no," says Moran. "The problem as I see it—you correct me if I'm wrong, Shem, Horvath—is that the Kaniks are extremely upset. My peregrinus tells me there's very ugly talk among them, and, well, when a wolf shows his teeth he isn't laughing, is he. There's a change in the rules, you see, and they don't understand. Alcheringians have never stolen horses in their raids. Now, suddenly, they do. Kaniks wonder, well, uh, how to right the balance. They examine their own code and—"

"What's it called, again?"

"The Regulae, sir. Well, uh, they examine it and begin to question the restraints. Only natural, isn't it? Too bad but true. They look for loopholes. They—"

"Can you be specific?" Horvath asks.

Moran's large frame quivers. His mouth turns down apprehensively. "Well, for example, they propose mounted raids beyond the Larl, into Alcheringia itself."

"Expressly forbidden," Shem says.

"Of course, but they feel provoked, don't you see. They feel justified. Why, the notion has even surfaced of forming an alliance with other tribes against the Alcheringians."

Shem snorts. "I can't imagine that! Kaniks are so proud and stiff-necked—"

"Just talk at the moment," Moran continues, "but nevertheless . . ." He lifts a finger. "The Kanik is clever, but it comes slowly—all the way from the back of his head."

"You've had a peregrinus report?"

"Several. Yes, indeed. Um-hm. They apparently have new young leaders, you know, who begin to question. To look to the future. To agitate. I'm afraid all is not well. Oh dear, no." Moran's gaze moves wide-eyed from one to the other.

"What do you suggest, Moran?"

The big man's body suddenly stops twitching. His eyes deepen into still pools behind their glasses. "End this dreadful liberalism," he says, flushing. "End this toying with the codices of the tribes as if they were simple regulations that could be altered at a whim. Remember the example of the Old Ones: First they killed their commandments; then they killed themselves."

Shem strokes his beard. "You think it's that important? You

think this business of the horses could jeopardize the Project?"

"It could. Yes. Rot beginning. Unless we stop it. Next thing you know they'll be going inside the Designated Zones. In fact . . ." His brow creases as he remembers something, and he begins to point to Shem, but Horvath interrupts him.

"Only the full Arborea could repeal that ruling. Do you recommend that they reconsider it?"

Moran nods eagerly, his jaws shaking *yes yes yes*, a parody of a small fat boy.

"You object, Shem?"

"No. It will be difficult, of course, if they *do* change their minds. It will exacerbate an already delicate situation."

Horvath's eyebrows lift. "Oh? Delicate? How so?"

"The usual Alcheringian problems."

"Anything your peregrinus can't handle?"

"No."

"Who *is* that peregrinus?"

"Jared."

"Still? Why, he's been there since your father—"

"Still one of the best. Perhaps *the* best."

"*Is* he, Shem? I thought I recalled some doubt about him years ago. Some hint of ambivalence, even subversion." Horvath's bright eyes shine golden amid the reflections of the sun. A small buzzer signals that the meeting time has elapsed. The eyelids close very slowly, musing. "But then, the Alcheringians have always been troublesome, haven't they? They are a people with an *art*. With a language." Horvath speaks softly, his tongue moving across his lips. "We must consider them another time. We must consider them."

The three men leave the sunlight of the meeting room and pass together through the outer offices, surrounded by the buzzing circuitry of myriad decisions. In the hall they go separate ways to attend to the business of the day. Wrapping each as he descends into the labyrinth of Yggdrasil is a cocoon of natural sounds—the calls of birds, the fluttering of wind through leaves, the hissing of a gentle surf on a languid beach—all subtly joined by the most tenuous of melodies.

In the elevator that bears Shem downward as he muses on Horvath's last remark are all these sounds of a timeless summer day. The air in the elevator is pure and sweet, and carries the scent of sea spray and of roses.

PART TWO

ALCHERINGIA

ONE

Asa's lodge stood alone on the extreme northern edge of Alcheringia. His mad mother had chosen the spot when he was only an infant, and in all the years of his life he had returned to this same spot every spring.

To reach it he passed through the center of the village. He could have followed the other path, the one which skirted the village on the landward side, or he could have walked up the beach; but tired though he was, he preferred to go through the lodges of his clan, and to hear the sounds of the place, and to know that he was home again.

It was a warm spring evening. Myriads of wild roses bloomed along the shore, and the sea wind bore the scent of them, blending it with the other odors of the camp—cedar smoke, and curing fish, and the pungent sweetness of tanning leather. People called and waved to him from the doors of lodges, and children ran to him and walked a little way with him, reaching to touch his bow, and his ax, and the sweat-hardened leather of his leggings. Asa in turn touched each child, walking a little distance with his hand on its head or shoulder. He remembered their names. He had a question for every one. Of all his Nine he was the most tolerant with children. Because he was an orphan, he had had as many mothers as there were women among the Cranes, and he had not forgotten their kindness. It would be a part of him forever. Anything that could be done to soften the harsh pangs of childhood, Asa believed, should be done.

Children had looked after his lodge for him while he was away. Children had gathered firewood for him, and brought him, now, choice bits of food sent by their parents. He ate sparingly in the last of the sunlight in the doorway of his lodge while the children sat at a discreet distance, sensing his exhaustion. Long after he had wished them good night and gone inside to his sleeping robe, he knew that the children were sitting where he had left them, and they would sit silently there until the last of the light died and they were called to the village below.

He fell asleep imagining the twilight over Alcheringia, and the mists that would move on such a night out of the marshes, joining with the smoke from campfires, weaving like soft fabric amid the firs.

He fell asleep listening to a woman singing somewhere, a bittersweet rejoicing for the memory of something forever lost, and to the strains of a solitary flute that at last grew so frail that they mingled indistinguishably with the calls of whippoorwills, and hoot owls, and other great-eyed birds of night.

For several hours he slept dreamlessly.

Then, at midnight, a storm moved in from the sea. Furtive breezes announced it, and faint thunder far away. The night birds fell silent. Thunderheads rose above the Islands of the Gods, crowding out the new moon, crowding out the stars. One by one the fires of Alcheringia flickered and died; the lodges were fastened shut. And the first rains struck with the hurricane.

The storm lashed the coast, raged up into the mountains, and then returned like a vengeful animal to growl and slap at Alcheringia again.

Huddled fearful in their lodges, the people said that the gods were angry, and Romoke said that this was but a harbinger of their rage, and that by and by when they could be approached he would make offerings to appease them and to learn the cause of their fury.

Alone in his lodge, Asa awoke several times screaming and gasping from nightmares of suffocation. In some, the thick walls of the lodge folded inexorably down under an imponderable weight of snow. In some, he was womb-bound, unable to be born. In some, the malicious and laughing gods crushed him under burdens he could not identify and from which he could not escape. In all, he pleaded for mercy in an unintelligible tongue.

Twice during the night he ran out into the storm and dropped sobbing onto his hands and knees. Once, desperate for air, he found that he had actually squirmed under the skirt of the lodge, lifting out two of the deep-driven pegs as he did so. Finally, toward morning, he built the fire and listened to the last vestiges of the storm trail eastward through the forest.

At dawn he saw the first light high above the storm clouds, and when he went down to the beach he found a freshet of rainwater splashing down where he expected it to be. He stripped and bathed in its little shower, gasping in the cold and scrubbing himself thoroughly with sand. When he had finished he walked naked into the cold sea and waded out until the surf foamed around his thighs. Offshore to the north, the Islands of the Gods were barely visible—three shadows on the dark gray of the horizon. He turned to face these islands, but he did not lift his arms in supplication as was proper when one was speaking to the gods. Instead, his fists rested on his hips. Nor did his speech lapse into the archaic diction and rhythms customary in prayers. He spoke plainly and directly.

"Listen to me," Asa said. "I am a man, nothing more. I have no weapons, no protection against you except the truth. I know that to be human is to be alone, and frightened, and preyed upon by what is inside as well as by what is out. I know that to be human is to speak little and speak the truth. I know that it is to laugh sometimes, and I know that it is to weep." He paused. "And I know that to be human is *to want to know*." He paused again, but the morning was quiet.

"As for you, I do not know who you are. Sometimes you move like men, speak like men. Sometimes you fly, or move across the land more swiftly than any creature. Sometimes you contain men. Sometimes you leap like silver spiders from hiding.

"I have watched you, and I shall tell you what I think. I think that to be a god is to be a coward. To be a god is to hide along the edges of a man's sleep and to curse him with dreams. To be a god is to hide from meeting men, to sneak along the borders of earth and heaven. I think you are *afraid*, and you hide behind your commandments in the places where you forbid men to enter. Do you hear? I think that to be a god is *to be afraid*!"

Asa waited. Exhausted surf fell on the Alcheringian beach and hissed back across the pebbles. Breezes stirred in the bushes. A pair of loons passed low, wings squeaking. But there were no other sounds.

A scimitar of sun suddenly lit the islands.

Asa laughed softly. "I pity you," he said. "For to be a god is *to be afraid of knowing*." A raven sloped down the hill behind him, announcing morning. From across the river a second answered. "Now," Asa said, his eyes narrowing, "hear what I will do! I will track you like a prey until I have found you and know you for what you are. No rules will prevent me. No Tabuly. No shouting of old men. If I must cross the Waysts, I will. If I must paddle there, to your islands, I will. It may be that I shall often be afraid, *but I will never stop*! I will seek and probe until I die, or until you destroy me, like Rusl." He leaned toward the islands. "Do you hear me gods? *You will have to kill me.*"

Again he waited, head turned. When there was no answer he laughed and waded out onto the beach. He had no feeling in his legs.

The huge warmth of the sun embraced him.

TWO

Horvath wakes.

He lies on his belly, hands flat on the hard bed, ready to spring. He has slept in this position.

Something has alerted him; he cannot tell yet what it was.

Everything is normal in the room. There is no movement. There is no sound.

He thinks of the order of the day's business. He thinks first, *Alcheringia*.

It is 0500.

Later, moving toward the privacy of his office, Horvath gives orders to assistants. Those whom they pass in the corridors catch only snatches of what he says—"Alcheringia . . . full review . . . scholars . . . A-One priority . . ." But the assistants, two young women who hear everything and record precisely what they have heard, need only a brisk conference after Horvath's door has closed to assess their task and go to work.

From the top level of the Yggdrasilian complex, where the narrow windows of Horvath's offices brood out upon the marshes to the south, their terse requests spread like electronic roots downward through living strata. One floor below, in the offices of the dream masters, screens blink alive with multicolored symbols. Secretaries rewrite appointment schedules at once.

Messages slide deeper still down concrete walls to the first of the technical levels, where the records of all missions to the mainland are stored. Signals go south, to Neffelheim, into the laboratories and workshops. Messages go north, to Jotunheim, into the silences of libraries and hushed rooms where scholars meet, where there are no clocks, no schedules; where the vital, timeless work of the Project moves forward. Other messages go deeper yet into Jotunheim, into the seabed caverns where all the records of the Old Ones lie accumulated, the archives, the heart of the Project, where archivists glide in soft-wheeled carts through the dozens of miles of stacks, and where technicians monitor constantly all the purring machines that maintain perfect warmth and perfect humidity. The orders are received, the swift carts dispatched, the materials gathered, duplicated, sent aloft.

No messages go deeper, into the reactor rooms, into the magazines, into the maintenance laboratories. No summonses go out, this time, to the barracks and the married quarters beyond the Center. No one is called from Val; no one, this time, from the Provender Section.

Only a few auxiliary requests are needed later that day. By then, Horvath's two able young assistants, with the careful help of scholars, have assembled for the Master of Norriya precisely what he has requested: a detailed profile of Archeringia, including a full history, a personnel survey, and several projected scenarios that take into account the most plausible variables.

Shortly after dusk, an assistant taps gently on the door of the master's office and enters. She is not surprised to find the room in darkness except for the palest light of the afterglow filtering through the western windows. Nor is she surprised to see the silhouette of the Master rooted in darkness beside those windows. Horvath is watching the mist fill the marshes and creep toward him around the trunks of the firs. So intent is he that he does not hear the woman enter, and when she speaks he is startled. Only his head moves—a quick sideways motion that exposes his small right ear.

"Excuse me, sir."

"Yes?"

"We have the dossier you requested. The scholars are ready, also. Shall we go ahead tonight?"

"No," Horvath says, turning back to the thick and gentle fog, swirls of which move against the window like beckoning fingers. "Tomorrow. We'll do it in the morning."

THREE

Asa WENT HUNTING.

His wounds ached and he was stiff, but he wanted to be alone. He did not want to have to retell the events of the last few days, or to listen to them being told by others. Besides, if the gods had heard him he wanted the confrontation with them or their messenger to occur away from Alcheringia; it was, after all, a private matter.

He dressed, gathered his weapons, and slipped out of the lodge. He took the back trail that skirted the encampment and joined the main trail near the pool at the foot of the waterfall. At this juncture he paused long enough to see that the Kanik women had not been left shelterless in the storm. Someone had raised an old lodge for them at the edge of the marsh, and even as he watched, two of them emerged, huddled wretchedly together, squinting into the sun, their backs to the sea.

He did not see Persis.

By the time he reached the crests of the nearest hills, more figures moved among the lodges and the scent of new smoke drifted up to him. A heavy, wattled barricade hung ready here above the narrow western end of the pass, in case of attack from the east, but there were no guards watching the approaches to Alcheringia. Asa frowned at this laxity, remembering again how easily they had entered the Kanik camp, and remembering also the thin gray eyes of Garm, and Garm's oath of vengeance. Sooner or later, Asa knew, Garm would come, bringing others with smoldering Kanik grudges.

But not now. Not today.

Another mile's light jogging with the full sun on his face brought him to the center of the hills, and here he left the path and angled up to his right through scattered cover. Around him the bald hills brooded. Once they had been raw mountains, craggy in their prime, but they were bent and eroded now, with fringes of forest rising almost to their crests and thick moss on the shaded banks of their streams. Countless rock slides and wild fires had opened new meadows where deer came to browse, tawny coats shimmering amid the fireweed and wild lupine.

By noon Asa was sweating heavily from his climb, but his wounds bothered him hardly at all, except for the slash on his thigh, which had been reopened and which now bled lightly into rivulets of sweat.

Shortly after noon he saw the buck whose tracks he had been following. It was standing on the far side of a large clearing. Nearby were two does. Asa began his stalk, circling downwind and then approaching his prey through thick underbrush. The buck was restless. Perhaps he had sniffed danger on some vagrant breeze. By the time Asa had crept within bowshot the deer had already located him and turned to face him, swinging his head. In seconds he would bolt, and the females with him. Smoothly Asa strung a shaft into his bow, and the next time the buck's muzzle lifted into the breeze he loosed it into the creature's throat. The heavy chert head plunged through gullet and jugular and buried itself in the vertebrae, severing the spinal cord.

The buck dropped. Its eye rolled to watch Asa as he loped forward and slit its throat. The does had vanished. A squawking jay exploded out of the forest as they raced away.

It was a perfect kill. Asa hoisted his bow and loosed an

exultant cry that was half laugh and half shout. Then he gutted the beast. Its entrails spilled steaming into the cool grass. The liver he set to one side, and when he had finished the butchering he sat in the shade on the edge of the forest, cut it into small pieces, and began to eat.

A curious hawk swept over a saddle in the hills, glided close, and slid away again. Asa called to it, but it did not respond.

He was utterly and mindlessly content. The whole familiar process of the hunt had satisfied him deeply. After all the turmoil of the events of the raid—the weird passing of the old god, the incident with Persis and Garm, the horror of the creature in the Wayst and what it had done to Rusl—after all of that it was good to return to this green world he knew well, knew on a level deeper than knowledge, knew in his very blood.

This is a sane world, said the hawk. *Sane*, said the cloud shadows on the slopes. *Sane*, said the pungency of the deep woods.

A stick snapped.

A partridge burst upward like an arrow.

Asa flipped backward off the log and in an instant was among the trees. Nothing moved in the glade. The hawk cried again and drifted out of sight. A deerfly settled on Asa's neck and bit. He didn't move.

"I thought I smelled liver," said a voice from the other side of the clearing. It was an amused and querulous voice, drawn thin by old pain.

Asa laughed and stood up. "Jared!" He was delighted. If there was one person with whom he would have chosen to share his pleasure in the day, it would have been this old man who had been like a father to the three of them—himself, Kenet, and Rusl.

Jared stepped into the clearing. He carried only a small bundle and the staff of the Wanderers, those who came and went among the tribes.

"Where have you been?" Asa asked, embracing him.

Jared raised his eyebrows toward the northern hills. *Somewhere up there*, his gesture said. *In the land*. He said nothing.

Asa did not ask again. Wanderers moved as easily as the wind through the wilderness, as easily as the ghosts of ancestors, bearing news, and advice, and wisdom, and sometimes stern commands. Legend said that they were nourished in the wild and in solitude, and that in the days before memory one of them had brought the Tabuly to Alcheringians. Legend said that Wanderers learned even the wishes of the gods.

Never were they questioned. Not ever. Not even in the smallest things. Asa's question was an impertinence that would be overlooked only because Jared had startled him, and because they were old, old friends.

Jared had overseen all of Asa's childhood. He had always been old. Sometimes he spoke in council, sometimes not. Sometimes he joined in the banter of the boys along the riverbank or the beach, sometimes not. Always he watched.

"And so," Jared said, breaking the silence in which he finished the last of the liver Asa had given him, "you have gone on your first raid and you have returned with wounds. I suppose I must call you a man now."

Asa shrugged and looked at his hands. "I do not feel like a man," he said.

Jared grunted. "You have a choice?"

"I thought things would be clearer. Instead, there are more questions."

"Poor Asa," said Jared softly. "You have always been troubled by questions, haven't you? You, and Rusl, and Kenet. Tell me, what questions are there now? What questions can come from a raid, where there is only action?"

"Jared . . . Jared, it was very strange."

"Tell," the old man said.

And so, sitting in the afternoon beside the carcass of the deer, Asa told his old friend everything about the raid, leaving nothing out. Somehow in Jared's presence the truth presented itself more plainly, more easily. So now. He confessed his fear of the thrashing god. He told the strange incident in the Wayst exactly as he remembered it. He confessed his horror and remorse at the slaying of the Kanik. Hesitantly, he even acknowledged his attraction to Persis, the girl with the eyes like peat fires in the dusk.

Jared sat in silence for several minutes after he had finished. Then he said, smiling like a man in pain and punching his palm, "Why is it that we cannot . . . simply . . . learn . . . forgetfulness? Well, what is it that troubles you the most?"

"The creature in the Wayst. And Rusl."

The old man nodded sadly. "There are some things with

which I cannot help you. When you three were very small I told you the stories of your tribe. When you grew older I and the elders taught you your Tabuly, and each year as you grew you acknowledged with the rest of us that you had not forgotten it and that you understood it. Before you set out on your raid you acknowledged again that you had not forgotten. Did you not?"

Asa nodded.

"And made certain . . . promises?" Jared was scratching the earth with the end of his staff. He glanced up ruefully.

Asa nodded again.

"We protected you in the only way we could, by showing you the limits of what it is permitted to know. If you transgress those limits we can no longer help you. We cannot protect you. It is very simple. Rusl has been punished. I cannot help. It is done."

"Jared, he isn't the first, is he?"

The old man closed his eyes. "No."

"I—I mean to have been punished in *that* way, so that parts of him—"

"I cannot help anymore, Asa."

"But you *know*, don't you?" Asa felt very small. He felt like a child with large, dark adults rumbling around him, saying things he didn't understand. "It happened to Romoke, too, didn't it? That's why he cries when he tries to remember sometimes. And it happened to my grandfather. Isn't that true? That's why Romoke came to see him so often. They each remembered little bits of what had happened. And that's why—"

"Asa," the old man said, shaking his head. "Asa."

". . . why my grandfather kept drawing that . . ."

"What?"

"That. That tree. The one you háve drawn there. In the dirt."

Jared sat unmoving. "I am a senile fool," he said.

"It is the same tree that my grandfather drew. Over and over. Where had he seen it, Jared? It is the same tree that was on the side of the god, or on the thing carrying the god. What is it, Jared? What does it mean?"

"A tree is a tree. It is an old sign. It means life. Life at the center. Life and world. Roots in underworld, trunk on earth, branches among the stars."

"Please, Jared."

"Tree. Nothing more. Look, here is a fox—"

"Jared, *what does it mean?*"

Jared's glance flashed a hot warning. "You are so keen to know what you should not!"

Asa was on his feet now, and crouched. His lips were drawn back. His empty bow punctuated what he said. "*Should* not? This is *my* body! This is *my* life! What are they doing to it, Jared? What are *you* doing to it? What are these god-games that we cannot know?"

"If there are things you should not know, it is—"

"For my own good. Yes. I know what you're going to say. But I am the one to decide that. I am the *only* one."

Jared stood. The color had drained from his face. "You forget who I am," he said quietly.

"My friend?" Asa stepped closer to him. "Are you my friend, Jared?"

"Yes. I am a better friend than you know! *You* will decide what is good for you? Nonsense! Who are you to challenge the gods, you who know nothing?"

"I know—"

"*Nothing* is what you know!" Jared's staff pounded the earth. "Nothing! Nothing!"

"Then you must teach me!" Asa blinked back tears of frustration and fury.

"*I . . . must . . . do . . . nothing!*"

"Ignorance—"

"*Silence!*"

Both heard the call of the circling hawk, but neither looked toward it.

"Now then," Jared said. "I am going to answer your question. You will find the answer unsatisfactory, but you will accept it. Is that clear?"

"I don't—"

"*Is* it?"

"Yes. Yes, sir."

"Good. Then listen to what I say. The tree-mark is a sign of the gods. There is a name for it which you may know someday, not now. It means life, and strength, and perseverence, and *immobility*. It means knowing that the place where you are rooted is the center of Earth. It means holding that center. It means . . . never . . ." Jared faltered, made a weak

gesture with his free hand, and sat down. "No more. Not now.
Later." He was holding his stomach.

"I'm sorry," Asa said after a moment.

Jared waved the apology away. "It doesn't matter. You have
no choice. Take your stag, now. Go home."

"Can I—"

"Go," Jared said. "All is well."

In the dusk, alone, Asa returned to Alcheringia. The lodges
glowed like weird beetles in the night. Outside the hut of the
Kanik captives smoldered a single fire, and he could see the
shadowy figures of the women moving against it. Persis was
among them, and only she saw him. He stooped and laid on
the grass at the side of the trail a choice cut of the brisket of
the deer. Then he went on without looking back to see if Persis
had picked up the meat or not.

That night he dreamed of Persis. So vivid and terrifying
was the dream that he awoke crying her name and could not
go back to sleep; he got up, built the fire, and went outside
his lodge to gaze down over the sleeping encampment and the
Alcher, gleaming in starlight.

"What?" he asked himself. "What is happening to me?"

In his dream he and Persis were lovers, though no physical
lovemaking had occurred between them. Asa saw all that tran-
spired as a mute and helpless witness, who longed with all his
might to shout warnings but was unable to do so.

Futilely Persis was looking for him, far away, as if from
the bottom of a deep well or canyon, or barely discernible
through the mist on the sea, or in a forest where he heard
nothing but her voice calling his name, saw nothing but her
face passing among the trees. Now she was so close to him
that he reached to embrace her, but she passed by him, or
turned away from him, and his arms hung empty. It seemed
desperately important for them to find each other before the
arrival of other people, but soon others did arrive, shadowy
figures at first, all smiling, but then growing more substantial
and gently insinuating themselves between Persis and Asa the
watcher; and as their numbers grew Asa was pushed farther
and farther back, always to the back of the crowd. He ran like
a small excluded child pushing at the obscuring legs of grown-
ups, and sometimes by jumping high or clambering upon some
object he was able to catch glimpses of Persis at the center.

White-garbed figures, all smiling, all ingratiating, had moved between her and the others, urging her into some arcane and votive dance which she apparently knew, for she began even as Asa watched, screaming soundlessly for her to stop and to come away with him to safety, to sway to the rhythms of music he could not hear. Smiling, dancing with her, the crowd mouthed silent words. Asa screamed and screamed, for it was clear to him that she was their sacrifice, and as he screamed someone turned and cut off his right arm.

He woke howling, clawing at the bottom of his lodge. He had thrust one arm under the taut edge and into the wet grass of dawn.

He sat up shaking, and fanned the embers of his fire, building them into a warming blaze. When the trembling ceased he went out into a morning of clouds dense as a nubbled ceiling, their undersides all rose and gold from a sun still hidden behind the mountains. Kneeling at the nearby stream, he bathed his arms and face and neck in the icy water, but even as he gazed into it the reflections of the clouds moved like dancing bodies, and he could not wash from his memory the vivid image of the woman.

Before sunrise he went to the marsh where the Kanik women were camped. As he drew close he saw the unmistakable hulking shape of Thorel moving off among the tag alders back toward the main camp.

Then he saw Persis.

Despite the cold she was bathing, rubbing herself with sand from the little beach that skirted that portion of the marshes. Nebulous mists drifted around her. Wakening blackbirds chuckled in the rushes. A raven croaked once in the hillside firs.

Asa stood watching on the bank. It did not occur to him to conceal himself, and when the woman dove and surfaced, turning in the sluggish current, she saw him. She continued her bath, and when she had finished she came back out onto the little beach and began to dress, her back turned toward him.

"I dreamed of you," Asa said.

She turned around then. Black hair hung straight. She had been lacing her dress, and she paused, holding the laces. "And so," she said, in a voice that was so light, so carelessly dismissing the ponderous works of fate that it sounded almost happy. "And so you have come to fulfill your dream, like your friends?"

Asa shook his head. "I would not want to live that dream," he said.

"Then why have you come?"

"To see you."

She laughed. "Well, you have seen all there is." She continued to twine the laces and to knot them, and when she had finished she brushed back her hair so that her face stood boldly out. She rested one hand on her hip. "No? Then you have come to see more than me, perhaps. You have come to see the results of your fine work in capturing me and driving me here like an animal. Do you want to see my lodge, how spacious it is? Do you want to see my friends, how happy they are among your gentle warriors? Do you want to see how well fed we are, with your bits of charity? No?" Her voice was so carefree, her laughter so light, that had Asa not been close enough to see the dark gleam in her eyes he would have thought she was speaking earnestly. "Perhaps, then, you want to see me closer, is that it, Asa?" She came forward slowly until they were almost touching, until he could feel her breath on his face.

"I wish you no harm," he said. "We are all captives. I did what I believed I must do."

"So will Garm," she said, smiling, "when he comes."

"But perhaps he will not come. And if you want to live—"

"Then I will be kind and friendly. I will acquiesce and make myself agreeable until some Alcheringian male claims me. Is that it? Is that what I must do?"

"There are other ways of saying it: Life goes on. Face facts."

She moved closer until her body touched his. "Here is a fact," she said, very softly. "Remember it. I am weaker, and I cannot stop your friends from doing what they will. But this is what I tell them: I wait for the right moment, and then—" Her fist struck hard on the left side of his back, beside the spine, under the shoulder blade, and Asa's breath left him in a rush. "And then I say, *Someday I will have a knife!*" She stepped back. "Someday. Some night. When you are least expecting it. That is how you will die!"

She stepped back and they stood facing each other.

Asa turned away first.

FOUR

W HEN THE CHRONOLOGIC VIDEO-BRIEF IS FINISHED, THE ELDER
of the two scholars says: "Historically, there has been a high
incidence of defiance among them. As you have seen, the
corrective measures required in only the last quarter century
are extensive—nine individuals in all."

"How do you explain that?" Horvath asks. He is listening
intently, his glance flickering between the two scholars, and
from them to the display screen, which at the moment shimmers
like green water.

The older scholar frowns, removes his glasses, squints at
them, and cleans them ostentatiously. He knows at least five
speculative answers to that question, and he is wondering which
to offer. Finally he says, "Abnormally high intelligence and
curiosity quotients."

The younger scholar bristles. He is perhaps sixty-two. His
speech is hampered by imperfect dentures which shift in moments of excitement, requiring rapid adjustments with his lips
and tongue. "Problematical! Highly problematical! Mumpp. In
fact, Heisenick's subjects were—"

The elder scholar glances heavenward. "My dear fellow,
you know that poor Heisenick's tests have been shown un-
equivocally to be culturally biased."

"But they have, nevertheless, provided frmmud the only
available Alcheringian data."

"Worse than useless!"

"Better than mere mmfhrup speculation."

"Speculation? Intuition! Intuition!" The elder scholar has
grown red in the face and is striking himself on the chest. "So,

89

after seventy-three years I rely sometimes on intuition! I'm entitled!"

Shem stares balefully at the two of them, and from them to the inexorable clocks dominating the wall of Horvath's office, and from the clocks to the fingernails of his right hand. Horvath's executive assistants take conscientious notes.

"Gentlemen," Horvath says, delicately lifting his pen from his desk, "I think I have caused the problem by asking a speculative question. Perhaps if we restricted ourselves to the demonstrable . . . Please refresh my memory. What precisely are the terms of the Alcheringian codex?"

Both scholars relax. Child's play, this. The elder explains, touching buttons to call up a prepared program, "They know it as the Tabuly, and of course there are many stories concerning it in their mythology. Certainly it is one of the simplest codices among the tribes."

All regard the screen, even the assistants, who know to a word what they will see:

1. YOU SHALL NOT LOOK UPON THE GODS.
2. YOU SHALL NOT MOVE ANY PLANT, OR BURY THE SEED OF ANY PLANT.
3. YOU SHALL NOT FEED ANY ANIMAL, OR USE ANY FOR BURDEN, OR KEEP ANY ENCAGED.
4. YOU SHALL NOT FEED UPON THE UNIMORPHS.
5. YOU SHALL NOT GO NEAR THE ISLANDS OF THE GODS, OR THE FORBIDDEN REGIONS—THE NORTHERN WAYST, THE MIDDLE WAYST, AND THE LANDS BEYOND.
6. YOU SHALL NOT LIVE IN ANY LODGE, IN ANY PLACE, MORE THAN SIX MONTHS.

"Class A Hunter-Gatherer," Horvath says.

The scholars nod. "Broad-scale polyandrous activity with subsequent pair-bonding," says the elder. "Patriarchal, quasi-hierarchical, shifting chiefship pattern."

"Pubescent promiscuity," adds the younger, careful with his teeth.

"Thereafter, the usual homeostatic mechanisms," the other scholar continues. "Prolonged lactation, occasional infanticide, group two euthanasia, and so forth. To maintain isolation, previous Masters have authorized maintenance of ancestral animosities with all neighboring tribes, Standing Order Number—"

"Yes," says Horvath. "Go on."

"Raids for the capture of young women were instituted as a measure against inbreeding."

"Recessumdghump. Recessive genes."

"Quite!" Horvath snaps, his temper flickering across his eyes. "I am not an utter fool!" He pauses so that everyone in the room—assistants, scholars, Shem, Moran—hears the snickering of the clock.

Shem thinks: *Forty-two years remaining. Forty-two years, twelve weeks, five days, one hour, nineteen minutes, and thirty-seven seconds. Thirty-six. Thirty-five. And we are being briefed on recessive genes!*

"Perhaps," Horvath says softly, "perhaps we are keeping the Alcheringians altogether too healthy. What do you think, Shem?"

"On principle I am against the use of controlled disease," Shem says. "You know that. Besides, you can never preclude the possibility of epidemics."

"Nevertheless," says the elder scholar, "there are several good precedents. Uh . . . uh . . ."

"File Number 357-HR-79," says one of the executive assistants, and the elder scholar touches buttons, calling the information up on the screen.

"Yes. Here is the one I was thinking of in particular. An outbreak of aberrant activity among the Abibones in 135. We quelled it by—"

"Influenza," Shem says with disgust. "Clumsy. Dirty. Unselective."

"Effective, nevertheless," Horvath replies, watching him closely. "The Abibones have been the most devout of tribes since then. Moran reports they still are."

"Yes. Yes, indeed!" Moran says.

"They have even eradicated the word *god* from their language. They make a circle sign instead."

Shem shakes his head firmly. "I won't sanction it, sir."

"Please remind us"—Horvath speaks to the scholars, but he is watching Shem—"what the alternatives are should all primary control methods fail."

The younger scholar counts them on his fingers. "One, disease. Two, regulated famine mumph. Three, warfare."

"Those are the secondary controls."

"Yes."

"And the tertiary?"

"Well, of course, they would never be——"

"What *are* they?"

"Final solutions. A strike from Yggdrasil. Genocide."

Shem's face is scarlet. "I know very well, sir, what the alternatives are!"

"You may leave," Horvath tells the scholars, the assistants, and Moran. "Thank you."

When they have gone he swivels his chair to face Shem. No part of him moves except his lips. Fixed on Shem, his gaze looks through him and past him, into the far reaches of time. He speaks softly: "Obviously you have some special attachment to the Alcheringians. Although I do not know what that is, I agree that they are an attractive people in the old sense— handsome, energetic, free-spirited, and, alas, inquisitive and inventive. Even I, were I to permit it, could feel an atavistic yearning toward them. However, I know that I do not need to remind you of the Project. Should the Alcheringians pose a threat——"

"They don't," Shem says. "Absolutely not."

"I hope not. I hope not. Otherwise, I shall use the alternatives." Something very like remorse flickers on Horvath's face and vanishes instantly. "I must. You know that."

Shem nods.

"I do not intend to sit in a meeting of the Arborea and humiliate myself by acknowledging a failure in simple *mechanics*, Shem. In the control of a *tribe*!" The skin on Horvath's neck quivers. A little shiver of anger slips under his collar, across his shoulders, down his back. "So I suggest that you make whatever arrangements are necessary with your peregrinus, whose name I can never remember——"

"Jared."

"Jared. Yes. That old man. I suggest you make clear to Jared that he not permit himself to be beguiled by these Alcheringians, and that he overcome his foolish scruples in dealing with them. However imperfect they may be, the clinicians are there to be used. Use them!"

Shem raises a hand. "Leave it to me."

The chair swivels silently and Horvath once again faces his desk. He makes a sweeping gesture. "Please take all this Alcheringian material with you when you go." He touches the CLEAR button on his console.

Shem's foot is a vortex of agony, but he walks back to his

own office, waving away the motor chair that an assistant is bringing.

Deeper than the pain is bitterness. He is sick of Yggdrasil, sick of power, sick of the dozens of expedients and compromises which the Project demands. He knows that if Moran were with him he would quote one of the grim old proverbs he likes so much—"A bad compromise is better than a good battle!" But Shem feels the whole, pure purpose of the Project being nibbled away, even as the clock hands nibble away seconds from the face of time. His faith in the Arborea, in the scholars, in his own ability, disintegrates, leaving nothing.

They will lose. He knows that they will lose. He knows that they lose a little more with every small decision like the one he is now being forced to make.

But he has taken an oath and he will keep it, not because of the gods, but precisely because there are no gods.

Among the signals he orders sent that afternoon is this: PEREGRINUS ALCHERINGIA. HENCEFORTH CLINICIAN NETWORK TO BE USED. ATTEMPT NO FURTHER LEVEL-ONE CONTROLS.

Shem imagines Moran smiling. He imagines Moran finding a proverb for the occasion: "You must walk with the Devil until you come to the end of the bridge."

FIVE

THE COUNCIL WAS NOT PROCEEDING AS JARED HAD HOPED.

He sat among the elders of the inner circle, close to the blaze. They faced south, according to the custom, and on the beach beside them and on the bank behind them stood both clans of Alcheringia.

The purpose was to celebrate the triumph of Asa's Nine,

and their entry as men into the tribe. The surviving seven had the place of honor to the right of the elders, facing the sea, and to the left, on the other side of the fire, listening wide-eyed to everything, sat the youths of next year's Nine.

The chief, Kurc, had begun. He spoke well, as usual, his kindness and humor rolling over them like a reliable succession of waves. He praised the dead first, Noxor and Sim, and then Rusl, who had led, although it was clear from Rusl's vapid smile that he understood almost nothing of what was said. Then Kurc praised them each in turn, growing wittier as he progressed, until, when he called on Kenet to tell the story of the raid, the whole assembly was chuckling.

Kenet had performed well, too. At first. He had found the cadences and phrases to make his remarks about his friends memorable, to insinuate them into the myths and legends of the tribe. He was particularly kind to Rani, and what he said caused the members of next year's Nine—and indeed all the assembly—to look upon the boy with new respect.

Kenet had grown into an imposing young man, a leader, incisive, thoughtful, quick and strong. He spoke with authority. But toward the end of his account, things had gone awry. Jared was not sure exactly where or why, but suddenly, when he should have been concluding, Kenet was saying, "Absurd! Absurd, that we should be doing these things as our parents did. As our grandparents did. Absurd that we should be traveling so far for game, so far to forage!"

Jared was instantly alert to danger. Kenet had opened baskets that someone had laid at his feet, and he was holding up potatoes and yams. He was holding up other tubers, too, and his cupped palms brimmed over with berries.

"When I was small," he said, "I rode on my cradle board for half a day and lay in it another half day while my mother gathered such foods. All grew high up in the meadows in the hills. Some beyond the hills. Sometimes we returned in darkness. All of these I gathered this afternoon along the borders of the river, and most from the refuse heaps and cesspools, where they were most numerous. Now: Why was this so effortless for me, when my mother traveled so far for so little?"

No one spoke. The mood of the council had veered suddenly away from amity. Such questions should not be asked. Never. They led to heresy, sacrilege, madness, death.

"My grandmother," Kenet went on, "had to go even farther,

and her mother before her even beyond that. Sometimes the foraging would last two days, or three.

"But now, the plants come close to us. If you do not believe me, ask your own women or look for yourselves. Now the food we need grows on the very borders of the camp, and the traveling is no longer necessary.

"Why?"

Kenet's listeners shivered as if a small cold wind had blown among them. Almost all looked toward the ground. A few shook their heads. "Do not ask, Kenet," they whispered. "Do not. There are mysteries—"

"Mysteries!" Kenet exclaimed. "Perhaps. But cannot voyages be made into mysteries? Can we not learn?"

"You know the injunctions," Kurc said quickly. "Stop now. Take another path, Kenet. This one will slip away beneath your feet."

"Beneath your feet," the elders echoed. "Cease now! Stop!" Some hissed in fear and anger, and some made the cut-off sign. "You know the injunctions," they said. "You know the taboos!"

But Kenet stood still. He lowered his eyes briefly, respectfully, but he remained standing, holding the speaker's staff. "I know what is said, that it is better to accept than to question, better to keep things as they have always been than to change, better to live with what is unknown than to know. But can I help thinking?" His eyes lifted and swept defiantly around the circle of elders. "Can I help wondering and asking? *Can you?*"

"Shame!" they cried, and a few began to rise.

"No shame!" Kenet answered, trembling. "For what is it to be a man? Is it enough to take what you are given by the gods and do nothing to improve it? Never to ask? Never to inquire or wonder?"

Swaying, Romoke had begun to lead the elders in the catechism of the Tabuly: "What is said of the gods that pass in the heavens, and in the sea, and on the surface of the earth?"

"Never to seek them," the elders droned, "never to look upon their passage, never to speak their names."

"What is said of the plants and earth?"

"Never to move them, never to break the surface of the earth."

"Who brought the Tabuly?"

"Oldin. Oldin."

"Whence?"

"From the gods, from the Islands of the Gods."

"At what price?"

"Nine days on the Tree. Nine nights on the Tree. Until he was given to himself. Until the laws were given."

"What is said of—"

Kenet flung his arm wide in the cut-off sign. "Do you think I was not sung to sleep with the injunctions? Did you say them at my circumcision, and Asa's, and Rusl's?" They all looked at Rusl, who was staring fixedly at Kenet, smiling, and a chill went through them. "Of course I know them! But it is absurd to ignore the truth. We *have* moved plants. We've brought the seeds back, and they're growing here, all of these." He gestured toward the filled panniers. "Can you deny it? Look around your lodges! Look at the edge of the encampment! The *women* know!"

"And never speak!" Kurc was standing with arms folded, and his voice in his great chest was like the roar of surf in a sea cave. "They are wiser than you, Kenet. They take what they are given and are thankful!"

"But if we could bring *more* plants, turn the soil, try—"

"Enough!" Kurc thundered, a cry echoed by all the elders of the inner circle, all of whom were now on their feet. "Shame!" they cried. "Cease!"

"Kenet," Jared whispered. "Oh, Kenet." The smoke stung his eyes, so he had to look away.

Asa stared at this friend. *You have gone too far*, he thought.

"Too far," said Kurc. "Now hear me, Kenet!

"We believed you would speak of the mystery that gave you triumph over the Kaniks. We believed you would tell of the mystery once again, so we could praise it, so you might be humble in its presence, remembering that it was not *you* who had done what you had done.

"Instead, you have forgotten yourself in the presence of that mystery. You have sought to violate it. You have grown *proud*."

Kenet flushed. "If we don't try things we'll never—"

"Silence!"

Asa heard only the fire, and Romoke muttering, and the snicker of the sea. *Banishment*, he thought. *Banishment and purge.*

"Now, Kenet, you will go by yourself into the wilderness. You will fast. You will place yourself at the mercy of beasts. You will go weaponless, and learn humility again. You will be afraid in that darkness and unknown. You will watch the stars and the god-lights passing, and know again that to be

human is never to know what they are. You will not return,"
Kurc said quietly, "until you have relearned the lesson of your
childhood, that *to be human is to leave mystery intact*!

"Have you heard me? *Have you?*"

Kenet lifted his chin.

"Then go!"

For a moment the two men were frozen in a tableau with
only the fire moving. Then Kenet kicked the baskets, sending
vegetables and berries spinning into the fire, and he strode off
into the darkness.

Gradually the congregation settled, the younger men last of
all, for they admired Kenet and his defiance had stirred similar
feelings in them. Each one thought of the old questions to
which there had never been satisfactory answers, only the weight
of tradition. *Why?* they wondered. *Must it always be so because
it has always been so?*

Restiveness lingered in the warm evening.

But Kurc had yielded his place to Romoke, myth-spinner,
map-drawer, who had told tales as long as any but the oldest
of the elders could remember; and soon again the rhythms of
his voice had beguiled them, drawn them into the fabric of the
tales they knew like the paths of Alcheringia themselves, tales
that bound them tight together, healed the wounds made by
death or by defection, and mended the frayed edges of their
uncertainties.

"Listen now," Romoke began in his reedy voice, smiling
at the flutist, who had struck up a tenuous melody to match
the tale. "Listen, and I shall tell you how in the beginning, in
the time of happiness, before either night or day, Dumineev
stole curiosity from the Islands of the Gods and brought it here,
to Alcheringia . . . ."

His tale cast its spell, wrapping them all so close that they
listened together, breathed together, thought together.

Except for three.

Asa had left the fire a few moments after Romoke's tale
began. He knew that his departure would be frowned upon,
but he wanted to find Kenet, to congratulate him, to wish him
well, and perhaps walk a little distance into his banishment
with him. In the darkness he had jogged along the main path
through the village and was about to call out to Kenet's shadowy
shape ahead of him when he stopped abruptly and crouched in
the long grasses at the edge of the path.

Kenet was not alone.

Squinting as his eyes grew accustomed to the darkness after the fire, Asa recognized the stooped form of Jared and heard his voice. Kenet was still shouting, but Jared's replies were conciliatory, and soon the anger began to drain out of their conversation. Asa was not close enough to hear what was said, but he could tell that the tone had shifted, and that Kenet had begun to receive answers to his questions that satisfied him, intrigued him, led him into further questions.

Soon they began to walk up the path and out of the settlement, Jared's arm around the shoulders of the younger man. Asa followed stealthily, crouching to all fours when Jared turned to look behind him. His heart was racing. He had a premonition of some fearful event, and yet he resisted the urge to shout a warning to his friend, or to jog forward on some pretext and join them. He hung back in the darkness.

At the top of the rise, before they reached the pass where the barricade hung ready against attack, Jared swung abruptly to the left, off the main trail and onto a lesser one that led north along the bluffs. Kenet followed eagerly, and it was clear to Asa that the old man had made some promise to the younger one which enticed him on—had promised, perhaps, to show him something that would answer all questions once and for all time. Pleasure and astonishment had replaced anger in Kenet's voice. It had become the delighted voice of a child discovering that the world was a far more wonderful place than he had imagined it to be.

They walked through the night along the bluffs. The trail dwindled down to an overgrown path, and at last seemed to Asa to have vanished completely, yet Jared's pace never slackened. He walked with the resolute gait of a man who knew precisely where he was going and what he must do.

Asa grew more alarmed. The route they were taking had led them around the deep fiord to the north of Alcheringia and across the neck of an isthmus which was part of the forbidden region of Gerumbia. In fact, Jared had already blithely passed warning signs that Gerumbia lay ahead—a bear's skull hideous atop its pole, and the weird Aeolian harps of the Gerumbians, moaning in the distance with the rising wind.

They should not be here. Not even Asa had come this far north on land, although he had passed the place at sea.

The flesh crept on his thighs.

He knew, now, where Jared was going. There could be no

question. It was a dark and remote beach on the north side of the isthmus, buried so deep in its cove and so overshadowed by brooding trees that the sun touched it only once a year. Only at the summer solstice, at the extreme limit of its journey north, did the sun reach far enough to fill that bay, and then the beach shone red and golden against the misty forest behind. On that day, if the sea permitted, the younger and more daring Alcheringians would slip away in their canoes to witness this phenomenon. For most, it was their first tentative challenge to the gods, for the place was not marked on any of Romoke's maps, and so was doubly forbidden.

Asa and Kenet had agreed that one day they would go there together; they never had.

At dawn, Jared and Kenet arrived on the bluffs above that beach. A gloomy and tangled forest tumbled down into the darkness, but from where he crouched among the wind-stunted spruces farther up the slope, Asa could see an old and narrow path winding down.

Jared's left arm encircled Kenet's shoulders. He was gesturing with his staff and talking animatedly, but the wind whipped all his words away from Asa. After a minute he and Kenet started down.

The path was steep and winding, and for a few minutes Asa lost sight of them. He went cautiously, careful not to dislodge stones. At the bottom, in a little meadow above the beach, he saw them again.

Kenet was smiling and entranced, utterly trusting, watching a patch of turf that Jared had found by probing amid the bushes with his staff. Jared was a little apart from him, now, looking at the same spot.

As Asa watched, the old man groped deep in his pack and drew out what appeared to be a small black box. He pointed it at the nondescript patch of turf, and above the wind Asa heard a single shrill cry, like the call of a searching hawk. For a moment the two men were frozen in a windswept tableau.

Then the earth opened.

Grasses, flowers, bushes covering a large square trembled briefly and unnaturally, and began smoothly to sink. In a moment they had disappeared, leaving a square black hole.

Through this hole, slowly, a silver creature rose.

It was spiderlike, delicately poised on the platform that lifted it. Its four legs were tipped with clusters of square pads. Two arms reached out. Red eyes glittered. A silver snout protruded, rotated, fixed on Kenet. The cry of the creature was the high-pitched whine of a wolf pup for its dam, unceasing and un-wavering, driving like new knives into Asa's ears.

Asa screamed.

He rose out of his hiding place screaming. "No, Kenet! No! Get out! Get out! Get out!" He lunged forward against wind and underbrush. He hit tree trunks, unaware of everything except the hideous mincing speed with which the creature ad-vanced on Kenet, and the pulsing red lights on its top. "Run, Kenet! Run! Get out!"

Reeling, screaming, he burst into the clearing.

Kenet saw him and extended his left hand in a brief wel-come. Jared saw him too, and even as Asa stopped running Jared pressed another button on the small black box.

The creature gently enfolded Kenet and drew him close. Its forepads pressed caressingly against his temples. Its sound changed from a whine to a loathsome purr. Its scarlet light dimmed.

Asa dropped to his knees. A gulf opened. He had seen it before; he had seen it all before. He knew exactly how Kenet would grope backward now, like a fighter perplexed by a blow from nowhere. He knew how the creature would half turn toward him, Asa, and hesitate. He knew how Jared would fumble myopically with the buttons on the small black box. He knew how the creature, in reluctant answer to some com-mand, would turn not with the silken sweep of a muscled thing, but with small and jerky movements, and squat again on the pad that had lifted it from earth. He knew how it would sink from sight, and how the swaying furze would hide its lair as if it had never been. He knew that he would see the pulsing light in the mists and in the sea itself long after the thing had disappeared.

Suspended, unable to respond, the gulf in him growing ever larger and the gods beginning to appear along its edges, he foresaw too how Kenet, suddenly finding his name, would bend with a vacuous smile and say, "Hey, *Asa*, are we gonna hunt now? Are we? Huh? Are we?"

And he knew at last how Jared, pale as a fish belly, his face the grotesque weeping mask of a man who has passed beyond all time, would kneel beside him, and embrace him, and say, "Be *happy*, Asa. Be satisfied with that!"

For a long time after they had gone, Asa sat unmoving.

Spells washed over him like fogs drifting from the sea. He might have remained at the dark beach for a day and a night. Or longer. He would never know. Deep in him, some kernel of awareness registered the passage of time, sensed the day's fading, and the seeping away of night, and the return of dawn. Something registered the odor of decaying leaves, and the sounds of a restless sea.

But that part of him was very small. Most of him was elsewhere, in a place where gods moved effortlessly through the sky, bearing him along, nodding sympathetically to his incoherent monologue.

At length he stood, walked. At length he found his way back through the tumbled forest to the bluffs above the beach. He was very weak. He saw that Jared had left signs so that the faint trail could be followed back across the perilous isthmus of Gerumbia to the safety of Alcheringia.

Kenet and Rusl sometimes sat together beside the sea. From behind they looked identical, two thickening men with their heads thrust forward into the breeze.

Side by side they would sit sometimes for hours, watching the play of ducks, and the passing of whales, but seeing only a small part of what they looked at.

No one included them in hunts. They were too unpredictable. They might leap up screaming maniacally in that tense last instant before the kill. Women rarely spoke to them, except to make jests, at which they, too, would laugh. There was a cruelty in these jests, but it was a desperate cruelty rooted in profound pity, and directed not against these child-man victims but against the random dark forces that had so diminished them.

Sometimes, sitting on the rocks, they spoke.

"Red eyes."

"A spider. Shining like winter sunlight on the sea."

"A singing."

"A warmth."

"Taking away a heavy load."

"Yes."

"Wonderful."

"Yes. Wonderful."

And both would smile at the skimming ducks, remembering the happiest moment of their lives and amazed that somehow, through some astonishing magic, they had shared it.

* * *

For several weeks Jared was not seen in Alcheringia. His absence was not remarkable. Wanderers came and went. They had many mysterious duties, duties which led them to rendezvous on lonely beaches, and on the trails that led through the wilderness to other tribes.

SIX

"EVERYTHING," JARED SAYS. "THE DAMNED THING TOOK *everything*! The man is one degree above a vegetable."

"The machines are deteriorating," Shem says. "They're erratic. If you want to know the technicalities—"

"And you ordered me to use one. Specifically."

Shem nods curtly. His face is ashen. "And you may have to again."

"Are things *that* bad? Am I *that* out of touch?"

"Their injunctions and taboos aren't holding. Their culture is cracking. You have a situation less manageable every day. *You* know that, and . . . and I have reports from other peregrini as well."

Jared's face becomes a mask of resignation. He sighs, and nods, and passes a hand across his eyes. "I've thought of breaking my oath to the Project, you know. I've thought of just going back. Into the wilderness."

"So have we all," Shem says quietly. "But we never do."

"You didn't know him as I did. You didn't watch him grow, watch the intellect just taking shape . . . And then, to have it all wiped clean so *carelessly*, like a wave across a beach—"

"You could have recommended him."

"To come *here*? No. Kenet didn't have *that* kind of talent. He was all open and honest. Like a moose. He wasn't a *pol-*

itician." Jared says the word as if it is something dead lying on the desk, emitting a bad smell. "Besides, after all your tests, how many apprentice peregrini have been approved for the field in the last twenty, thirty years?"

"Only a few. You were one of them."

"Yes. And do you know, Shem, I wish to heaven now that I hadn't been. I wish your father had just let me be, left me alone. A happy animal. I had my boat, a sail, the sea . . ." He smiles faintly. "I had Yura. What else does a man need? I wish he had let me be, even if I had lived only a quarter of this life."

A buzzer on Shem's desk beeps insistently, and he answers it. Engaged in the conversation which follows, he does not see that Jared has suddenly tensed, momentarily paralyzed with pain.

Death closes all . . . The old man rises and crosses slowly to the window, so that he may look down upon the sea . . . *but something ere the end, some work of noble note, may yet be done* . . . The spell passes. He surreptitiously wipes away the sweat that has sprung out above his beard.

"The others have arrived," Shem says. "We should go."

Together they slowly make their way toward the room where the other peregrini are waiting, and toward the meeting for which Jared has been brought to Yggdrasil.

SEVEN

THE KANIKS CAME UNDER A FULL MOON, ON A HOT AUGUST night.

Shocked and bleeding, one of the old men whose task it was to watch over the retreat of women at the first waterfall

on the Larl ran stiff-legged into Alcheringia wailing that the
dust raised by Kanik horses had been a whirlwind in the moonlight, and that the earth had trembled under their hoofs.

They were led, he said, by a young man with fair hair and
terrible pale eyes.

By the time Kurc and Thorel, roaring like bulls, had gathered
the warriors and led them up the hill, the Kaniks were already
in the pass. They had paused only long enough to refresh their
horses and themselves at the Larl, polluting it with their presence, before plunging across the ford and along the main path
to Alcheringia. Had the Alcheringians delayed only a few minutes longer, the Kaniks would have been fanning out across
the slopes that descended on both sides of the Alcher, and there
would have been no way of preventing them from sweeping
through the village. As it was, Thorel arrived in time to drop
the barricade across the pass, and the Kaniks were checked.
Alcheringian fighters spread like quickfire up the steep hills
on either side of them, and Alcheringian arrows began to find
their marks. Men shrieked and horses whinnied like stricken
birds.

But the Kaniks were ferocious warriors with old scores to
settle, and although several fell, the others were soon bound-
ing up the hillsides, war cries splitting the air. Some wheeled
around, stayed with their mounts, and began to outflank the
Alcheringians.

After the initial volley, Asa had time to loose only one
arrow, at a lean figure attacking in tremendous leaps, and he
had the fleeting satisfaction of seeing that man spin uncon-
trollably, clutch his neck, and sag against a tree trunk. Then
there were so many bodies and the quarters were so close that
the combats quickly became hand-to-hand, and Asa found himself part of a small band that included two of his own Nine
and some older men as well. He heard Thorel laughing insanely
and bellowing his rallying cry, "Brothers! Brothers!" Above
the melee Asa glimpsed the unmistakable head of Garm, like
white foam on a dark and racing sea.

Then he had no time to think. Kanik knives flashed around
him, and suddenly he had closed with a warrior whose weight
and momentum bowled him over, and whose awful quickness
let him stab twice before he and Asa hit the ground. Asa dodged
one thrust, but the second sliced deep into his thigh. Despite
the pain, he managed to bring his knee up into the Kanik's

groin and his knife down into the Kanik's back at the same instant. The man arched in agony, groping futilely for the hilt of the obsidian blade buried in his spine. Suddenly his legs were useless; his face was filled with wonderment. Asa rolled him off. Gasping with pain, he pulled the Kanik's knife out of his thigh and plunged it into the stretched throat of his enemy. The man's life came out in bright red gouts that mingled with the darker, slower blood that coursed over Asa's knee and calf.

He rose clumsily. His leg felt numb and unreliable. He had to look down to see that his right foot had actually swung forward and stopped where he wanted it to stop. He was drenched in blood, his own and his enemy's, and his throat was so dry that the first time he tried to shout he made a sound like an old raven. He swallowed, swallowed again, worked bitter saliva into his mouth. Then he shouted into the chaos the hillside had become. Through the smoke and the drifting dust, over the shrieks of the wounded and the berserk, he shouted a name: *"Garm!"* He kept shouting, and he hobbled forward on the numb leg, slipping in the blood that had filled his moccasin.

Briefly he glimpsed Garm's pale head above the fray, bobbing and weaving as the man fought, disappearing and reappearing as he twisted and thrust at the growing throng of Alcheringian warriors. Once he saw Garm look directly at him, his gray eyes pale with fury. He saw him raise his lance in challenge. But then the tide of battle separated them, and even while Asa cried, "No! No!" and hobbled forward, the Alcheringians with Thorel roaring at their head had rallied, and counterattacked. The Kaniks fled. The battle broke into a dozen skirmishes along the path and across the Larl. Some of the Alcheringians leaped onto captured horses, and the curses of pursuit faded into wind and distance.

"No," Asa said. Nothing had been more important than fighting Garm, although he did not know why.

He sank. Earth tilted. Pain came like the steady breeze and pulsing waves that announce a storm. He tried to sit, but he could not. The wings of the hillside rose and enfolded him, and he dropped forward and laid his face gratefully on the warm breast of earth.

With infection came fever, and Asa knew that he was dying. He had seen many others die this way, of suppurating wounds turned gangrenous and reeking. Then, delirious, he had no recollection of a long period in which he drifted, sometimes silent, sometimes raging and burning, except for that moment when he grew conscious of the chanting of Romoke, and lifted his head to find the old shaman's solemn face bent over his leg, bent to the sucking pipe that brushed the angry edges of his wound. A soft drum thumped somewhere outside the lodge.

"No," he said to Romoke, quite distinctly, although the sweat beaded on his brow with the effort it required to focus his eyes. "Even if I die, do not take off my leg."

He had had a premonition. He had seen himself running free along a sunset beach; and then, suddenly, an old man with a stick and a single leg, hopping heronlike backward from the rising tide. Somehow he lifted his hand to point at the shaman. "Even if I die, Romoke. On your honor!"

The cadaverous old shaman had nodded, furtively slipping back into its sheath the keen obsidian knife he had brought to do the job that very night, when the moon was right.

Then for a long time Asa knew nothing.

When he grew conscious again he was lying in the sunlight in the doorway of his lodge. There was no more pain. He felt light and cool, and he knew that he would live. He was hungry.

Aware of someone else, he turned his head, expecting to see Romoke perhaps, or Rani, or another of the Nine.

Persis was with him.

She sat cross-legged beside the fire, wearing a fresh garment made from new, clean buckskin. She was sewing. When she saw him move, she smiled. For several moments neither spoke.

Then Asa asked, "Why?"

"Say that I dream," Persis said, setting down her work and leaning forward to offer him cool water. "Say that in my dream you called me."

Asa tried to sit up but could not. She cradled his head and brushed away with the back of her hand the trickle of water that spilled across his cheek when he drank. "Dreams," he said when she had laid his head down on its cushion again, "are not enough."

"Also, the old man came." She smiled and mimicked a beard, a staff, a stoop-shouldered gait.

"Jared."

"Yes. He said you had need of me, and he brought me here. He is a very wise old man."

"Even that is not enough," Asa said.

Persis set the bark cup back on its shelf. She gathered her sewing into her lap. "When I heard you had been hurt I was afraid. I wanted to be with you." She brushed the hair back from her face. "It is something I cannot explain."

Asa wanted to keep looking at her, but his eyes would not stay open. Her features blurred. Streaming through the smoke flaps, sunlight lit her hair like the sea. "Garm?"

"He is very far away," she said, "and he has put a great gulf of pride between us. I no longer think of him."

Asa extended his hand into a growing darkness and felt it taken gently in both of hers. He slept.

When he awoke he was much stronger and could prop himself up on an elbow while Persis fed him broth. He found that his leg was healing well, and although he would always carry a livid scar he would not be crippled; he would run again. Gently he raised the leg and flexed it. He laughed.

"Jared did that," Persis said.

He looked at her.

"Jared cured you."

The laughter ceased. "How?"

"He brought medicines. Two were for your wound, a powder and a salve. And he brought little pebbles"—she made a small circle with her thumb and forefinger—"that crumbled into water. He named these things, but they were strange, like the names of old gods, and I do not remember them. They came in strange containers—such things as the Old Ones might have used. He said to tell you that they were gifts from another time."

Asa struck the earth hard. "Mysteries! Where are they, these containers?"

Persis pointed to the sea. "He said that if you got well I was to destroy them, and never tell anyone but you. I have done that."

Rage was a hot flame in the center of Asa's chest. So, now he owed his life to Jared! To *them*! "What else?"

"He said you would be very angry, but that he would return and talk with you, and that he would answer all your questions then."

"When?"

Persis shrugged and opened her hands. "When you were well."

* * *

He came on the ninth day. Through the doorway Asa saw
him approaching slowly up the path from the main encampment, saw him stopping to speak to children, saw him pausing
with Rusl and Kenet where they sat together staring at the sea.
Rani had been sitting with Asa inside the shadow of the lodge,
but he moved out and away at the old man's approach, angling
across the meadows toward the hills.

Because they came and went in mystery, wanderers brought
unease to an encampment—unease but also a lifting of the
spirit, for as long as they traveled they bore hope with them,
hope that beyond the Waysts, beyond the sea, there was something more than chaos.

They were never asked questions.

Jared stood in the doorway, blocking sunlight.

Asa asked, "Why did you save me?"

"Say that the gods have plans." He stooped and entered,
settling himself with difficulty.

"No! I have my own plans! I have no need of the gods'!"

"Then say that I love you," Jared said quietly. He seemed
very tired. He dipped water from the hide bucket and drank
deeply.

"Why? . . ."

"Ah. *Why?*" The old man's eyes flickered under their heavy
brow. "The most dangerous word. The most dangerous question."

"But if I ask it, Jared? If I keep asking, will I become like
Rusl? Like Kenet? Will you do *that* to me? Will you make
me—*happy?*"

"Is happiness so terrible, then?"

"For some. Some ought not to be merely happy, for their
life is in the quest. To receive is to die."

"Hunters," Jared said.

"If you like."

Jared smiled and nodded. He was caressing the palm of his
left hand with the fingertips of his right, and for several minutes
he gazed down, contemplating this circular action. "Imagine,"
he said to Asa at last, "that you begin a long journey with three
children—"

"Oh, no! Please. No stories. No parables!"

Jared's head snapped up. His eyes were no longer smiling,
but were as stern as black agate in the wild gray of his hair

and brows. "I thought you were interested in the truth," he said
very softly.

"The plain truth."

"Plain truths," Jared said unblinking, "are like arrows meant
for enemies. Fool! Do you imagine that any truth can be *told*,
like a mere fact? Are you so innocent that you think stories
are meant for children, and not for wise men?"

Asa flushed. "I'm sorry," he said.

"A journey," Jared continued, "with three boys. You do not
know your destination, but you know the direction in which
you must go. You know also that time is very important. There
is no time to be lost.

"Your way is rich in diversions, and the children are lured
to them. One sees, far off, a delectable enticement. Perhaps it
is a waterfall splashing. Perhaps it is easy food, when there
has been none for days. *You* know, although he does not, that
danger lurks in the valleys between, perhaps predators, perhaps
the perils of the land itself, perhaps the poisons of the Old
Ones.

"So, you stop him. For his own safety, and for the good of
the journey. How? Perhaps you drive him ahead of you, or
leash him and drag him behind. Perhaps you make him content
with what he has, so that he remains docilely on the path.

"You continue, and in a little while, farther on, the second
child is enticed as the first had been. Again you see that the
journey to what he wants is fraught with dire peril, for him
and for you all. In fact, if he leaves, the journey must end.
So, once again, with love and regret, you restrain him. Perhaps
you show him that there are other delights near at hand, or . . ."
Jared hesitated, rubbing a pain along his ribs, along his belly.
". . . perhaps you blinker him so that for the rest of his life he
will see only one road, straight ahead, and only one reward at
the end of it."

"Perhaps a sunrise," Asa said, thinking of Rusl and Kenet
beside the sea. "Perhaps a seal on a rock. Perhaps a loon."

"There are worse things, Asa," Jared said, watching him
intently. "But I have not finished my story.

"The journey proceeds. The third boy is the most curious
of all, the most observant, perhaps the brightest. Also, he
knows something of human pain.

"You come to a fork in the trail. Here the boy stops and
will go no farther. He wishes to travel alone. Once again you

know that there is great peril in this, both for him and for those who will follow him. You urge him to stay with you. You remind him that you have safely traveled this far together. You do all you can, but at last dusk comes and you have no more time. You ask him then what he will do. And he replies . . ." Jared raised his eyebrows, waiting.

"With a question," Asa said. "He asks, 'Is your way more interesting?' "

Jared laughed sorrowfully. "Oh yes, you assure him that it is infinitely more interesting. But you tell him, also, that the Old Ones had a curse: *May you live in the most interesting of times.*"

"Then he will go with you, because he wants to know."

"Because he *must* know. Because unknowing is like a gnawing in his stomach. Because," Jared said, "he is man, a wondering animal."

Through the doorway Jared saw Persis returning across the meadows, and he smiled wistfully watching the youthful ease with which she moved as she bore the panniers of food she had gathered. For a few moments the sight of her wafted him far, far away, to another place and another time. "Yura . . ." he said, so softly that Asa scarcely heard him. Then he sighed and stood up. "Get well. I shall be back in twenty days, perhaps before, and then we shall travel together."

He embraced Persis as she arrived and he made some remark about Kanik passion, rolling his eyes heavenward, and for the first time Asa saw Persis laugh. Still with his arm around the woman, the old man reached down for Asa's hand, and he was suddenly serious again. "Stay together! Whatever else happens, do that! Only if you contrive to stay together, in spite of everything, will all the mistakes, and false starts, and terrible accidents finally make sense." Then he raised two fingers to them, and bent down to pass through the doorway.

They watched him cross the meadows and slowly ascend the hillside to the pass.

Later that night, when the door had been fastened shut and the fire had crumbled to embers, their bodies joined in what for both was but another stage in the most natural of all progressions. Her arched fingers pressed against that place where she had once threatened to sink a knife; and Asa realized, among many other things, why it was that in the battle which had nearly slain him, he had wanted so desperately to conquer Garm.

EIGHT

COMPARED TO OTHER OFFICES IN THE ASGARD CENTRAL COM-
plex—Shem's, for example, or Horvath's—Moran's is opu-
lent. Lush plants festoon its windows and flourish around the
whirlpool bath which awaits him, idling under its starlight, in
the adjoining living quarters. Deep couches reach languorously
from the walls, and a real fire, feeding on sticks laboriously
gathered by a foraging patrol, flickers in the fireplace directly
across from the desk. "We all have our little peculiarities,"
Moran replied to the patrol leader's disgruntled comment about
adequate central heating, and although he chuckled his little
eyes shone bright. "Live and scratch, Captain, live and scratch!
When you're dead the itching will stop!"

He specified cedar. Cedar asserted itself satisfyingly with
myriad tiny explosions and released in its smoke the perfumed
memories of other centuries.

Kanik lances hang above the fireplace, together with a large
Montayner alpenhorn and a selection of choice Abibone boom-
erangs. Thick carpeting muffles all sound in the room except
the relentless, silken ticking of clocks and the occasional whisper of the radio monitor.

The dinner he has ordered sits ready on its warming plate,
for he did not answer the bell and go with the others at 1700
to dine in the refectory. He prefers his own silences. When he
has assimilated the information he received from his Kanik
peregrinus that afternoon, and when he has decided on a course
of action, then he will eat the dinner before his fire, and he
will take his bath, and he will go to sleep under the skylight
that permits him to watch the stars turning through their seasons.

111

Moran has been sitting immobile for over an hour, his fingertips touching contemplatively. Occasionally his index fingers brush his lips and his fringe of auburn mustache. At last he sighs heavily, presses buttons on his desk console, and speaks into its small microphone.

"Request to SKULD, please."

"Yes, sir?"

"Two-year projections on three hypotheses:

"First, effects on Kaniks assuming that Regulae is kept strictly intact and that Alcheringian horse/women raids continue under Arborea Dispensation Number SGU-18-rt-64.

"Second, effects on Alcheringia assuming repeal of that dispensation. Extend that: effects on Norriya.

"Third . . ." There is a long pause.

"Sir?"

"Third, effects on Norriya and on the Project if Alcheringia were obliterated."

"Very good, sir."

"Please see that SKULD has access to the following files . . ." Moran reads a series of numbers.

"Very good, sir. Shall I call you later this evening with the projections?"

"Yes," Moran says. "Yes. Do that."

And so, shortly after he has eaten and bathed, his monitor summons him once again. "I have the SKULD printouts, sir."

"Go ahead."

"On Number One, SKULD projects increasing restiveness and internal fragmentation within the twenty-four months stipulated. Beyond that, SKULD projects severe stress on Kanik mores, possibly leading to terminal disruption."

"Two?"

"Inbreeding is inevitable, with obvious results beyond the two-year limitation."

"And three?"

"Stabilization."

"What?"

"Stabilization of Norriya, sir. You *did* request effects on Norriya?"

"Yes."

"And that is SKULD's projection. Norriya would be stabilized if Alcheringia were obliterated."

Moran sits. He is hot from the bath. He is not sure whether

the moisture streaming down his ample neck is sweat or bath-water.

"Do you want the full printout tonight, sir?"

"The morning will be fine."

"Very good, sir. Have a good night."

In bed, Moran watches the stars. An onerous load has been taken from him. He wishes, briefly, that the strict oath of the dream master permitted female companionship. He recalls fleetingly agreeable sensations when he was young, in the skin days, among the tribes . . .

He sleeps.

NINE

DESPITE HIS PROMISE, JARED DID NOT RETURN IN TWENTY days. Or in thirty.

Asa's wounds healed and he gained strength rapidly, but his leg remained stiff and only gradually loosened with exercise. Each day he walked on the beach, each day a little farther, until at last he could run a few hobbling steps. Sometimes Rani came to walk with him, and sometimes one of the others. Kenet and Rusl would come together and sit or walk with him in silence. Other Alcheringians of both clans brought meat to supplement what Persis had gathered, until Asa could hunt again.

Quietly, watching Rusl and Kenet, Asa made a resolution: If Jared had not returned by mid-September, he would go alone back to the forbidden beach, and he would somehow draw the silver spider out of its lair, and he would fight it and destroy it.

Thorel's visits disturbed him. Others had accepted Persis

and acknowledged their changed relationship. Thorel did not. To him she was still the Kanik slave, and common property. He watched the woman in such a way that Asa finally had to say to him, "My friend. Thorel. Things have changed with Persis. She is no longer one of the Kanik women. She has made a decision." Thorel had smiled and nodded, but Asa grew even more uncomfortable, for he had seen many times before how words could slide off Thorel and lose all meaning. After a few such visits, Persis would leave the lodge and not return until after the big man had gone.

One evening in the second week of September, when Asa's leg had healed completely, he returned from a day-long hunt. He had shot two rabbits. Laughing, he held them up so that Persis could see them through the dusk. She was sitting hunched over, close to the lodge, and she did not move. When he knelt beside her he saw that her mouth was swollen and bleeding. A raw bruise covered her cheek, and there were ugly red welts on her throat and neck. She sat with her arms folded across her belly.

Asa touched her hair. He touched her cheek.

A gulf opened. He had done this before. He had knelt before to comfort a hurt woman. He had . . . *NO!* he said to the spell that was claiming him. *NO! NOT YET!*

He stood and strode back down the path to the camp, breaking into a run as he drew closer to Thorel's lodge, and beginning to shout the other man's name. He was aware that people were speaking to him, but he did not hear what they said. He was aware that someone reached for him, sought to hold him back, but he broke loose. He was aware too of Thorel's laughter ahead, and he saw him rising up, still smiling, from beside the fire where he had been crouched talking with other men.

"Brothers!" Thorel called to him, holding up his palms, appealing to all the rules of the Nines, all the rules of sharing. He was still smiling. "Brothers, Asa!"

But when he saw that there was no placating Asa's rage, Thorel moved fast. His charge was a bear's, shoulders dropped and arms hung low until the last instant when they rose to crash down on his victim. Asa waited for that instant, and when Thorel's paws groped for him he hurled himself against the big man's pumping shins. Asa grunted with the pain in his ribs and shoulder blades, but when he leapt to his feet, Thorel was sprawled in the dust. He came up fast, roaring, and lunged again. Again Asa dodged, dancing sideways, and brought clenched fists down on Thorel's neck, once, twice, as he reeled past. The blows were glancing, weakened by Asa's backward momentum, but still strong enough to knock Thorel off balance for several awkward strides, his feet slapping the packed earth, until he crashed down once again.

This time he rose more slowly and advanced more warily. Asa knew that he must at all costs avoid those arms, but he could not. When he feinted, Thorel anticipated him, and he could not pull back fast enough. Thorel's arms locked around his waist, and he roared with triumphant laughter. He turned slowly, showing his catch to the crowd, and as he turned he squeezed. Breath left Asa and he could not draw it back. Thorel's fists crushed his backbone. The world spun, trees, lodges, sea and sky, and all the watching faces, like objects jumbled in a child's rattle. Silence came. Color drained out of the earth. He knew that in moments he would lose consciousness.

Desperately he groped for the tendons of Thorel's neck and squeezed with all his remaining strength. The big man bellowed, and his arms slackened just enough to let Asa draw breath, to send sudden energy coursing like flames through his muscles, and when he squeezed again his grip was strong enough to paralyze Thorel's upper body. He held that grip until Thorel fell to his knees, and he released it only to deliver a bludgeoning neck blow that flattened him.

Asa fell on him as he tried to rise, slamming his head against the packed earth. He seized Thorel's hair and shoulder and hauled him over on his back. The man's beard and throat were slippery with blood and his eyes rolled groggily, but enough comprehension remained that Asa knew Thorel heard him when he hissed, "I . . . *love* her!" Then his hands closed around Thorel's neck and he began to beat the great head rhythmically on the ground, and long after Thorel's tongue had lolled out of his bloody mouth and his eyes had lost all consciousness, and long after the other men had dragged him off, Asa was still shouting as if the three words were a magic formula which must never be forgotton, "I *love* her! I *love* her! I *love* her!"

The hands that restrained him had done so before, in another time, and the faces, and Thorel trying to sit up, and the shouts— all, all were familiar. He was aware of the gods moving on the edges of the abyss that he contained, and then he was aware of nothing else . . .

* * *

That summer had been fruitful for the clans of Alcheringia. Halibut abounded. Salmon swarmed into the river weirs, and only a few were morphs, unfit to eat. Sea hunters had killed several porpoises, enough to cut into several hundred long, thin strips that they had cured over the slow fires. Other hunts had also been successful, so by the time the geese and ducks began to move southward, filling the morning marshes with cold cries, the families were well provided against the coming winter.

One by one, over the weeks of autumn, after the last of the council fires, the lodges were taken down and folded, and the poles stacked where they could be found in another spring. One by one the families filled their packs and baskets and turned inland, up the trail that wound beside the river. Some would have a two- or three-week journey to their traditional winter hunting grounds. No ceremonies attended these departures; a family simply decided when to go and went, usually at daybreak, swiftly, saying good-byes to whoever else was up and about.

By the end of the second week in October, only a single lodge remained standing in Alcheringia—the lodge of Asa and Persis. They were waiting for Jared.

He came in late October; there was ice on the pools among the rocks. He was startlingly changed. Seeing him descend the path beside the river, Asa thought he had aged twenty years. Time had caught him. He had grown bent, shriveled, myopic, hopelessly enfeebled. He cradled a pain in his belly. Every step hurt.

Asa would never know where he had been or what had brought on this change. He went out to greet him, and when he heard his name called Jared stopped walking. Had anyone been close enough to him they would have heard him say, his voice as small as a bird's that has dropped out of the wind into a great forest, "Well, then, I have arrived."

He was almost blind. At most he could distinguish a paleness with shadows moving through it. Asa broke all decorum and protocol by embracing the old man. His cheeks were wet. "You told me twenty days," he said gruffly.

"The trails have grown longer," Jared said.

"We were afraid—"

"That I was human? That I might die? We think alike. I was worried about that, too!" His laughter was the startled cry of a bird discovering beneath him a feral presence.

He slept for a night and a day in Asa's lodge, rising only to take a little broth that Persis had prepared for him. "He is going to the place of no deciding," she said. On the second evening he had energy to talk.

"Not long now," he said.

"You have medicines," Asa said, showing the cleanly healed wound in his leg. "Use them."

Jared wheezed in laughter. "There is no medicine for age, nor will you want one when you come to this place." He stretched cramped hands into the warmth of the fire and massaged them gently. He was alternately smiling and grimacing. "Oh dear," he said. "Oh dear, oh dear."

Asa drew a warm robe around the old man's shoulders.

"I have not forgotten," Jared said suddenly, as if reading his thoughts. "That is, I have not forgotten that I promised to answer your questions. But I'm afraid I'm forgetting the answers."

"No matter," Asa said.

"But it *does* matter." Jared's eyes opened unnaturally wide and searched until he had found the contours of the fire. He drew the cloak tightly around him, as if he were girding for a struggle. "Yes. And we should wait no longer. Let's begin."

Asa hesitated. "You . . . you'll tell me the truth?"

"Of course."

"You told me once that truths were arrows, and not for friends."

"Some truths." Jared smiled. "Sometimes. Not these. Not now."

"Very well. My father." Asa watched closely, but the old man's expression never changed.

"Yes?"

"My mother said that he was not Alcheringian."

"Well, that is possible." He laughed abruptly. "Such a beginning! Next you will ask me if men and women are human, and have passions."

"My mother said that my father came . . . came from the sea."

"So," Jared said. "A Yulok? One of the sea traders?"

"No. She said that he was brought to land by a strange beast such as she had never seen. She said that it growled constantly, and that its eyes gave their own light."

Jared sat unmoving. He said nothing.

"It was one of the god-boats, wasn't it, Jared? Wasn't it?"

Jared frowned, gathering memories, faces, fragments scattered in time. His trembling fingers reached out to touch Asa's face, across the brow, across the eyes.

"You know my father."

"Perhaps," Jared said. "Soon, in time, you shall meet him." His head suddenly tilted forward, and he lacked the strength to lift it. They laid him down. Persis tucked the robe around him, and it seemed that he had fallen asleep; but then a scrawny hand emerged from the covering, beckoning to Asa. "There is a place I would go," Jared whispered when Asa leaned close. "You must be my legs."

They left at dawn. It was a dismal morning, with a chill, wind-borne drizzle off the sea. But Jared had weakened even further overnight, and he did not want to wait. Dying, full of bone-hurt, he said that any weather, even the rain on his face, was the last of his blessings.

So they went. Persis had made a kind of sling, and Asa carried him like a child on his back. Persis wept. Jared took her head in his old hands and kissed her. "All is well," he said. "Truly. Death is the least of my worries."

The way led north along the coast, through the meadows. "Tell me all you see," Jared said, his head on Asa's shoulder, and Asa did that, describing the gusty gray of the sea, and the seals on rocks below, and the clusters of late ducks browsing. He was not sure whether the old man heard, because when he paused Jared said, "She is a good woman. She will change with you, and you will have splendid children. But you must keep together and beware the world! Do you hear? Do you? The world will dull you, if you let it. Sometimes you may be unsure of your love. Then above all you must stay together by habit, by rote, blindly, until the storm has passed. Sometimes you will feel nothing at all, and then you will think your love has died. You must keep together then above all, and the air will move again, and your love will return. Promise me you will do that."

Asa nodded.

"Promise!"

"I promise," Asa said.

They were following the same path by which Jared had led Kenet across the Gerumbian peninsula and out to the place where the silver spider had risen from the moss. For a time Asa thought that they were returning to that spot, but Jared gave him very precise instructions which took them instead along the south shore of the peninsula and by late afternoon brought them to a secluded upland meadow.

An overgrown ring of stones marked the place where a lodge had once stood. In the center lay the charcoal of a very old fire. "Around the corner of the north side, there is a little stream," Jared said. Sure enough, a rivulet tumbled off the rocks there and fell into mist toward the sea, a hundred feet below.

"And at the back there is a little cairn. It will be beside a small pine."

Asa found the cairn, tumbled by frosts and animals, overgrown. The pine was no longer small; it was a proud tree with forty years of growth between its present state and Jared's recollection of it.

"The cairn," Jared asked. "There is a small space to the north?"

"Yes," Asa lied. To the north rose a dense tangle of bushes. "It is just as you remember it."

"Bury me there," Jared said. "When the time comes."

After a while, the path to the waning moon stretched on a languid sea. Side by side they faced this immense serenity that Jared could not see. "I promised to answer your questions," the old man said, "and now I no longer have time to do so. But you must not stop asking. Never. You are right: That is what being human means. Another will come after me to answer your questions. And some of those answers will be satisfactory." He released a burst of the old laughter that Asa recalled from childhood. He had thought then that the laughter was mocking; he thought now it was full of surprise.

Later, Asa slept. When he awoke the fire had crumbled to embers and the night had turned high and cold. To the northeast, the aurora flickered like lambent milk in a bowl of stars. At the base of this majesty rose an edge of destroying dawn.

Jared was reciting his death chant in a frail and wavering voice, and Asa knew that when he had finished he would never speak again.

> "My Yura, my love,
>   Is it your voice calling in the seawind,

Calling in the boughs of the tamarack?
Call louder, love,
So I may be small in the greatness of your
  voice,
So I may escape this prison.

My Yura, my love,
Is it your body running in the white sand,
Lying amid the boughs of the tamarack?
Give me your body, love,
So I may be whole in the wonder of your
  passion,
So I may escape this prison.

My Yura, my love,
Are these your tears on my hands?
Do you weep for the drifted time?
For the counted years?
Smile, love. Hold me, love.
We shall pass beyond all seasons, now,
And escape this prison . . ."

It took Asa most of the overcast morning to clear away the
tangle of bushes and to hollow out a grave. He laid the old
man in the flexed position he would have kept in his mother's
womb, and beside him he placed the few tools and amulets
that he found in his pack, keeping out only one item. Over the
body and possessions he sprinkled the red ocher that Jared had
kept ready, and then he filled the grave, using stones to dis-
courage animals.

By the time he had finished, a drizzle had again begun to
sift through the evergreens. In the rain he labored through the
rest of the day to haul stones from the beach and construct a
second cairn beside the first.

At dusk, he built the fire again and kept his vigil beside the
burying place throughout the night.

The one item he had kept out of Jared's grave was a little black
box festooned with buttons cunningly inset so that they could not
be accidentally moved. Asa placed this box beside the fire and
sat regarding it for a long time before he touched it. The button
he selected moved down, up, and nothing happened.

Nothing at all.

He tried another, and another. Still nothing.

He then tried a switch, and this time, wrapped in a sound
like a small fire crackling, a voice spoke to him. "Come in . . ."
it said. "Come in . . ."

Asa recoiled from the thing, and as he did so he heard a roaring behind him, a roaring that he thought at first came from deep in the hillside but that a moment later swelled into a thundering, hissing swoop like a hundred owls, sending him frantically tumbling into the underbrush in a bright white light, scrambling from the god-talons that would seize him.

But there was no shock. No pain.

The light blinked out. The roaring diminished as the thing passed out across the ocean, low over the water, and Asa saw eyes that were red and green and white revolving about each other and lifting in a measured dance until they vanished among the clouds.

The box continued to squawk. Asa flicked the little switch with the tip of his knife and the words ceased. He sat quietly until his fear and his anger had subsided. Then he picked the box up and put it into his own pack.

Early the next morning, he said his final good-bye to Jared and turned back up the trail. But when he reached the fork in the overgrown paths on top of the bluffs, he headed not south, toward Alcheringia, but north, across the neck of the Gerumbian peninsula. At noon he reached the place where the spindly silver thing had risen from the moss. Cautiously he made his way down the hillside to the little plateau and stood where Jared had stood. Before him the ground lay serene and apparently undisturbed; nothing indicated what lurked beneath.

Softly he laid down his pack and removed the black box. He switched it on, and a tiny red eye glowed. He slipped out of his jacket. He pulled the battle-ax from his belt and gripped its stout ash handle. He braced himself.

He said, "Now, gods, this is a thing between you and me. If you would kill me, then try to do it now. If you would make me childish like Rusl and Kenet, then do it now—*if you can!*"

When he said this, he leaned forward and touched the first button. Nothing happened. He touched the second. Nothing happened for the first eight buttons.

But when he touched the ninth the ground moved.

Precisely where it had opened to Jared, ten paces in front of Asa, a rectangle of earth sank and vanished. Coiled and gleaming, the silver spider rose. On its top a small sensor revolved, swept past Asa, hesitated, then came back and fixed on him.

The thing stood and, with horrid grace, ran like an effete dancer across the intervening space, its arms outstretched.

Asa did not wait for it to reach him. He ducked beneath the extended arms, feinted to his left, lunged forward, and struck the creature a hard, two-handed blow on what, on an animal, would have been its knee. He felt the ax go in and heard a squeal as the torn edges of the silver stuff rasped on stone. He pulled away, rolled, and was on his feet before the creature toppled.

It had half turned to follow him, and it did not collapse all at once, for the shattered limb still partially supported it. The whirling sensor had rediscovered him and continued to whisk signals into the creature's brain, signals to which it tried desperately to respond. The good leg pumped futilely as it went down, and the shattered stump clawed at the foliage, hopelessly entangling the trailing shank.

Asa danced around it, looking for his opening. The sensor was still twisting to follow him, and the groping arms reached out with venomous pads. The things was on its back, still thrashing. Asa danced in, struck once, twice, and dodged away, but not before one of the pads had brushed his shoulder. It was very cold, and in moments his upper arm had lost all feeling. However, he had chopped an arm off the creature—not cleanly, for the severed portion flapped from bright ligaments. On his next attack he severed another arm and smashed the sensor, and the creature lay at his mercy.

He crushed its head. Its eyes shattered, pieces of the sensor whirled away into the grass, and the skull buckled and split, spilling a thousand woven wires. Blow by blow he tore and severed these, until the motions of the thing dwindled to spastic twitches and finally ceased. A hiss of something escaping came from its breast.

Gasping, Asa bent over with his elbows on his knees until he had recovered his breath, and then, still wary, slowly rubbing the feeling back into his shoulder, he circled the corpse of his enemy.

From the tip of a nearby fir, a raven that had witnessed the whole conflict made a single monosyllabic comment and flapped away.

Without ceremony Asa kicked the remains of the thing onto its platform, keeping out only a few pieces that he gathered into his pack. Then he pressed buttons on the little box until the platform began to descend. At the last moment he tossed the box in as well.

The ground closed.

"Asa!" he said, turning to the Islands of the Gods, lying like gray giants in the mist. "Asa!"

He gathered his pack and his jacket and headed back up the trail. He went slowly at first, because of the heat in the open places, but when he reached the cool forest he began to run.

Once he leaped high. Once he clapped his hands and shouted.

TEN

AT 1600 HOURS, SHEM RECEIVES THE FIRST OF THREE MES-SAGES.

Sunlight has begun to bend through the tall pines beyond the western windows, and to splash in mottled patches across the carpeting of his office. All is quiet except for the music by which he is working, the Mozart bassoon concerto. The bassoon romps with the sun. Shem follows its dance and smiles. He has a special fondness for the bassoon, the most grotesque of the Old Ones' instruments.

A small bell rings.

"Yes?"

"Sorry to disturb you, sir. This is the peregrini monitor. We have an anomaly."

"What's happened?"

"It's what *hasn't* happened, sir. We've had no signal for twenty-four hours from the Alcheringian peregrinus."

"Jared."

"Something's wrong, sir. He's never missed."

"You've tried emergency procedures?"

"Yes, sir. No response."

"I want a close air search of the following area . . ." Shem consults his map and gives sectors. His foot has begun to throb with a dozen separate agonies.

"The *whole area*, sir?"

"Yes, dammit! Can't you read the order?"

"Yes sir. Very good, sir."

"One other thing. I want to speak to the pilot."

"I'll establish the link, sir. One moment, please."

Static clicks and murmurs like insects in the speaker, and while he listens to it, and to the voice of the controller reaching out to a patrol somewhere over the mainland, Shem remembers precisely where Yura was buried, so that when the pilot's voice comes through he is able to take over from the controller.

"Hello, Yggdrasil Control, this is Hugin Four Five. Go ahead, please."

"Hugin Four Five, this is Yggdrasil. Your position, please."

"Coordinates sixty-five dash four by D for Devil two. Course two six four. Over."

"Stand by, Four Five ... Alter course to two three two. Make a low-altitude pass across the coast at coordinates sixty-four dash nine by D one. Lights and camera. Transmit, please. Over."

"Roger, Yggdrasil. Here goes. Lights. Camera. Are you receiving? Over."

A blurred line appears at the top of Shem's screen, separating a pale darkness from a deeper darkness. "Receiving," Shem says. And then, as the aircraft loses speed and altitude, and as the powerful searchlights in its wings and belly touch the forest, Shem sees details of individual hillsides, copses, and plateaus.

The pilot is good. He holds his course and drops as low as he dares to give his superiors what they want, almost brushing the treetops on the last hills and crossing the small nest of meadows on the Gerumbian isthmus at under two hundred feet.

Spotlights flood these little pockets of night with a sudden blaze of high noon, and in the moment of their passing, Shem's attention is caught by the glow of a campfire on one of them. Peering closer, he sees two mounds or rocks, one old and overgrown, the other fresh. He sees also a figure scrambling for cover. Then the land vanishes off the bottom of the screen, and there is only the sea and the cloud-flecked horizon.

"Hello, Yggdrasil. Shall I make another pass?"

"Negative, Four Five. Thank you. Out."

Shem stills the voices and slumps heavily into the silence and the dusk, waiting.

The second message comes half an hour later.

"Sir, we've received a signal on Jared's frequency."

"What was it?"

"Unintelligible, sir. Just a fleeting signal."

"An accident."

"I think so, sir. Yes."

"Thank you."

Shem sits in darkness. The bassoon has gone, and the hastening away of seconds has replaced it. He says, "Old friend, one day when there is time you will have a proper tribute. I promise."

The third message comes next morning.

"We've lost a clinician, sir."

"Earthquake?" Shem asks. "Flood? Landslide?"

"None, sir. It was an attack. Deliberate aboriginal attack. See for yourself."

The screen lights even while Shem struggles into his gown and limps across to peer at it. A young man approaches in a fighter's crouch, dodges, moves in fast under the eye of the camera. Then the camera lurches violently, tumbles earth and sky and, quivering, shows nothing but a close-up clump of milkweed. "How did he get it out . . ." And then he remembers that garbled signal, and he knows the answer.

Shem holds his breath as he watches the short, lethal battle through the dispassionate eye of the clinician-victim as it expires, sees twice more the attacking man laughing, and finally the flash of something descending into the lens. Then nothing—except, for a few moments, an eerie blip across the screen like the electronic fluttering of a dying heart.

Shem exhales in a long, soft whistle.

"Lord!" says the controller, forgetting that his microphone to Shem is still open. "How about that! There is one freaked-out aborr!"

Shem draws a note pad toward him and on it he writes the name of the young man whom he has recognized: ASA.

He writes it large, like a shout.

He circles it.

ELEVEN

IN LATE OCTOBER, ASA AND PERSIS AT LAST FOLDED THEIR lodge and turned toward the interior. Gales and flood tides had already begun to scour all traces of human occupation from Alcheringia, leaving only the charred stone fire rings and clusters of lodgepoles leaning forlornly against swaying trees. Leaves and needles covered the paths. Scavengers and incessant drizzle crumbled the garbage heaps back into earth.

The land was being cleansed.

The evening before they departed, Asa and Persis walked through the campsite and a mile up the Alcher. Light snow glittered in the air.

"Why do you move?" she asked, huddled against him as they turned to look down over the empty meadows.

"The Tabuly," Asa replied. "The sixth law: It is forbidden to inhabit one place more than six months."

She wasn't satisfied. "But there must be more reason than just the *law*. There must be a *real* reason."

They both laughed.

"You've heard what's said at the council fires. You know what the elders think. For them, the law *is* enough. It must be obeyed. Besides, it's become a custom. It's the way we live."

"And die," Persis said, hunched against the cold wind, bobbing on her toes. "Wouldn't the sick and the old live longer without these journeys? And wouldn't you *all* be better off together, instead of breaking up into so many vulnerable little groups?"

"Shh," Asa said mockingly, peering around for gods eavesdropping. "You're talking heresy! You'll be expelled!"

She was suddenly serious. "I wouldn't want that," she said. "Not unless you came too."

The next morning they left together, carrying what they owned. Their journey to the southeastern foothills would take three days. Some Alcheringians had gone even farther east, to traditional wintering grounds in the plain itself—sheltered little valleys through which flowed tributaries of the Larl. Sometimes their winter hunts brought them close to the Montayners; sometimes, to the Kaniks.

Asa's place was among the foothills, beside a little lake. Asa's grandfather had always brought him and his mother here, but Asa would never know whether the old man had chosen the place himself or whether it had been picked by some remote ancestor. In any case, it was good. It was sheltered from all winds, and had adequate supplies of water and fuel close by. Deer yarded in the thick forest not far off, and caribou sought refuge in the forest. All the winters that Asa could remember had been good, for the family had been warm and well fed.

This year, hard frost came early. Asa had trouble driving pegs, and only a few days after their lodge was erected it was wrapped in snow waist-high. More came, and more, and by the shortest day the lodge was covered to its smokehole, and Asa and Persis entered and left through a long tunnel.

Inside, all was comfortable. They had food, they had fuel. A thick, springy pad of spruce and tamarack boughs insulated the whole floor. Persis changed it frequently, so the warm air inside was always sweet and fresh. Over this carpet lay a blanket of soft hides. Despite the vicious cold beyond them in the forest, and the hungry winds that came searching across the plains, they were warm and content. Their metabolisms slowed, like hibernating animals'. They spent much time in their sleeping-robe, embracing, mesmerized by the shadows among the lodgepoles. "We are learning what it is to be a man and a woman," Persis said one night, pressing his face against her breasts. "There is no longer anyone between us and the thing to be learned."

They told tales. They told each other all that had happened in their short lives, for it had suddenly become very important that their lives intertwine as their bodies had done. And so Persis told him of her parents, and of her longing for horses, and of her dreams of them galloping across the plain in the moonlight, their manes adrift.

Once, during a long and hungry storm, when the wolves in desperation had grown more bold than ever before, and had come so close that their calls shredded his dreams like keen knives, he had awakened and, for the first time, asked her about Garm, for his eyes had joined the wolves' eyes in his dreams. She had swum up out of her sleep and murmured, "Asa, Asa, it was so long ago..."

But it was not long ago—less than a year—and for several nights after that he dreamed of Garm. Rather, he dreamed of the eyes of Garm, and of the way Garm had said, "I shall find you and kill you!" Always in those dreams, Garm was sleek and strong and well fed, a lithe, quick hunter who moved like a shadow among the trees. Always he took Persis back, laughing. Asa would waken sweating in the middle of a storm, or in the depths of a night so cold that trees burst open, and he would grope frantically for her beside him and then, unable to sleep again, feed more fuel on the fire, and draw his weapons close to him, and listen.

When at last she spoke of Garm and of what she had once imagined to be her love for him, she gave Asa insight into Kanik society that he had lacked—a society propped up with pride and with taut, neurotic notions of personal honor. If Garm came, she said, it would not be because he wanted her, Persis, but because Asa and the Alcheringian Nine had insulted him by stealing his property. It would be because of pride. Kanik pride.

And Asa understood that someday he must face that pride head-on and defeat it, for it would never rest, so long as both he and Garm lived.

Three times in the depths of that winter he had spells. When the walls of the lodge began to lift like wings, and the howls of the storm stretched into eerie god-calls, and the sense that he was infinitely old and wise overwhelmed him, then Persis would hold him close and rock him like a child as his mother had done when he was very small, and sometimes she would sing Kanik lullabies and kiss him while he sat frozen rigid in the grip of his spell.

Sometimes, she told him, he called his mother's name: Marieke.

Sometime, she said, she would like to know about his mother, and about what had become of her.

One night, Asa told her the story his mother had once told

him. He had never repeated this story, not even to Jared; all his life the story had seemed the one secure thing amid whirling uncertainties, for he believed his mother when she said, "Those of us who travel between two worlds know that it is only the *story* of the voyage that is real."

Marieke had often left him during his childhood. Her madness made her do it. Her madness made her wander off through the meadows and along the sea cliffs, drawn to the wilderness, and to the space, and to the tempests. "Marieke of the storms," the others called her, and those who had grown up with her recalled that she had always been pensive and withdrawn, given to unpredictable bursts of laughter and to strange moods of despair that would sweep over her even in the midst of play.

At such times she would simply go off by herself, and as she grew older her absences grew longer. The strange child became a strange woman, and although she was attractive and as skilled as the other women, no man had taken her for a mate. The young men shied away. "It is as if," one of them had once mused, "she has already been taken by another. It is as if she is married to her storms."

Some of the women, the truly superstitious, believed that Asa had been conceived by a storm, and they shunned him as they had shunned his mother, turning away their gray heads at his approach. Older and kindlier women, however, looked after Asa during his mother's absences and sometimes, by the firelight, searched the boy's sleeping face for the features of their men.

No one knew who Asa's father was. Marieke had never told. And for this reason, and because of his odd affliction, the boy had grown up in an air of mystery, set apart from the other children.

One night when Asa was ten, Marieke told her son very gently that she would soon be leaving him and that she would not return. She opened her jacket and showed Asa a place beneath her breast where there was a tumor the size of a gull's egg.

He knew that he was looking at her death, but he said, "Romoke..."

She laughed and shook her head. "No. Nothing will help."

And it was then that she told him that it was important that he know, now, about his father.

She said that his father had come from the sea.

She said that his father had been a god.

She said that there was no question, because she had lain with only one man in all her life.

This was what had happened: She had gone alone far north along the cliffs looking for the eggs of seabirds. She had intended to return long before sunset, but the day was cool and clear and she had kept walking through the beauty of it until sunset found her deep along the south shore of the fiord that penetrated Gerumbia.

She had simply stayed, rather than return in the dark. Often she had spent the night alone in remote places. She loved the night, the sounds of night, and its creatures. She loved watching the sea turn silver-black as the night spread over it.

She had built a small fire and had cooked some of the eggs she had gathered. Later, she slept. When she awoke the fire was cold and a thin moon hung above the sea. Her hair and clothing were wet with dew. She had been awakened by a sound like the droning of a mosquito, but louder, stronger. Only the gods in their journeys made such a noise. It came from the sea. At first she saw nothing, but then two stars appeared, red and green, moving on the surface. A third soon joined them, a bright, white star that swept the bay like a long finger. When the humming ceased, a dull little line of orange stars had appeared as well.

Despite all taboos and injunctions, she had gone down the bank and out onto the beach. But the thing had turned and returned the way it had come, its sound fading down the long fiord. Then, just as she was turning away in disappointment, a man had waded in through the surf, pulling a small leatherlike boat. The sea glittered against his thighs. She knew that he was a god, and she knew she had been brought to that place, that night.

She went forward to meet him.

She said that he had laughed first with surprise, later with pleasure. She said that he had been very gentle for such a large man. She said that he was young, only a little older than Marieke herself. He was on an errand for the gods, he told her the next morning, but he would return to this place, and she was to wait for him. He spoke her name in such a way that she knew he would not forget it.

She had waited, but he had not returned. She had waited two days, three days, a week, two.

At last, fearing that he had been slain among the Gerumbians, and that she would meet the same fate (for she had seen Gerumbian hunting parties moving toward her along the far cliffs of the fiord), she had returned to Alcheringia.

Later, when she went back to that place and looked for his boat in the little cave where he had hidden it, the boat was gone. Always afterward she believed that he lived, and would one day return for her.

She believed that with such naive trusting faith that Asa could not look into her eyes when she told the story; young though he was he knew enough of human callousness to see that his mother had been used, and at that moment, with this sudden new reason to despise the gods, a terrible dilemma was born in him, for *he found himself hating the father he did not know*!

Not long afterward, when Marieke did not return from one of her excursions into the storms, Asa knew where she had gone, and he knew that she was dead.

He was ten years old.

He had gone up onto the bluffs where he could get a clear view of the Islands of the Gods. Rubbing away his tears with a fist, he had sworn that when he was a man he would force those gods to notice him, and he would go to those islands, and he would find that man . . .

When Asa told Persis this story, she said immediately, "You must do it!"

"You sound," he said, smiling, "like a Kanik. I was going to say that it doesn't matter anymore. That you have replaced that oath."

"No! There are some things, for each of us, that must be done. You must go there, somehow. Otherwise you will not be content, not ever, and all your life you will take more than you give."

That winter they grew so close together that talk became unnecessary for anything but the sharing of the most personal and secret memories and dreams. In all routine matters, they thought together.

In April, the streams began to open little by little, permitting fishing. Birds returned, and some fell to Asa's arrows. By the middle of May they were able to shed their winter clothes, and they waded shyly, laughing like children, into one of the pools near their lodge. They were both thin still, but the cool water cleansed them and revived them, sharpening all their senses.

At the end of that month they returned to Alcheringia.

Most of those who had survived the winter had arrived before them and pitched the summer lodges. The campsite seethed with activity. Already they had gathered a rich harvest of *latchons*, the rich and oily pelagic smelt, and the salmon run was starting. Winter-damaged weirs were being repaired, smoke scaffoldings built, canoes refurbished. Children frolicked. From the falls, from all along the river, came the laughter of women. A little crowd gathered when they arrived, inspecting them, seeing how they had wintered, and it was clear that Persis was no longer simply a captive, a Kanik woman, but one that had helped Asa to survive.

She had earned a place. Women called her by name.

What the Alcheringians could not know was that Asa had made certain decisions that winter. He had decided to ask the questions that Rusl and Kenet had asked. He had decided to keep asking them until the gods took action. And he had decided that he would never, whatever happened, end up simplified and grinning like his two friends. He would die first.

Asa looked for the faces of strangers, but no one had replaced Jared. Not yet.

TWELVE

"That," Moran says, "is skuld's projection, not mine. I must say I don't like it. Not at all." He appears genuinely uncomfortable, shifting his bulk, squinting through the windows of the conference room at the winter brilliance beyond. "Genocide violates the Principle of Diversity. Nevertheless, that principle is programed into skuld's ROM, and it still—"

"Absurd!" Shem says, very flushed. "Absurd even to think of such a thing! Even to request such a projection!"

"A final solution," Horvath says, touching a finger to his lips.

"No!" Shem is on his feet. "Never!" We shouldn't even *think* of it!"

Silence. Silence. Water drips from a melting ledge.

"We should think of everything," Horvath says softly. "Particularly the greater good. That is why we are here. We have not taken an oath to be afraid; or to be emotional, or to turn away from what is distasteful! We have taken an oath to *think*." His eyes widen slightly. "And to act wisely."

"SKULD is a machine—"

"Oh, quite right, of course," Moran says. "A tool, only a tool—"

"—that can only *measure*! It is merely *rational*! It is incapable of humane thought, because you cannot measure love, or compassion, or humor, or creativity, or wonder, or even, dammit, animal attraction!"

"My dear fellow . . ." Moran lowers his eyes.

Horvath says, "Perhaps we should postpone this meeting."

Trembling, Shem sinks into his chair. "I'm sorry," he says. "Sorry."

"We are painfully aware," Horvath says, after another short pause, "that databases are incomplete. Imperfect. That is why, of course, SKULD is not usually used in problems of this sort. Ethical variables are ephemeral—is that not what you intended to say, Shem? Motivating emotions are unquantifiable?"

"Yes."

"At the moment. Yes. However, as procedures are perfected—"

"I think," Shem interrupts, "that I am saying more than that. I am saying that diversity is essential to the Project. And we cannot have diversity without risk. Controls are never perfect. Chances must be taken. The horror of the Entropies was that they were a period of *radical simplifications*. We are managers. To manage is to protect, not to eliminate, not classify and cut to fit! All questions of humanity aside, Horvath, you are talking here about *raw material*. Data."

"That, of course, could be compiled," Moran says, hesitantly glancing from one to the other.

"Never! That's my point!"

"Gentlemen," Horvath says. His voice is a sibilant whisper, almost pure exhalation. "I have something to say to you both." His glance flickers sideways to include Moran, and then turns to the window and settles somewhere beyond the conference room, beyond the window, where the marshes of Asgard glitter in the new sun.

"This question of Alcheringian heresy is taking a disproportionate amount of my time and yours. I am weary of having references made to it in the meetings of the Arborea, and of explaining that it is an isolated occurrence which will not infect other tribes and which will soon be controlled. I dislike explanations, I dislike excuses. I dislike also emotional tension between my dream masters." He says the word *emotional* as if it were venemous, poisoning all language. "I have no doubt that when the scholars have completed the Project, if they ever do, we shall learn that it was precisely such drivel that led directly to the downfall of the Old Ones. And so, Moran"— Horvath raises a finger without looking—"your job is to regulate East Norriya. Kindly limit yourself to that formidable task, and leave the SKULD projections to me and the Arborea."

Moran flushes. Parts of him, overflowing the armchair, move independently of other parts. "Sir, as a matter of policy, the bringing forward of proposals concerning the adjustment of territories—"

"Did you hear me, Moran?"

"—within the scope of regulations as I interpret . . ."

Horvath turns his gaze upon the man. His eyes are yellow, his pupils unhumanly narrowed. It is a gaze older than all time. It is infinitely older than all caring, all pity, older than rage or fear. It is the gaze of a sublime bird gliding above the marshes of a bubbling earth, indifferent to all but that which must and will be done.

Moran pales and blinks and falls silent. He thinks, *The future is his who knows how to wait.*

"As for Alcheringia, Shem," Horvath continues, turning again to the window, "as you know, it will be the Arborea's task, not SKULD's, to weigh uniqueness against the threat of aberration. However, if it comes to that, you cannot deny that what the Arborea will be asked to deal with is a managerial failure."

Shem nods wearily.

"A year. One year. That is what we have, according to the

SKULD projections. At most. After that, this Alcheringian heresy will be spreading like a corruption through all of Norriya." Horvath pauses. He is very pale in the harsh winter light, and he is immobile, except for the tongue which flickers across his lips. "I will give you one-half that year, Shem. Six months. No more. If in the autumn this bothersome Alcheringian matter is not in hand, it goes to the Arborea. And I must tell you now that I will recommend the SKULD solution." He rises. Moran rises. "It's in your hands. I suggest you find yourself a genius of a peregrinus to replace that dead old man—"

"Jared."

"Jared, yes. Who let things slip this far."

"He was human," Shem says.

Horvath turns in the doorway and emits a sound like laughter. "Whatever that may mean," he says.

THIRTEEN

SHE CAME ALONG THE BEACH AT THE EDGE OF THE WATER, and the wash of the incoming tide obliterated her footprints behind her.

Persis saw her coming, and felt the feathery brush of fear in her belly. It was not the same kind of fear—half rage— that she knew well from other incidents—the time, for example, when Thorel had strode huge and laughing out of the underbrush and the wind had carried her cries away. This was slower, deeper, such a fear as a woman might know when she senses that something beloved will be taken from her—when she sees the shade of death in her father's eye, or touches the constricting swelling in the neck of a child.

She straightened from the hide she was scraping and called Asa.

He came and stood beside her. Mists raveled between them and the approaching figure. At first they could not be sure even that it was a woman, for the pace was not a woman's, but rather the rolling gait of a squat bear.

When he went down through the mists to meet her, Asa found himself face to face with the ugliest woman he had ever seen. She was very short—hardly five feet—and very squat. Bulky garments and a bulging pack thickened her even more. Lank black hair framed a face oddly compressed, perhaps by some accident of birth, so that both nostrils were fully exposed. Above them, small eyes shone bright and unblinking. Hair fringed her upper lip and the edges of her jowls. Her right hand held a staff; her left was hidden in the folds of her cloak. Her brow was furrowed and she was smiling with what seemed to Asa incongruously intense pleasure and surprise.

"Who are you?" Her voice was very low.

"Asa."

"Good. Later we shall talk, you and I. No? Later you will have some questions for me, is that not true?"

"Yes. Why have you—"

"But not now. Now I would like to eat, and talk to Kurc and Romoke."

"That way," Asa said, and he pointed down the beach to the main body of Alcheringian lodges, lost in the fog.

Her name was Alva.

For three weeks she watched.

For three weeks she walked the beaches of Alcheringia and watched the fishermen putting out to sea. She watched how they assisted each other, and whose suggestions were most often taken, and who returned most regularly with fish and porpoise. For three weeks she watched the Alcheringian hunters come and go. For three weeks she sat on the banks above the river weirs, and heard the women laughing and gossiping at their work. Sometimes she helped, but her left hand stayed hidden always against her breast. She knew wonderful new games to delight the children, and strange stories to widen their eyes. Parents knew when their children came home placid and bemused that they had been with Alva. Outposts in the hills or at the falls of the Larl would be startled to find her suddenly beside them, peering with them into the mists for signs of raiders, and she would stay for hours to ease the boredom of their watch, talking and listening. She seemed content to listen to anything, no matter how trivial, and very often she gave advice in the subtlest of suggestions, so subtle that the recipient believed he had thought of that solution for himself.

For three weeks she sat on the edge of council fires, listening, and although it appeared she must be drowsing, yet under the lowering brow her eyes were wide open. She heard everything that was said, and occasionally she lifted her head just enough to gaze long and thoughtfully at the speaker. In three weeks she grew to know them all, the brash and outspoken, the witless and senile, the meditative and introverted. She lived a day or two in many different lodges, as Wanderers often did, and learned about the occupants—strengths and weaknesses, passions and oddities.

Asa watched her watching. He watched also as the others, nervous, circumspect, and politic in her presence, sidestepped in council the issues raised by the Tabuly. Their evasions disgusted him.

Finally, he rose to speak.

The occasion was the council dedicating the Nine of that spring. Through the ceremonial stages of the evening, Asa had gazed across the smoke and the heat haze at their eager and youthful faces, and he had felt old and angry. He watched Romoke dutifully preparing his three maps for the raid, which this year was to be against the Montayners, and he grew angrier. He saw Kurc and all the elders nodding soberly through the ritual chanting of the Tabuly, and he grew angrier still.

When at last he signaled for the speaker's staff a hush fell over the council. It was the first time he had done so in a year.

Asa stood, bright eyes squinting against the smoke, black hair disheveled as ever, feet evenly planted in a fighter's stance. He bent forward a little from the waist. His left fist rested on his hip, his right gripped the speaker's staff. The scar from the Kanik knife shone livid across his thigh.

He pointed the staff first to the elders on his extreme left and drew it slowly down the sitting line, past Tanis and Urc, past Marshal, past Leec and Kurc, past Quiner, Paj, and Romoke.

"All of you," he said, "all my life have taught us to respect the Tabuly."

"True," they murmured, nodding, all self-righteous and devout.

Asa waited until the muttering had died away, and then asked, "Why?"

There was a shocked moment of silence.

"It is done!" old Quiner said indignantly in his stringy voice. "It has always been done."

"Yes. Tradition," said several of the others, nodding jawfirm.

"What sort of question are you asking, Asa?" Kurc spoke low in his throat, warning. "It is the law. It is from the gods."

"These gods." Asa grinned, squinting against the smoke. "They are greater than men? Greater than we are?"

"Omniscient, omnipotent, ubiquitous . . ." the elders began, lapsing into the rhythms of an ancient chant.

Asa waved them to silence with the staff. "Nonsense!"

Kurc's fists pushed into the ground, lifting his great body. "Asa-a-a . . . if you speak heresy . . ."

Rusl had covered his ears and sat wide-eyed and moaning softly.

"I'll speak the truth," Asa said. "You call it what you will. But if it is heresy for me to say that we are hedged in by foolish rules, by foolish customs and traditions, then so be it. For that is what has happened to us. Gradually. Year by year we have acquiesced, grown fearful. Look at us! Yes! Afraid even to speak! Afraid even to *think*, lest we offend the gods and their precious Tabuly!" He gripped the staff tight and probed forward with it into the smoke. "If that is what piety does, then *give me heresy!*"

"Oh oh oh." Rusl rocked like a frightened child. Horror rose in single gasps out of the assembly.

"Shame!" said the elders, peering at the darkness, peering at the star-shot sky. "Make penance, Asa! Plead forgiveness! Quick!"

Asa laughed and motioned to Rani, who scampered forward with a knapsack he had begged Asa to be allowed to carry, then scuttled crablike back into the crowd. "As for those gods who hold us in thrall," Asa said, opening the pack, "would you like to see how invulnerable they are? How omnipotent? There. There is a piece of one. And there is another." The chunks of metal spun and clattered on the packed earth, gleaming, some trailing multicolored bits of wire. The gathering recoiled from them, hissing and shielding their gaze but looking anyway, looking surreptitiously at the god-bits inert and harmless dropped among them.

Everyone was standing, now. The circle had grown wide. They had even helped old Quiner to his feet, and he stood tottering and baring his gums this way and that like an ancient turtle with clouded eyes, smelling danger, smelling fear.

"Silence!" Kurc was roaring. "Silence!" And others of the elders had joined in that chorus, some shooting pure gouts of sound as if this way, howling shut-eyed, they could wipe the horror of what had happened from the slate of memory. But some of the younger warriors had stepped forward too, beside Asa, facing the elders across the fire.

No one noticed in the confusion that Alva had slipped away.

The new Nine looked at Asa with dismay and admiration and he was speaking now to them. "Gods die. You know it. We all know it. Everyone has seen their brown corpses rotting in the wilderness where they have fallen. Yet we are so crippled by fear that we never *say* what we have seen. Well, let us say it now. Plainly. Gods die!"

Silence followed this, a shocked silence broken only by the soft whimpering of Rusl.

"They die!" Asa repeated. "They die by falling out of the sky, and by getting old, like men, and"—he raised his war ax—"they die when men *decide to kill them*! Like this one." He gestured to the scattered pieces.

The elders were no longer listening, but had gathered in an agitated huddle. Some were shouting orders that no one was obeying. Kurc pushed through them, roaring.

The hubbub dwindled, except for Asa's voice, a single voice clear and calm in the silence. "Do not be afraid," he was saying to the pale young members of the new Nine. "Remember, you are *men*!"

"One month's banishment," Kurc roared. "One month!"

"Go where you want to go. Look at what you must."

"Two months!"

Asa faltered. He looked for Persis, but he could not see her in the smoke and the confusion. He thought fleetingly of her lips and her warm body in the cool of the August nights. Two months!

But there was something more that must be said.

"Above all, think free of the old restrictions. Try to understand, without the gods, what is best for us—what is best for *man*."

"Three months!" Kurc was livid and there was dire warning in his eyes. It was within his power to order even death, although Asa knew that he would not do that.

Asa had finished. He stood silent, calm, facing the wrath of the chief.

"You have spoken," Kurc began. "Now hear me!" He blinked, and seemed in his fury to have forgotten the Article of Banishment.

"For three months . . ." Romoke prompted softly, surreptitiously gathering the pieces of the god for later use. Some would find their way into the unguents and talismans of his trade.

"For three months," Kurc said, recovering himself, "you will keep farther off than one day's travel from Alcheringia, and have no meetings with our people . . ."

"Unclean in mind and . . ."

"Unclean in mind and soul, you will seek to purge yourself in the purity of the wild places, and to return with clean thoughts."

"And may . . ."

"And may the gods have mercy on you."

Asa turned away, turned through the furtive touches of well-wishers, and at the edge of the crowd he found Persis' arms, and her hands in his hair, and her wet face.

"Unclean," he said, trying to smile. But she clung to him anyway, clung to him weeping as he gathered what he would need from the lodge, clung to him until at last he turned and embraced her, and told her that he loved her and would love her forever.

"I'll be all right," she said then. "Go now. Do what you must do."

On the hill beside the first waterfall, he paused and looked back on Alcheringia, looked back on the resuscitated council fire where Kurc and Remoke and the elders would be healing over the rift he had created, soothing, soothing, but seeing in the gazes of the people that his words had stuck and rooted, and that ideas continued to grow.

He smiled.

When he turned back to the path he could not continue, because a squat shape was blocking his way. He reacted instinctively, reaching for his knife, but then his eyes grew accustomed to the starlight and the dim reflections of the fire.

Alva stood before him.

She was gazing at Asa's face, not his knife. "That was quite a speech," she said.

"How do you know?"

"I heard it. Enough of it."

"And now?"

"Now we talk."

She was holding the staff in her right hand. It was topped with the three-root tree-symbol of the gods. *Another will come,* Jared had said. *Another will answer your questions.* Her left hand remained buried in the front of her cloak. Asa motioned with his knife for her to draw it out.

She seemed at first not to understand him. Then she said, "Oh. That. I'm not armed, and even if I were . . ."

He motioned again.

"My dear boy, you're not going to like it."

He jabbed out with the knife.

Slowly she exposed her hand.

It was not a hand. It was a paw, broad and coarse-haired, with long-webbed fingers tapering into cylindrical nails. Asa saw, as she slowly rotated it, a pink and wrinkled palm.

"We all have little misfortunes," she said, shrugging at his expression of shock. "All of us. Some bear them outside, some inwardly. I told you you wouldn't like it much."

"You're a Gerumbian!"

She nodded. She waited for him to speak, in the silence slipping her hand back into her jacket.

"They've sent you for me, haven't they? They know I killed one of them." He was still gripping the knife, although it now hung at his side.

She snorted. "Don't be silly! Of course you didn't kill a god. You killed a machine. A robot. And a very old and decrepit one at that. You think *that's* something to be proud of? Foof? A child could have done it! So don't pretend you're an intrepid warrior. And put away that wretched knife! Do you really think you could stop me if I decided to kill you now?"

Asa's anger spiraled up into a tight sneer. "You *morph*! You couldn't—"

Her staff flicked out faster than a newt's tongue and sent

the knife spinning into the underbrush. In an instant her bulky body lunged forward with astonishing speed. In one swoop the terrible paw had caught him behind the knees, and he was on his back with her foot on his chest and the sharp point of her alder staff only an inch above his eyes.

"Couldn't what?" she whispered.

"Let me up."

"More insults?"

He shook his head. "No."

"Good. Come then. Let's move." And stepping off him she turned and led the way eastward up the path, away from Alcheringia.

Asa followed.

In an hour they reached the first of the broad valleys. Around them in the starlight the old hills rose like protecting bosoms. Alva slowed her pace and motioned for him to walk beside her. "You have questions," she said. "Ask."

"Questions are dangerous," Asa replied, glancing sidelong at her.

She chortled. "Oh yes. Always. But you have no choice, have you, Asa? Some people can keep silent. You cannot."

"No more than Kenet."

"You are more circumspect."

"No more than Rusl."

"You are more clever."

Asa saw that she was smiling, and again anger flashed across his belly. "Are we *always* watched?"

"Not always." She laughed. "The gods are human, too."

"When, then?"

Alva shrugged. "What answer do you want? When it can be done? When it is necessary to manage? Whenever they are bored?"

Asa danced backward. "You're trifling with me! You're playing! You invite me to ask you questions and mock me when I do."

Alva turned, holding her pathetic paw with her good hand. She moved close, close enough for him to see into her eyes as into darkening pools of wisdom, sadness, and profound unknowing. "I am not trifling with you, Asa. I will answer your questions. That is why I am here. I will tell you the truth, and the first truth you should know is that there are many truths and many ways of answering. *Do you hear?*" Again, she moved forward with amazing agility and her paw seized his chin, shaking him gently. Its claws touched his throat. *"Learn that first!* If you are not to grow stupid with knowledge, learn first that there are many answers, and when you choose one you kill the others."

They walked for a time in silence, a little distance apart. Asa asked, "What do you watch for?"

"Among other things, for wanderers."

"And when you find them, what do you do?"

This time there was no answer, nor any sign that the question had even been asked. He tried again. "Do they always feed the silver spiders?"

She shook her head. "Not always."

"What are my choices?" Asa asked.

There came no answer. The woman walked doggedly.

"It occurs to me," Asa said, his voice the high singsong a frustrated child might use to strike at parents, "it occurs to me that there are better ways to live. Yes. Not only ourselves but the Gerumbians and the Yuloks and even the Kaniks. Look at us. We spend half our lives in traveling to our food and returning it to camp. But supposing . . ."

Alva stopped walking and listened attentively, her eyes fixed on the ground.

"Supposing we brought the food to us and kept it there. Supposing we built corrals for the caribou—pens where the meat might be kept fresh, where they might even be bred. Supposing we planted the nuts, and berry bushes, and tubers on which we live, and created around them the conditions under which they might prosper. Oh yes, I have done that," he said quickly in answer to her sharp and questioning glance. "I have tried in secret places in the forest, and I have seen what occurs. There is no mystery. There is no magic. It is predictable. I *know*."

"What do you know?"

"I know that I can cause plants to grow where I want them, provided the soil is rich and black."

"Yes," she said. "You can."

"And . . . and that if we plant enough we shall have no shortage, no winter famine, perhaps no need to move."

"Yes. And then?"

"And then we shall be happier." Alva raised her eyebrows at his use of the word, and he flushed, remembering his outburst to Jared: *Is there nothing better than happiness?* "Life will be better." He shrugged. "Richer."

"Bah!" Alva flicked her hand at him as if he were a troublesome fly. "You are a child! You know nothing!"

"I know—"

"Nothing!" She sat now on a smooth rock, feet spread wide, fists on her hips. She thrust her face forward and touched her pig's nose. "You see this far, no farther."

"I see—"

"Nothing except what you imagine to be good. You are like a blind man feeling his six feet of tree trunk and describing a tree. Everything above is a mystery to you. Everything below is a mystery to you. Everything *inside* is a mystery. And yet you claim that *you know the tree, and that there is no mystery*! Pah!"

Asa moved close, his jaw set. "Then you must *show* me! *Teach* me! You and them." He pointed to the Islands of the Gods."

"We must do *nothing*."

"Like Jared!" he said, recoiling. "You'll delay. You'll say that another will come. Then another! And then it will be too late!"

"Asa, listen—"

"No! I've had enough listening. I'm sick of it, all the talk that leads nowhere! If I am ignorant it is you who keep me so, you and your kind!"

"*Listen!*" Alva hissed, and her alder staff rose menacingly. Her eyes were beads, all black. "You asked me if all those who wondered and searched came at last to the silver spiders, as you called them. I told you no. Some do and some do not. You are one who will not."

"What, then?"

She grunted. "What do you think?"

He flung his arm toward the islands.

She nodded.

"When? Tomorrow? Now?"

"Patience."

"You know that if you don't take me, now, I'll go alone. I'll paddle out, just as Kenet and Rusl and I always planned to do. I'll—"

Alva was laughing as she rummaged in her pack, and her laughter was so like coughing and snorts that Asa thought she might be choking. "You'll do nothing that we do not want you to do. That we do not *permit*." Again the alder staff pointed at him, and again the black beads that were her eyes shone bright. "Here are some words for you. Presumptuous. Bumptious. Impertinent. You don't know what they mean, do you?"

Asa shook his head.

"You'll learn. Because you *are* those things, I have been sent to take you where you're going." She had drawn out of her pack a small black box festooned with buttons, similar to the one that Jared had carried.

Asa smiled then, remembering the creatures that had passed above him. "Through the sky!"

But Alva shook her head, pressing buttons and summoning the voices of ghostly insects out of the box. "That is an unnatural way that I detest. We're going through the sea. *Through* the sea, do you hear?"

Her guttural laughter mingled with the cicada voices from the box, and then she spoke into it in a language Asa could only partially understand. It answered. "Come on," she said when she had finished, snapping the box shut and dropping it back into her pack. "We have to hurry."

FOURTEEN

—HELLO, YGGDRASIL. THIS IS MUNIN FOUR.

—Hello, Munin Four. We have a request from a peregrinus. Rendezvous at Location Two Nine, twenty-one hundred hours tomorrow. Can you comply, Munin Four?

—Stand by, Yggdrasil . . . We are nine hours' surface time from that location. Charts indicate navigational hazards at the mouth of the bay and heavy-sea condition when winds are southwest. What is your forecast, Yggdrasil?

—High pressure for twenty-four hours. Clear skies. Winds from northwest at six knots. It should be calm as a fishbowl in that bay, Munin Four.

—Very good, Yggdrasil. Will proceed to rendezvous. How many personnel?

—Two. One peregrinus, one aborr.

—Yggdrasil, about that aborr—

—Peregrinus will take precautions, Munin Four.

—Very good, Yggdrasil. Out.

FIFTEEN

"HE'S GONE ALONE."

"Yes."

Kenet nodded into the sunset, toward the islands. "There." He smiled.

"We should, too," Rusl said. "We should."

Kenet nodded again.

But neither moved. Neither moved from the rock on which they sat, yet their two stout bodies expressed the longing to rise and go down the darkening beach to where the canoes lay like drowsing seals, and to drift into the last of the light, westward, until they reached the islands.

Then they did. Like one body they rose, lumbered down the beach, selected the best canoe. They slipped it into the froth of the sea, slid their paddles up the gunwales to steady the craft while they stepped in, and then, doggedly, they moved

out, moved north, moved up the coast to that point where the
Islands of the Gods were closest.

Occasionally, from both ends of the canoe, came a sound
like laughter.

SIXTEEN

LIKE THE WAYSTS, GERUMBIA WAS A FORBIDDEN REGION.

Asa had entered it twice, once when he had followed Jared
and Kenet to the dark bay where the silver spider waited, and
later when he had carried the dying Jared to the south shore
of the Gerumbian Peninsula.

Now he was going a third time.

It was impossible to enter Gerumbia by mistake. Its boundaries were marked by myriad warnings left by hunters, and
shamans, and travelers who had wandered too far and wanted
to save others from seeing what they had seen. In fact, these
danger signs began well south of the actual boundary of the
region, so for at least a mile south of Gerumbia the forest
through which the trail passed had been transformed into an
eerie no-man's-land. Girdled trees were the commonest sign,
lifting stark and lifeless branches. Faces of agony had been
hacked into the trunks of some, and many had been hung with
grotesque and unspeakable totems—atrophied animal parts and
grim puppets warning of horrors ahead.

Aeolian harps of many tones hung in the stark branches,
and when the wind moved among them they moaned like lost
souls with a plaintive cacophony that chilled Asa's blood and
prickled the flesh on his thighs and scalp. Occasionally, in
some twist or breeze, one of them would utter a shrill, demented
shriek before lapsing again into the doleful chorus, *Keep*

awaaaaaay . . . Staaaaaay off . . . Turn baaaaaack . . .

Asa doggedly followed Alva's round back through it all, until they came to the bear's head.

It hung impaled on a stake, and rose up out of the fog only a few feet in front of him.

He sat down abruptly. He was a child again, in a nightmare. The familiar gulf began to open. He had been less afraid in battle with the Kaniks. He had been less afraid killing the silver spider.

The head had hung there for months, perhaps years. The stake was winter-bleached and smoothed by wind and ice. The skull had not been picked clean; rather, the head had mummified in such a way that the skin had shrunk tight against the skull, until it was hard as the bone itself. Eyeless sockets glared their warning, and exposed fangs gleamed in the twilight of the forest.

Alva contemplated it in silence and then reached up to touch it gently on the drum-leather cheek, as one might caress a lover. Then she shrugged and walked on beneath it. She went several paces before she realized that Asa was not following, and turned around. "It is a dead thing," she called back to him where he sat trembling in the bushes at the side of the overgrown path. "Dead things cannot hurt. Get up. Come on."

But he could not. He sat hunched, hands clasped between his knees.

She came back, sat beside him, saw the fear. "Look at me," she said. "Not at the head."

He did as he was told, and the image of the totem faded gradually into Alva's face.

"Why are you afraid?"

"I—I fear what I do not know."

"No. You fear *what you think you know*." Behind her the wind harps moaned and shrieked in the wilderness. "Asa, Asa! Do you think you would be here were it not for your *vulnerability*? Come now! Come!" She tugged him to his feet and nudged him on ahead of her, under the skull and farther into the region of monstrosities. "What do you think," he heard her muttering behind him, "what do you think it *is* to be human?"

Soon they left the totems. A bit farther and the mournful singing of the harps, and the flat tinkling of clay bells, had faded and died. With the setting of the sun they came to the outskirts of Gerumbia itself.

There was no mistaking it. For some time the vegetation had been dwindling, and at last only sparse and dwarfish bushes remained. Farther on even these died out, and rank sedges and crusty lichens became the only living things.

The path they were following had long since vanished, but here no path was necessary, for the soil—what there was of it—was parched and caked mud, curling like scales on the hide of a sickly beast.

Nothing grew higher than half a hand. No birds flew. No creatures left their marks and droppings. For as far as Asa could see beyond the baked mudflats there was only rock, smooth and undulating, like a sea magically frozen in the aftermath of a great storm. Except for the plaintive sounds of breezes in the mouths of crevasses, the place was silent utterly.

Alva grunted. "This way," she said, and they moved toward the last crescent of sun. In the afterglow they crossed a strip of rock that lay flat and smooth under Asa's moccasins and stretched as far as he could see on either side. They traversed it in a few strides, but so strange was it that he turned back, crouched, and touched its pebbly surface. End-to-end, running precisely down its center, lay long oblongs of pale gray. "Come," Alva called to him. "Hurry. There's not much time."

They began to descend an ancient cobble beach, sloping steeply half a mile to the sea, like the brow of a giant. In a clattering of stones and driftwood, they slid down together, and stood on the largest beach Asa had ever seen- a huge crescent that stretched away and vanished into the gathering darkness on both sides. It was awesomely still. Even after sunset, most beaches were busy with the cries of shorebirds and the occasional soft calls of seals offshore; this beach was barren, part of the devastation through which they had traveled all that day.

The skin tightened in Asa's groin. His back felt cold. He felt that he was being watched—watched not by living eyes but by the eyes of the Old Ones who had once laughed and played along this beach, and who then had gathered their belongings in the dusk, in just this kind of dusk, and returned to the homes where death had found them. Thousands were watching him, perhaps tens of thousands. He could feel them lining the brow of the ancient beach, gray as ash. Those behind pressed forward so inexorably it seemed impossible that the mass did not begin to overflow the slope. It thickened, increased its ghastly weightlessness, trailing cerements.

"What is it?" Alva asked, shaking his arm. "What do you see?"

"The dead."

"Still!" she hissed. "Stand still! Of course it is a haunted place. Of course the gaze of the dead is on you. But what will they do if you make a spectacle of your terror? Be still!"

Holding his arm, she turned to face the mass of translucent bodies and suddenly flung her arms into the air, loosing the wordless guttural roar one utters at a nuisance. The shades sagged back like limber bushes in a sudden wind, sagged and separated, crumbled into fragments.

Asa's trembling slowed. "Why . . . why do they come to us?"

"They are filled with remorse, the dead. They want to make apologies."

"Apologies? For what?"

"That you will learn, Asa. That is one of the reasons we are going to the Islands, so that you may learn why they want to apologize." As she spoke she took from her pack the small black box and pulled up from one corner a slender silver branch. The box squeaked like an exotic bird, and she listened intently. When the cries ceased she pressed a button, grunted with satisfaction, folded the silver arm back into itself, and sat down on the beach. "Now we wait," she said.

Asa sat beside her, drawing his knees up like a small boy under his chin. Chill breezes began to sneak off the sea. The first stars blinked on above the afterglow.

"Your woman," Alva said suddenly. "Persis. Do you miss her?"

"Not yet. Not here."

"What is the name for what is between you?"

"Love," Asa said.

Alva made a low sound in her throat, but he could not tell whether it was laughter or a growl. "Do you remember the old story of Orfus and Urdcy?"

Asa nodded. It was one of the basic myths, told by all mothers, told by shamans and by wanderers. In the myth, a beautiful young woman whose name is Urdcy is taken away to the Islands of the Gods and kept there. Her lover, Orfus, driven by grief, ventures in search of her against all reason and all taboo. His canoe is swamped in a storm, but he is miraculously saved, cast up more dead than alive on the shore of one of the islands. Nearly slain by the guardians of the place, he is saved again by the intervention of a god who takes pity on him because of his courage and the intensity of his love. Protected by this god, Orfus is shown many wonders on the islands, and many ways of improving mankind and its lot. He sees such possibilities as he had never imagined. In the end he is told that what he has seen is nothing compared to what might be known. But in order to learn more he must make a choice between living within the life of his beloved Urdcy, a choice which would mean warmth, comfort, and all things good, or self-consciously pursuing knowledge, a choice which would mean uncertainty, risk, suffering, and certain loneliness. His fate will be determined by whether he gratefully and unquestioningly accepts the return of his beloved, or continues to inquire. Orfus asks, "But how do I *know* that knowledge will end in pain?"

All Alcheringian children learned this myth, the point of which was that Orfus was a fool, fatally enticed by knowledge, who sacrificed the vital for the ephemeral.

In his fatigue, Asa wondered briefly why Alva was telling him the story again now, when there were obviously no choices to be made . . .

But she was going on. The next story was longer, and when she finished she continued with another, and another, interspersing them with the lullabies his mother had sung, wrapping them both in a cocoon of tenderness against the encroaching night. Her voice was soporific, borne on languorous rhythms, and soon Asa slept like a child, head on his knees.

When he woke, the sea had darkened until he could no longer distinguish even the nearest headlands. In fact, everything beyond the gentle rhythmical breaking line of surf a hundred paces away was obscured. Something else had changed as well; the beach was no longer silent. From beyond the headlands came a sound he had never heard before, yet knew. *It was like the droning of mosquitoes*, his mother had said, *but louder, stronger, steadier* . . .

Then there were the lights, exactly as his mother had described them, like stars close together on the surface, and as the droning grew louder the lights brightened and one began to sweep like a probing finger across the sea.

Asa sat fascinated. He was not at all frightened now. He was filled with awe and curiosity.

The humming ceased.

Clanking sounds followed, like those made by the cold, heavy sticks they had once found and knocked together in a childhood forest clearing.

He heard voices, clear over the water, although he could not understand what was said.

He heard the familiar, rhythmic dipping of paddles, and he knew that a canoe was on its way to the beach.

"Come," Alva said, and they both walked to the water's edge.

It was not a canoe that loomed out of the darkness, but a more cumbersome craft. Bulbous, it looked more like a sea mammal than a boat. Like a sea beast's, its sleek hide gleamed in the starlight. A single paddler worked two paddles simultaneously, for they were hinged on the flanks of the boat.

He greeted Alva perfunctorily and steadied the boat against the gently rocking surf while they climbed in. When they had settled, he swung the craft back out into the bay. As he rowed he stared at Asa.

They were about the same age, but the resemblance between them ended there. The stranger was clad not in skins but in a black, tight suit. His hair was closely cropped, and he bore neither tribal nor clan tattoos or insignia. The greatest difference, however, lay in his pallor; his face was so white that Asa thought at first he was wearing ghost-paint for some arcane ceremony. His hands were the same color and, when he loosened the throat of his jacket under the exertion of rowing, so was his neck.

They approached the lights. The bright one had caught them in a brief wash of brilliance that was, Asa thought, like the inside of a star. He squinted into the glare of it. When they were still a hundred yards off, the beam swung away to sweep the shore, and for the first time Asa saw the creature from which it shone.

The thing was like a whale inert upon the surface, rocking in the swell. Yet it was not a whale, for there were no animal signs of life about it, no languorous sweeping of a tail, no steady gaze from a lidless eye, no rhythmic whoosh of breath through the blowhole. It was rigid. A squat tower hunkered on its back, and a sporadic, hollow clanking echoed from somewhere inside.

Their small boat bumped alongside, and as it did so, two

men appeared as if by magic to help them up. They were dressed like the one who had rowed them out, and had the same beardless faces. They knew Alva and exchanged friendly banter with her, although so quickly and in such an unusual dialect that Asa could not understand everything they said.

They led Asa toward the snout of the craft, then through a hole and down a ladder. He found himself in an area so bright that for a moment he could see nothing. He was guided to a seat, and gradually his eyes grew accustomed to the glare.

Once when they were children, he and Rusl had fallen by accident into one of the caves of the Old Ones. It had been dank and gloomy. Vinelike filaments dangled through the broken ceiling and through a mesh of hard, orange tubes, like the calcified entrails of some monster. They were cold, these tubes, and the orange had rubbed off like a stain on their hands. They had scraped off some of it for paint pigment, but when Romoke had seen what they had brought back to Alcheringia he hurled it with a curse into the fire and began a series of long, purifying rituals, one of which had involved opening their wrists so that the cleansing blood streamed over their palms.

They had never returned there.

The place where Asa now sat reminded him of that other cavern. Here were the same vinelike filaments running everywhere along the walls and roof; the same tubes with patches of the same orangeness; the same rock-hard floor.

But while the other place had been dead, this was alive. Light blazed everywhere. People moved constantly. Disembodied voices spoke magically from elsewhere. As the craft began to stir itself for its journey back to sea, buzzes, hums, clicks, rings, and hisses raced throughout it. The door above them clanged and sealed itself. The craft rumbled, and the rumbling sent reverberations along its length.

They moved.

In the low doorway at the end of the narrow room, the young man who had rowed them out appeared and beckoned. He was smiling. Behind him, a man and a woman sat side by side, before an array of multicolored lights, switches, levers, and wheels. They greeted Alva warmly and raised their hands to Asa in the signal of friendship; then they turned back to their work.

Through an opening ahead of them, Asa saw the sea, gray on gray. He knew they were moving very fast, and it wasn't long before they had left the mouth of the bay and the Islands of the Gods loomed ahead through the raveling mists. In less than an hour they had drawn close enough to distinguish the hills of three islands against the sky. They were headed toward the central one, but even as Asa peered forward to see it better, the floor of the craft tipped, water washed across the glass, and they submerged.

The boat glided midway between the surface and the sea floor. Powerful beams of light swept across the sandy bottom and along jagged cliffs, startling creatures into motion. Lobsters raised huge claws. Clouds of mackerel and herring shimmered into the light, then away, then back again. Startled squid left black explosions spreading in ultramarine.

Asa knew these creatures. He had drawn them from the sea, he had seen them dead on beaches, and he had sometimes seen their vague shapes when he opened his eyes underwater. Always they had been alien and threatening, but now they were suddenly vulnerable, extraordinarily frail and beautiful. He thought how strange it was that of all the charms and placating prayers used in the course of a hunter's life, none was directed to crustaceans or to fish, but only to the mammals of the sea, only to those closest to man himself.

Their course narrowed to a tortuous passage among granite crags. The craft slowed. The two helmsmen grew more intent on the job at hand. Asa could no longer see the surface, which had hung like a translucent sheet above, and he knew that they had entered a submarine cave. A solid wall of rock loomed ahead. The craft slowed further and hung still in the sea, with a sound like the thrumming of tiny fins. The helmsman spoke, and a voice like a raven's answered.

The cliff opened into an oval portal.

The craft moved forward.

Behind, off the southern headland of the great bay from which the submarine had departed, a canoe rode the dark swells. Its occupants sat immobile, silent. In a little while they would be roused by the nearing sound of sea on rock, and without speaking they would begin to dip their paddles. But for the moment the canoe drifted, and Kenet and Rusl sat rapt by visions of the god's rumbling passage and the beam of his dreadful eye. Both knew the god had swallowed Asa and had borne him beyond mortal reach. Both knew the god had warned them not to follow.

They did not follow. After a time they turned silently back to their own dark coast.

Later, in Alcheringia, Romoke strove to draw meaning and comfort from the tale they had told him. He used all his skill, all his cunning, and with Rusl he succeeded. Rusl was beguiled and satisfied and laughed like a child again.

But with Kenet he failed. Kenet wandered off in the night, and searchers who followed his trail the next day said that he had passed on beneath the bears' heads of Gerumbia, on beneath the sighing of the distant harps.

PART THREE

YGGDRASIL

ONE

"THE MUNIN PATROL IS ARRIVING WITH YOUR PEREGRINUS,
sir. You wanted to be notified. Bay Seventeen."

"Thank you." Shem presses and releases a button on his
console. He moves closer to the screen, crossing the soft beige
carpeting of his office. He limps heavily, despite the cane.
Inside the felt boot his toeless foot, a mass of unconnected
bones, muscles, and ligaments, twitching spasmodically, struggles to help him. Parts of it grind together.

He refuses to acknowledge the pain, although it is surging
in waves over his knee and into his thigh. "Have them taken
to a briefing room," he says.

On the screen, a small submarine breaks the surface and
maneuvers into a cavernous docking area. Hatches clang open.
Deckhands run to secure lines. A gangplank drops into place.
Down it, crew and passengers descend to the jetty—the offi-
cers, the unmistakable Alva, and Asa.

The boy draws close to the camera. He is clearly afraid,
but the fear is kept in check by determination and anger.

Shem holds his breath and peers hard at the screen. Again,
something about this boy—perhaps the high cheekbones and
the frank eyes, perhaps the long black hair, perhaps the proud
tilt of the chin—something has evoked a memory long dormant, a memory from dead days before he was either dream
master or peregrinus, but only a young courier to the Gerumbians. In fact, what he recalls is less than a memory; it is
an impulse suppressed by a holy oath; it is a woman's name.

He calls other monitors into use as the group passes through
the docking area. Each time he stares hard at Asa's face. Then

he clicks off the monitor and turns away. He is caught for a moment by a glimpse of sunrise on a sea as clean and sparkling as if it were the first day of creation, and for a moment its beckoning is almost irresistible.

Then he turns away from it to the files on his desk, to his schedule of appointments.

TWO

THE CAVE WAS VAST AND UNLIKE ANY HE HAD SEEN. IT WAS brilliantly lit by hundreds of stars—not real stars, as Asa could see, for they all burned from the same height with the same intensity. It was swept by strange, warm winds which hummed from long ducts. Peering up, past the lights, Asa could see myriad catwalks and galleries intertwining with each other and rising until they vanished in the darkness overhead. Men moved on them.

Men moved everywhere. The place was alive with activity and urgency. Other vessels like their own moored in and departed from other bays, and teams of men swarmed over them, carried to them by humming carts that halted obediently, waited passively. Acrid odors drifted from these bays, from substances that spilled down long tubes, longer and thicker than the arteries of any animal Asa had ever seen.

What disturbed him was not the strangeness and novelty of these things, but the fact that he saw others like himself, men clad not in sleek fabric suits but in skins; men who were not working but were—as he was—being led by others; men who, staring across the spaces at him, wore the same shock of recognition that he must be wearing. He glimpsed them here and there, being led up ladders, down stairways, along galleries,

and all, all in unhuman silence, a silence underlined by innumerable unnatural sounds. Twice he almost called out to
them, "Wait! Wait! We do not belong here! We belong where
there is wind, and sun, and a moving sea! Not here! Not in
this frenzy! There is some horrible mistake! Don't go farther!
Don't!"

But he did not call out. Curious, he kept silent, and the
others like himself moved on with their puzzled eyes and their
strange, fixed smiles. They looked across the spaces at him,
and their eyes said, "Well, yes, we know you. You are one of
us. But we can't stop now. We must keep moving because
what we don't know interests us more."

So they kept moving, all of them, moving up staircases and
along catwalks and galleries, moving on their ways to separate
destinations.

The guide leading Asa and Alva took them away from the
great cavern, down a short corridor, and into a small closed
room that moved upward in response to the touch of a button.
In a moment its door opened into yet another corridor. Alva
trudged forward with the same rolling gait with which she had
crossed the miles of country between Alcheringia and the great
beach. Thirty paces down the corridor she paused in front of
a door marked with the tree-symbol and a number. She glanced
at the note the guide had given her, and placed her good palm
on a pastel square beneath the number. The door opened. Behind it was a small room filled with the sun of the new morning.

"Whew," said Alva, collapsing. "What a relief to sit in a
civilized chair again. Go ahead. Sit down."

Asa stood.

"Suit yourself."

He had moved so that his back was to the solid piece of
wall, the door on one side and the sun-filled windows on the
other.

"Idiot child!" Alva closed her eyes and sighed heavily. "Do
you think we brought you this far to *attack* you?"

But the room was full of menace, full of alien objects that
seemed to Asa the playthings of demented children. All its
surfaces were unnaturally flat and gleaming. Opposite the windows was a parody of the sun with symbols inscribed at intervals around its periphery and two slender sticks, fixed at the
center, pointing to two of these symbols at once. He had noted

in the short time they had been there that the larger of those sticks had moved. He had noted also that despite the fact that one side of this space was apparently open to the weather, there were no natural sounds here, no wind-whisper or bird song. Nor could he hear the crash of the surf that he could see plainly, behind the swaying trees, less than a hundred paces away. Instead of the proper sounds, this place had a plethora of un-natural ones—rings, buzzings, rhythmic ticks, the distant hum and bustle of subterranean machinery.

Asa kept his back to this solid place in the wall, his ear turned warily toward this rustling cacophony of urgency and unease.

Alva half lay in the chair with her eyes closed. She might have been sleeping. Like Asa, she was filthy from the long journey; her furs had left smudges of dried mud and grime on the upholstery, and the tracks of two sets of moccasins could be traced clearly across the pale gray carpeting.

They waited.

The door hissed open and a man entered. The door slid shut behind him.

He was tall and broad-shouldered, with red hair and a red beard. He walked with a heavy limp. He did not look at Asa, but went straight toward Alva, smiling. "Hello, Gerumbian morph."

"Clubfoot brute," Alva said, pushing herself out of her chair. "You've no idea the trouble this little excursion cost me."

"It will get worse," he said. "I promise."

They embraced so warmly that the man hoisted the little woman completely off her feet, and she patted him affection-ately on the back, causing puffs of dust to rise from her de-formed paw and diffuse in the beams of sunlight. "Oh Shem, Shem," she whispered against his shoulder, "I'm not sure I can go through with this."

"You can," he said quietly. "You will."

He turned to Asa then, and made the Alcheringian gesture of welcome. His cheekbones were broad and high. His eyes were wide but wary too, like those of an animal that would be friends. Asa had a reeling moment of *déjà vu*. He was sure that he knew this man, but the man apparently did not know him. "This is Shem," Alva said.

Shem offered his hand. "We have much to talk about," he said in the Alcheringian dialect. "I have much to explain."

Asa remained immobile and watchful, his back to the wall. He asked Alva, "Where are the gods?"

"There are no gods," she said quietly. "Only us."

Shem spread his hands, smiling. "Only us. Sit down, Asa. We'll talk."

But Asa kept standing. "Only you," he said.

Shem nodded. "And others like us. All mortal."

"But the things that carry you . . . the spiders . . ."

"We call them machines. And they wear out, as you know. They die, too." Shem indicated a chair, and now Asa came forward slowly and sat down.

Alva laughed and touched his shoulder reassuringly. "I'm leaving. I want to sleep if I'm going back to the mainland in two days, and I want to get cleaned up. We'll see each other tomorrow. If he doesn't treat you properly, let me know."

"You'll go back, too," Shem said to Asa when she had gone. "I promise. You'll be here only a little while, and then you shall return to Alcheringia. But you will go back changed."

"Like Rusl? Like Kenet?"

"No. I promise that, also. You will be changed by *more* knowledge, not less. Isn't that what you want?"

"Yes."

"Good. Now, because time is short, we should begin soon. I shall call someone to take you to your quarters so that you can bathe and change into the clothes we wear here. Then we shall eat together, and then we shall go to work."

Asa sat unmoving. He asked, "What is time?"

Shem looked puzzled.

"Time," Asa repeated. "You said that it was short."

Shem laughed abruptly. "Very rude of me! I had forgotten that you do not have that word in Alcheringian. Let me tell you what time is, since it rules all our lives here, and will govern your stay with us.

"Imagine that you have taken the circle of all life and all days, this circle"—he made the sacred sign with two fingers—"and you cut it here, or there, or anyplace. You stretch it flat, then, like a length of sinew. Imagine that it is longer than you can see. Neither you nor anyone knows where it begins. You know only that it will end. Here is the end. Here. And here you are now. Here. Time is a way of measuring the distance between where you are and the end."

Asa thought. The idea was absurd to him, but out of courtesy he did not laugh. "And at this end, which you have made by severing the circle, what will happen?"

"It will be death. The death. Of everything."

Asa laughed now. It was too ridiculous. "No," he said. "Who could believe that? It is impossible that all things should die. They are reborn constantly out of themselves. We all know this."

Shem shook his head. "Our knowledge is greater and sadder than yours," he said. "You will see."

"And so," Asa asked, "is this what it means to live here— to enter into time, and to be sad?"

"Yes," Shem answered. "That is what it means. But come. Enough for now. We'll talk more later." He pressed a button on the desk and the door behind Asa hissed open. A young man in a pale blue uniform entered, and Shem gave him a series of orders.

The young man led Asa to a room where he instantly felt comfortable. It was round, and only slightly larger than his own lodge at Alcheringia. As in his lodge, daylight filtered in from above. Its walls were the hue of smoked hides, and he walked on a floor like smoothed sand spread liberally with furs. In one corner a mass of granite had been hollowed into a large bowl to receive the water that trickled through it constantly. From the distance came the roar of the sea.

His guide indicated that he should take off his garments. He showed Asa that the water in the pool was warm. He explained the use of the toilet closeted behind the pool, and he pointed out that the bed and the clothing laid ready on it were for Asa's use. Then he left.

Asa bathed. The water was deliciously warm, and it soothed away the strain of the journey. Afterward, he put on the soft clothes and pressed the button as he had been instructed to do when he was ready. His guide returned and conducted him to Shem.

He was shown to a different room this time, a room that opened on a broad patio overlooking the sea, and on this patio he and Shem shared food. Some of the foods Asa recognized; some he did not. In reply to his question, Shem explained that some food was grown on Yggdrasil and some was brought from the mainland in what he called the forager shuttles.

As they began to drink their tea, Shem said, "Your people are turning away from their law and their traditions."

"If you had asked me," Asa said levelly, "I would have said

they were turning away from superstition and dumb fear."

Shem raised his hand. "Please. Hear me out. You have been brought here to learn, and there are some things I must simply *teach* you. What you and I are going to do in the next few days is too important for us to argue or quibble. Really, we do not have the time. Agreed?"

Asa smiled.

"You must simply accept my word, for now, that the Alcheringians are in great danger. Truly. They are, in fact, on the verge of a disaster. Their leaders are aging men, and their young ones more and more lack respect for the traditions. I know all about Rusl and Kenet. I know all about you, and Rani, and the others. I know that Kurc, in banishing you, has acted as you have forced him to act, in the only way he knows. I know that Romoke has advised you and I know that you have gone against his advice. And I know that Jared, your old friend and mine, did his best to warn you and you refused to be warned. I know that you buried Jared and I know what you did after Jared's death. You see, we received your message.

"That is partly why you are here, that message. It would have been easy for us to neutralize you as we had to neutralize Rusl and Kenet, and send you back as yet another warning to the Alcheringians. Had we done that, we might have increased their fear of us, but we would also have increased their anger. These tactics of force have a way of "escalating," as the Old Ones used to say. Believe me, we prefer the quiet ways." Shem paused and looked out over the sea, his hand in his chin, for so long that Asa thought he had lost his line of thought. Then he said quietly, "At least, some of us do . . . In any case, your message told me that you would be a useful ally."

Asa's jaw clenched. "Not as long as—"

"Please . . . please . . . In the next few days I am going to tell you who we are, and what we do, and why. It will be strange to you, all of it, stranger by far than the journey through the sea by which you came here this morning. It will be so strange that when you return to Alcheringia you will believe sometimes that you have dreamed it all. But I know that you can understand what you are about to see, even though it will mean taking a giant step from one age to another. In the days of the Old Ones, men did such things."

"How do you know?"

"I know," Shem said, "because there is something called *history*."

* * *

On that first day a small cart was brought to them, and they rode in it along the seacoast and around the perimeter of a large complex of buildings. Those buildings were set so skillfully into the brows of hills that they seemed part of the landscape, places where the rock had fallen, or where glaciers had knifed out a perpendicular slice of hill. Some were set high, and provided views of the sea over the tops of trees; some were low, opening onto the meadows that sloped to the beaches, or onto the misty swamps that bordered the southwestern side of the complex. Through a window on this side, Asa saw a lean figure watching them go by.

As they rode, Shem explained that they were on Asgard, the central island of Yggdrasil. Asgard curved S-like from Jotunheim, the northernmost island in the Yggdrasilian Archipelago, to Neffelheim, the smallest and most southerly.

The building complex on Asgard contained the administration center for all three islands, and for much more as well. These buildings were fairly new, for they had grown to the surface only within the last century and a half, like cautious flowers, from the hollow shelters of the Old Ones underneath, a labyrinth of caverns deep in the bedrock of the islands, linked by tunnels through the sea floor itself.

Asa laughed in disbelief at this, but Shem told him once again to be patient; told him, smiling, that he would see for himself in good time.

The little cart hummed magically along paths constructed for it, taking the hills in its stride. Here and there they were given vistas of parts of the island and the sea. In the distance, along the southern and western slopes, Asa saw larger buildings with people moving among them, and Shem said that these were lodges, the homes of those few who, over the last few generations, had gradually learned to like weather. There were, Shem said, six thousand Yggdrasilians. Most of them lived underground.

Strange food, strange sights, strange conversation and ideas—all of these exhilarated Asa before his fatigue from the journey began to catch up with him. By suppertime he was yawning, and by sundown he asked to be taken back to his room. Alone, he watched the last of the afterglow from the little balcony that jutted out high above the sea cliff. He watched the last of the gulls swerving back to nests in the cliffs. He thought of Persis. A question, the last of a hundred he had asked Shem, half formed in the back of his mind, something more about *why* ... But then, just before falling asleep in the bed that was like September meadow grass, he had the child's thought: I will know the answer to that question when I am old enough, when my elders have decided that it is proper for me to know it.

Then he slept. For ten hours he would know nothing at all.

He would not know that while he slept the wall above him would open and through it would come a large and extremely delicate silver spider, a spider of multitudinous arms and accouterments, a spider that would pause before descending, its sensors extended. He would not know that for an hour the spider would hover above him, touching with the greatest delicacy, sensing, measuring, analyzing. He would not feel hollow needles thin as gnats' stings slide through his flesh to sample the juices of his body. He would not know that the most sensitive of monitors had eavesdropped on his dreams. He would not know that the information gathered by the spider would pulse through the cat's-whisker filaments to awaken a computer, to cause it to separate, synthesize, correlate, and file; or that, even as it was doing its job, the information would be sliding, green and silent, across the terminal in Shem's office.

Despite fatigue that lay like lead in his bones and turned his foot into a gelatinous mass of pain, Shem sat up very late into the night, drinking tea, watching the information about Asa unfold on the screen beside his desk. Twice he touched buttons ordering a replay—once when the blood type was determined (RH POS), and once when a scan revealed a brain anomaly. Apparently this anomaly was bothersome, for it took the computer several minutes to search its databanks and produce an explanation. Even then the diagnosis was tentative:

SUBJECT: ALCHERINGIAN MALE. ASA. #A 8746.

LIMDIS: DREAM-MASTER LEVEL.

SUGGEST PREVIOUS DIAGNOSIS (I.E. CLASSIC GRAND MAL) INACCURATE. SUGGEST LIMBIC ANOMALY HIPPO-CAMPUS AREA.

SUPPORT: HISTORY FEBRILE CONVULSIONS (FILE HJ 4839 [M]). HISTORY ERRATIC BEHAVIOR TYPICAL PARTIAL COMPLEX SEIZURE (FILE IF 4857 [E]).

Shem watched the unrolling of further data until it ceased. Then he touched the buttons which permitted him to watch the silver spider delicately fold in upon itself above the body of the sleeping boy and retreat through the wall, which sealed in total, hermetic silence.

Then he clicked off the monitor, swallowed the potion which would permit him to sleep, and went to bed.

THREE

Garm lay on his belly in the brush.

He had lain so still for so long that even the jays had ceased to pay attention to him. In front, a precipice sheared away three hundred feet to a rubble of scree and detritus barely covered by high tide. Above, gulls and cormorants hung placidly in the updrafts off the cliffs, searching for scraps in the incessant currents.

It was a good height from which to search.

Since crossing the Larl far to the south of Alcheringia two days before, Garm had searched constantly as he and his small band made their way through the coastal mountains. He had searched for Alcheringians.

Now he was overlooking Alcheringia itself. Now he was searching for particular Alcheringians.

He had seen Asa's lodge, apart from the others. He had seen Persis working beside it. But he had not seen Asa.

"Tonight!" whispered the young man beside Garm. He was a good hunter, and he would be a good warrior. But he was impatient.

Garm shook his head absentmindedly. His thoughts were on the encampment.

"But why not? We can go in *there*, across those meadows on the north. We can take her when she is sleeping. The others will never know. The fools have no guards, except at the pass!"

"No," said Garm. "Not yet. Not yet."

"But *why not*? There are five of us. We can . . ."

Garm turned his gray eyes on the young man as if seeing him for the first time. In his gaze there was no anger, no impatience, but only an intense curiosity, as if this person were suddenly less, unaccountably and infinitely less, than he had seemed.

The young man fell silent and turned his attention back to the encampment.

Cumulus clouds blossomed over them and rolled serenely out to sea. From the woods behind, the song of a cerulean warbler told Garm that all was clear—the report from one of the three lookouts he had posted along the cliff.

He saw Persis, but his gaze drifted over her, searching, into the main body of the camp.

He did not want the woman; he wanted the man.

FOUR

"PEOPLE," SHEM SAID THE NEXT MORNING AFTER BREAK-fast, "have not always lived as you live—the Alcheringians, the Kaniks, and the other tribes. You have seen the things that have come from the Old Ones. In fact, you have seen one of the cities of the Old Ones, haven't you? In the Wayst. You and Rusl."

"So. Even that you know."

Shem nodded. "You remember. Rusl does not. Furthermore, you know that those things were made in the time before time."

Shem made a curving sign, back and down. "'In the dark backward and abysm of time.'" Asa's brow furrowed at the strange words, and Shem smiled. "Poetry," he said. "In that time, there were many places like this. In fact, much grander. In that time, men passed easily through the air, as well as upon the sea and under it. In that time, they talked to each other by means far beyond the reach of voice and drum. This place, and the "spiders," and the aircraft that you have seen all your life—they are all left from that other age."

"And they are dying," Asa said.

Shem nodded solemnly. "Yes. They're wearing out."

"Sometimes magic dies with the magician," Asa said. "I have seen the corpses."

"Yes. And it is because you have not been frightened, like the others, that you are here."

"But—"

Shem made the sign for silence. He looked very weary and, Asa thought, a little frightened himself. "There will be a time for other questions," he said. "For now, I want to answer this one: Why, if the Old Ones were such cunning magicians, did they destroy themselves and their magic?

"There are many ways of answering that question. For now, let me tell you only that it was because they grew to hate the products of their cunning. They saw themselves as a flawed species, and their artifacts as corrupt. They wanted them gone, and set about to destroy them. But it was too late. Those things had taken on their own life, grown strong. And the Old Ones found too late that they could not destroy them without destroying themselves.

"Only a few survived. Those who built this place were among the few, and we are their descendants. We have all their skill, know all their magic. Some of it we practice; some we do not, either because we choose not to, or because we no longer have the materials required."

Shem sipped his tea before continuing. "If you live, there will come a time when you will hate me for what I am about to do. If you live longer, you will come to see that it was necessary. Please understand that I have no choice."

"What is it you must do?"

"Give you history."

"History," Asa said, trying the strange word. "Is it a way of knowing?"

Shem nodded.

"Then why should I hate you? I came here to know."

Again Shem nodded, smiling ruefully. "Let's begin, then. You asked me what time was, and I told you that it was the cutting of the circle of all life and stretching it straight." He drew an imaginary line on the table. "It is like a path. We are here, at the center. What is ahead of us is the future. What is behind us is the past."

"And history?"

"It is a way of remembering the past—as much of it as possible."

Asa laughed. "And so, to journey in your 'time' is to roll up the path behind you and carry it on your back!"

"Very like that," Shem said.

"How foolish! The load will grow too big. It will crush you! Besides, we do not all travel the same path."

"What I must show you and tell you now will convince you that just such absurdities are necessary. Come. We are going to make three visits. The first is into the past, into history."

They entered the underworld of Asgard. An elevator took them silently down out of the sun and the odor of the sea, into a deep and restless world of labyrinthine caves and tunnels. Pale light flooded these spaces, making all those they met seem white and harrowed, with cavernous shadows where the eyes should have been. Muted sounds, infinitely mingling, radiated outward in a sibilant plethora of activity such as an insect might have heard from the center of a hive. People moved in urgent little carts along passageways. Pausing at intersections, Asa saw men moving also on far and shadowed galleries. He lost all sense of distance and duration. He went along with Shem in mingled horror and incredulity at those forces that had created such a place, had turned men and women into such pitiful bundles of anxiety and haste.

Their cart carried them swiftly down a long tunnel. Occasionally other carts passed silently, and their occupants acknowledged Shem with movements of their pale hands or glances from cavernous eyes. "The Old Ones made this place," Shem said as they rode. "They saw the time coming when their fear of others would grow to such a pitch that they would attempt to destroy them utterly. And they knew that the others would attempt to destroy them, also."

"Many raids," Asa said, frowning, knowing that this was

an inadequate phrase for the cataclysm that Shem was describing. "Many raids all together."

"They called it war."

"But," Asa said, shaking his head in horror, thinking of Persis and the weird turnings of fate that had made them lovers, "but if you kill your enemies, you cannot marry them."

"That was not important to the Old Ones. They were interested in power. In ways of destroying. They even had a word, *holocaust*, the destruction of everything. They believed that they had reached the point where they could do that—destroy the entire world in which they lived. At the same time they believed they had reached the highest point in their culture."

"Mad," Asa said.

"Yes."

"In their madness they must have hated themselves very much." He had seen such self-loathing, in which men stabbed themselves and hurled themselves off cliffs.

"A few," Shem continued as the cart ascended an incline and the muted buzz of new activity drifted down to them from the complex that lay ahead, "a few recognized that madness for what it was and knew that it could not be cured in time. Knew," he said more softly, "that perhaps it could *never* be cured, that it might be part of humankind. They caused this place to be built so that something might be saved when the holocaust project was complete. They were very wise. It is fortunate that they did. They gave us—you and me and all of us, all of humanity—another chance. Come, here we are."

Another short elevator ride brought them to a large, quiet room. A woman turned from a desk as they entered. "We've been waiting for you," she said. "We're ready."

"This is Urtha," Shem said.

In the weird light it seemed to Asa that she was constantly changing, now young, now old; now beautiful, now haggish; now smiling a welcome, now grimacing with baleful threat. "Come," she said, and her voice too shifted like the lighting, distorted and protean. She led them past the desk cluttered with spools from which snakelike strands of transparent ribbon unraveled, and into a smaller room where they were seated facing a large rectangular space that shimmered magically. The woman left, closing the door behind her, and the light in the room faded.

"You will see history now," Shem said. "But first you will see how man lived *before* history, before the round was cut and straightened out in the way I have described to you."

The image of a man in skins appeared on the screen, and Asa gasped in recognition. He did not know the man, nor the type of skins he wore, but the weapons he carried could have been made by any Alcheringian hunter. Also, the hunting and gathering of the man and his family were thoroughly familiar. The film showed them now with black skins, stalking exotic prey in a place where there were no shadows; now with tattooed cheeks, gliding in long canoes through forests where birds cried like lost souls; now insignificant on endless ice, rotund and motionless figures crouched above the blowholes of seals.

"Man has always lived like this," Shem said, as the ghostly images passed. "I cannot tell you how long because the numbers would be meaningless. As long as there have been men and women. As long as there has been what the Old Ones would have called *Homo sapiens*, knowing man, they lived this way."

"So do we still. What other way is possible?"

Shem glanced at him sharply in the darkness. "What other way? Why, the way you have been suggesting, you and Kenet and Rusl. Did you think you were alone? Did you think that such ways of living were never *tried*? Look!"

The shifting images moved from the familiar to the strange. Asa saw others actually doing what he had proposed, planting the seeds of grains and gourds, and impounding caribou in corrals of stones and wattled fences. He saw them working the ground with hooked sticks, and singling animals out of the herds for slaughter. He saw a different way of living emerge before his eyes. He saw special buildings constructed not for living but to hold the fruits of harvest, to hold the *surplus* food. He saw lodges clustered around these granaries and stores, never moving, because there was no need to move. He saw the lodges changing for that reason, growing larger, built of more permanent materials such as stone and logs.

He listened to the debates in the councils of these villages and he found that the concerns of the people had changed, that men were less worried about the common good, more preoccupied with private matters, with families, and with the use and acquisition of what they called *property*. Where previously men had shared for their survival, knowing that fate did not treat all equally, now they did so grudgingly, with the sense that those in need were less deserving, less provident.

The gods changed, too. No longer were they the fickle manlike gods of the hunting trail and the warpath, gods of the elements who could kill or preserve a man, gods of sacred stones and brooks, gods of tabooed places. Like men, the gods came to the plantations and the corrals. They became shepherd gods, farmer gods, gods of fertility and harvest. And the ways of honoring them changed accordingly. The impromptu ceremonies for each particular occasion gave way to an annual round of planting, harvest, and fallow waiting, with festivals at each stage, some orgiastic, some sacrificial. Shamans became priests. The shaking tent that had once moved like a ghost across the countryside became a church with fixed symbols, fixed designs, and static ceremonies. Flexibility and invention became repetition, repetition became habit, habit became routine, and routine hardened into ritual.

The pace quickened. With increased security came increased numbers. Permanent settlements soon dotted the countryside, and the dots changed into blotches, and the blotches spread, and joined, and the hunting trails became wagon tracks, and the wagon tracks roads, and the roads highways on which metal creatures hurtled with men inside. No one hunted any longer, except some who killed for the sake of killing, and some of the hives in which people lived were over a day's journey in one of the hurtling machines from the fields and pastures where the food was grown.

Hives was the word that came to Asa's mind, for the dwellings now contained more people than he could count, and their lives resembled nothing to him so much as the frenzied scurrying of bees and ants, except that while the activities of insects had purpose, those of men had none. Most were not only far removed from the sources of their own food and incapable of gathering it, but they lived lives caged and circumscribed, lacking all contact with nature, never breathing the fresh air of a forest morning, never bathing in a cold stream, never warming themselves before a fire of driftwood. So poor, so lost, so barren were the lives of the people whom Asa watched that had he not been horrified, he would have wept for them.

What they had done to the earth horrified him most. Much of it lay covered by a concrete crust in which the people lived and on which their vehicles dashed about, so it had ceased to be earth at all and was only a sterile slab. Over it the air had grown so foul that it could not be breathed in safety. People coughed their lives away with hideous diseases, especially the most vulnerable, the very young and the old. And the rivers that coursed through the land, and the lakes that lay tranquil in its bowls, once the home of fish and the refuge of myriad birds, were no longer crystalline and vibrant. They lay sluggish, dammed with sludge, opaque and bubbling with poisons. Ranges of hills and mountains lay stark and bald, all their forest cover gone, cut away, burned off. No animals moved upon this land except in cages, and these turned dumbly until the time came for their slaughter, gazing at an empty heaven through eyes bereft of wilderness.

"No!" Asa cried, pounding the arm of his seat. "Why do you imagine such horror when it can never be? It can never be! Men would never permit it!"

"It *has* been," Shem replied.

The images moved relentlessly. On the screen now, men were destroying the places where they lived. They had found the means to puff large parts of them into airborne blossoms. In these blossoms people died horribly. Metal insects screamed across the sky, diving and rattling.

Afterward, for a little time it seemed that there might be peace and green again; but then the building recommenced, a scab on the body of earth. Then, a little later, the destruction also recommenced, until finally the blossoms in the air grew much larger and, at last, erupted like gigantic mushrooms feeding on corruption in the earth.

After that came a long period of stillness. Nothing moved. The buildings did not grow again. Instead, in time, a kind of green returned where they had been. In time, animals returned. In time, a few men in skins crouched on the edge of a clearing . . .

Asa's brain reeled. He choked.

"They're called films," Shem said. "Some were made by the Old Ones, some by us."

"Horrible! Why do you keep such stuff?"

"Because we learn from it what is in us."

"Learn?"

Shem watched him intently. "Because it has happened, as I told you, surely there's a question in your mind."

"How to prevent—"

"Yes," Shem said, smiling sadly. "Of course. And now there is no going back."

Urtha was not at her desk when they left.

"What is it that you want, now?" Shem asked when they were once again in the silent cart. "Do you want to forget?"

Asa shook his head.

"Good. But what, then?"

"The sun," Asa said. "And the sea. And the tracks of a deer across a beach."

"Ah. I can give you all of that, and more." Shem touched buttons on the controls of the machine and leaned back. "We are going to a place called Val. I promise, you will like it."

Later, after Asa had allowed himself to be taken by the smiling attendants of Val and sent gently into sleep; after the Analysts had sorted out the most intricate and perplexing of his desires, and the Programers, quicker than the flutter of a wasp's wing, had drawn the myriad subtle ingredients from their memories and melded them into the necessary composite; and after Asa, in precisely the right stage of REM sleep, had begun to dream the prepared dreams which would give ultimate satisfaction, purging all disquieting memories and repressions; then, alone, the Dream Master of West Norriya moved with difficulty along the darkened corridor to the viewing room on his ruined foot, and sat in the darkness watching Asa's dreams as they crossed the monitor in the slow dance of dream time. Much of what he saw was incomprehensible, unique to the sleeping youth, and there were some things he did not see at all—the watching wolf's eyes, for example, set in the cumuli above the sea. But most of the images were familiar. They depicted a lonely childhood and were peopled by those he knew—an old man with a staff who drifted wraithlike in a futile attempt to replace the missing father; and a raven-haired young woman with the wind tugging her clothes on the bluffs above the sea, watching, walking forever through the meadows; and another young woman, on a beach, weeping, moving forward with her arms outstretched . . .

Shem was alone in the viewing room. Perhaps for that reason he made no attempt to hide his tears. On the other hand, perhaps he was simply unaware of them, so absorbed was he in the simple images that passed before him across the screen. Had anyone entered and asked him why he wept, he could not have said whether it was for the destruction of his own innocence, or for that of the dreaming boy, or for them both together, inextricably caught as they now were in the coils of time and knowledge.

FIVE

THE KANIKS HAD KINDLED ONLY A SMALL FIRE, AND THEY huddled close to it against the chill of the August evening. They were growing surly. "Tomorrow," one of them said, jabbing at an ember with a smoldering stick. "Tomorrow!"

"Not yet," Garm replied.

"Yes! No more delay! Let's take the woman and be gone!"

"No," Garm said very softly, looking up in surprise. *No.* He mouthed the word, shaking his head.

Another suddenly flung a handful of pine needles into the fire, causing it to sputter furiously. "Why not? Why do we wait? You owe us an answer!"

Garm turned cool eyes on him. "I owe you nothing, but I will tell you that we wait for a man who is not here."

"You risk our lives with this hatred!" the other hissed.

Garm's smile chilled all who saw it. For a year there had been no humor in it. For a year he had not laughed. His smile now was the grin of a coiled wolf whose eyes are the last sight its prey will see. "And which," he asked, "do you think is more important—my hatred or your life?"

The other did not avert his face, but he looked away, at the fire. His throat was exposed. It was so still in the Kanik camp that the hiss of air escaping from a firelog sounded like a snarl from the edge of an ancient darkness.

"Three days," Garm said. "If the man has not returned by then we shall take some other action. Be content."

SIX

SEVERAL DAYS PASSED BEFORE ASA MET WITH SHEM AGAIN. He was told that Shem was occupied with urgent and unexpected business. In the meantime, others attended to his needs, answered his questions, and escorted him on tours of the service areas of Yggdrasil. They showed him the island's tidal generators, its airport, its submarine bays and hovercraft hangars. They showed him the greenhouses and the gardens, and explained the workings of the fertilizer plants where wastes were recycled. Curiosity soon replaced any lingering fear he may have had.

"Remember that you, too, will go back," Alva said when the time came for her to leave. "And what then? How will you *use* what you have learned? Think!"

He thought. Always at the back of his mind were the grisly images Shem had shown him from Urtha's files, and when he and the dream master met again over breakfast several days later he said, "What you showed me are shadows. Dreams. They are like the mists, there, that the sun will soon burn away. Why should I believe that such things really have been?"

Shem smiled. "Are dreams not real? Because a dream is insubstantial, because it comes in strange forms and changes, even as you look upon it, into something else, does that mean that it has not existed?"

"History is insubstantial, then?"

"As frail as language," Shem said. "As frail as thought, or honesty. As frail as trust."

Asa considered, staring at the large man, and finding his gaze levelly returned. Shem's right eyebrow was lifted quizzically. It asked, *Shall we continue?*

Asa shrugged and nodded.

"Later," Shem said, "it may be necessary to go deeper into the past and to question those small bits of it we have chosen to call history. There are people who do that. There are people who spend their lifetimes on *one year* of the past, or one *event*, or one *person*. We call them scholars. They are essential. They are the reason for our existence, and everything we do is designed to protect them and allow them to work as long as possible. Perhaps later you will learn more of them and of the terrible beauty of what they do. The question they must answer is the same one you asked when you saw the films: *How to prevent the horror that once occurred from ever happening again?*

"Remember that question. Believe that what you have seen is the truth, if only a very small part. Believe that the question is the most important anyone can ask." When he saw that Asa had finished eating, Shem stood. "Come now. I have more to show you. Time is short."

Again the elevator whisked them deep into the bedrock beneath the sea. Again the cart was waiting, and in a few moments they arrived at another complex of offices. Here was none of the leisure and silence that had characterized the place where Urtha had presided. Here, people walked hastily with their heads down, and when they consulted they did so earnestly, with furrowed brows. There was no laughter. People talking on telephones pushed their fingers through their hair, and looked down at their desks, or at one of the ubiquitous clocks, or punched computer keyboards or calculators, or doodled in jagged lines. A few nodded to Shem as they passed, but neither he nor they had time to talk.

"It is as if," Asa said, "they believed time will end, and soon."

"It will," Shem said. "They know it. We all know it. We have only forty two years left to do what must be done. Already we are beginning to run out of some things. We have to send foraging parties to the mainland not just for food but for other things as well."

They passed through the hubbub toward a distant office, an island of relative calm.

"Why do you not allow it to end? What can be so important?"

Shem did not reply.

"Is it not an illness?" Asa persisted. "All this busyness?"

"Yes." Shem nodded. "It is. But a sacred illness. An illness that everyone here has taken voluntarily. You see, *they believe that they are responsible for all those who will come after them.*"

"And you would have me catch this illness, too."

Shem grunted. "You *have* caught it. There is no going back."

Asa thought of the sea at evening, and of Persis' laughter, and of the joy of the hunt. He thought of the brush of a dewy branch across his wrist, and the firm set of the path beneath his moccasins. He thought of the smell of woodsmoke and meat cooking in the evening. He thought of children playing on a sandbank at the edge of a river.

He thought, *I will go back!*

They had reached the office and were immediately shown inside. A woman was speaking into a telephone nervously, tapping a pen as she did so. Her desk was strewn with files, records, and stacks of computer discs, as was a long side table against the wall. A very large clock dominated the room.

The woman herself was perhaps fifty. Her black hair was generously streaked with gray. Time had etched delicate networks of wrinkles into the folds beneath her eyes, which she made no attempt to conceal. Time had dried and crinkled the skin on the backs of her hands, so it hung slackly over the atrophying muscles beneath. Time had taken all warmth and questions from her voice and left it hard and abrasive.

Time passed under her impatient gaze as the hand of the clock jerked from second to relentless second.

"Do that," she was saying into the phone. "Do that and call me back . . . I can't talk now . . . No . . . Right!" The phone clattered into its receptacle, and she swiveled, back straight, and extricated a file from the stack on her desk. "Everything—" she began.

"This is Verthandi," Shem said at the same moment. "She is in charge here. This is Asa."

"Hello." The slightest smile flickered across her mouth. Her eyes did not change. She pushed back a strand of hair and laid the file on her desk. "It took time to bring this together, believe me. But I think it's what you want."

"Thank you," Shem said. "If—"

"Shem, there's got to be a better way of arranging these tours. This is the fourth request I've had this month, do you realize that? If they really are necessary—which I doubt—then some other procedures will have to be established. I can't keep asking my staff—"

Shem was nodding with his eyes closed. "I know. Leave it with me. It will be on the agenda for the next Arborea. Meantime"—he lifted the slim file—"thanks for this. I see that we start in the map room."

The telephone was ringing and Verthandi was reaching for it. "Right. Right. If there's a problem call us. Bye. Bye, now." Her glance flickered to the clock and then slowed, froze, listening to some request from the other end of the line.

"This way," Shem said outside.

A short walk took them through a series of pneumatic doors and into a quiet room. Projected on a screen which covered one entire wall was a huge diagram. "Map," said Shem, but Asa had already recognized the undulant coastline of Alcheringia and its rivers, recognized them from Romoke's bark and sand drawings. This map, however, was much larger than he had ever seen, and showed details of the coast farther north and south than he had traveled or known anyone to travel, except the sea traders.

"We call this the Master's Map of Norriya," Shem said. "Here we are, at the center." He pointed to the Yggdrasilian Archipelago, tiny in the sea, insignificant against the looming land. "And here is Alcheringia, almost opposite us. Here are the coastal mountains. Here is the Larl, here the Em. Here are the lands of the Yuloks, the Montayners, the Kaniks, the Abibones, the Gerumbians. Here are the northern tribes, and here are the southern ones. Yes"—he followed Asa's gaze into the center of the map—"that is the Middle Wayst, where you and your friend Rusl rode. It's grown fairly safe since the Entropies, but if you had kept going you would have come to one of the cities of the Old Ones, and had you gone there and stayed you would have died."

"We saw it," Asa said. "It was gray, and pink, and purple, like a strange flower."

"I have brought you here to show you what is happening now—not in the past or the future, but now. As I speak to you, keep in mind the question that we are striving to answer:

How can man live without destroying himself and his world?
In other words, *How might man be cured?*

"I have told you that the Old Ones, when they knew that
their behavior had grown so aberrant that a cataclysm was
inevitable, stored in this place everything that they knew.
Everything. There are hundreds of depositories beneath the
deepest chambers we have visited. It seems that long before
the cataclysm occurred they had replaced wisdom with knowledge. And then they exploded knowledge, and gathered the
pieces—millions and millions of pieces. They called those
pieces *information*, and it is that information that is stored
beneath us. It is that information from which our scholars are
striving to assemble sanity again—decoding, assimilating, always searching.

"They now know, as you have seen, that in all man's history
and prehistory, he was most successful when he was part of
nature. Dependent on nature and not dominating, not making
nature do his will."

"Hunting," Asa said, watching the older man's face carefully. "Gathering."

"Exactly.

"Toward the last, the Yggdrasilians knew that some main-
landers would survive what was coming. They knew that these
people might carry on with life with no way of knowing, except
in legends, what had gone before. They saw that these survivors
must at all costs be prevented from taking the step to what they
called *agriculture*, and to congregating in hordes in vast, permanent settlements. They saw too that if we here in Yggdrasil
were to have a second chance to do what they had failed to
do, then we must have time for our scholars to work.

"Therefore they devised two plans. The first, in which they
created the space and the time—five generations—for the
scholars to work, they called simply the Project. The second,
in which they devised the means to control the mainland tribes,
they called the Gaian Expedient."

"I know some of those means," Asa said bitterly.

"Tell me."

"Fear." Asa raised one finger. "Fear of superstition and
taboo." He raised a second finger. "And the spiders."

Shem nodded. "There are others that you will learn about
now. One is persuasion. Logic. Reason."

"What is *Gaian*?"

"Gaia. A very old name for Earth."

"Earth?"

"This." Shem touched buttons on a console at the side of the screen. The map vanished. In its place rose a blue circle wreathed in mists, magically turning, the toy of a delicate child. "We are here. Here."

Asa laughed, but Shem nodded soberly. "It's true. Once, in the days of the Old Ones, there were people all around Earth."

"And now?"

"Now we don't know. Somewhere there may be others still."

The door of the map room opened cautiously, and an anxious young woman peered in. "Excuse me, sir. I hate to interrupt, but we have the map room booked for oh nine-thirty."

"Just leaving," Shem said. He shrugged to Asa. "Time." He led the way to a moving corridor, and consulted Verthandi's file as they rode along on it. Soon they came to another quiet place, where the workers wore loose green suits and caps. They spoke softly to one another. Gauze masks hung at their throats. One, a woman, looked inquiringly at her clipboard and then at Asa as they approached, but Shem shook his head.

"The devices that you called 'spiders' were aging rapidly, like all of us. Like this place itself. The fact that you could attack one and destroy it is a sign of their decrepitude. The command to destroy them all was issued several days ago, and their self-destructive mechanisms were activated. They no longer exist. As a result, we must use other means to do what they did."

They entered a darkened room. Ahead of them, on the other side of a transparent wall, a small drama was in progress. Asa saw a man and a woman, aborrs like himself. They obviously believed themselves to be alone. They were engaged in intense conversation, and embracing. The man touched the woman's hair, and it seemed to Asa that they were deeply in love.

Suddenly they parted. Apparently a knock had come on their door, and when the man opened it there was an attendant waiting. The man was being summoned, and he went willingly, reassuring the apprehensive woman that he would return to her very soon.

"I must tell you," Shem said, touching a series of buttons on the wall, "that he believes he is going to become one of us, a Yggdrasilian. He is a man of huge ambition, a Yulok, and he would do anything to satisfy that ambition. He has made a choice now, for power." He twisted in his seat to stare at Asa. "He is therefore a very dangerous man."

"He loves the woman," Asa said.

"Perhaps, but he loves power more. Power over people. Power over animals. Power over the land itself. He would not hesitate to sacrifice her, or anyone, to that lust for power. In fact, he has just done so, or believes he has, for he thinks that he will not see the woman again. He has traded her for power. What you just saw was a pretense, an act."

The image through the transparent wall faded, and a new portion of the wall lit to reveal another room at the moment of the man's entrance. In the room was a small group of men and women like those they had passed in the corridor. All were dressed in loose-fitting clothes of pale green. Gauze masks hung at their throats. They welcomed the Yulok smilingly. In the center of the room was a thin white couch on which the man at once reclined. Arrayed around him, hanging from the ceiling and hovering on rubber-wheeled carts in the background, were a number of thin, articulated devices so much like miniature clinicians that Asa actually shouted a warning. "No! Don't do that! Get out!"

"He can't hear you," Shem said calmly. "And even if he could it would make no difference, for he believes that what will now happen will give him that power he so badly wants."

The team operated with brisk efficiency. For a short time they clustered so closely around the man's head that Asa could not see what was done. Various pieces of apparatus slid silently forward or descended from the ceiling to perform their function. Attendants brought trays of tiny, precise instruments and took away stained pads. Very soon the Yulok was sitting on the edge of the couch cautiously touching a bandaged area on his skull. Solicitously the group helped him to his feet. The operation seemed no more serious than the removal of an arrowhead from beneath the skin.

And yet, when they returned the man to the woman, he no longer recognized her. When she embraced him he seemed embarrassed and looked around at the others for some explanation. Whatever the two of them had once shared had been taken forever.

Asa went cold, and when Shem said, "I think we've seen enough of that," and left the room, Asa could not speak for several moments. The place was full of perils! It was a vast and darkened forest where gods hung waiting in the trees, omniscient, and where men crept fearfully in their little beams of sun.

"Perhaps you're wondering," Shem said as the moving corridor took them softly back to where they had parked the cart, "why we bother with that sort of thing at all, when it would be far easier simply to kill. The answer is that life itself is precious to us, as it was to those who built Yggdrasil and established the laws by which it is governed. There is so *little* of life now, you see, that we cannot risk reducing it by even a single soul. That is why the injunctions of all the tribes prohibit killing, although we know that it must occur in the heat of emotion, in battle."

"But what," Asa asked, "what if your devices don't work?"

"They always have . . . with individuals." Shem added the last phrase so softly that Asa almost did not hear him.

"What do you mean?"

"The problem of a tribe, that's another thing."

"Why?"

"We do not have the means, you see. It's as simple as that." They had reached the cart, and Shem kept silent, thinking, while they climbed into it and he swung it back into the tunnel on the return journey. "Supposing that for any number of reasons, any number of human failings or circumstances beyond his control, a peregrinus (Wanderers, you call them) loses control of a tribe and permits it to drift beyond fear of the taboos, beyond awe of the myths. Supposing too many individuals have strayed that far to permit any 'clinical' corrections to be made without endangering the whole fabric of the tribe. Supposing we see that tribe beginning on the downward slide toward the horrors you know about. And supposing we see the danger of that rot spreading to other tribes and endangering the whole frail Gaian Expedient. What would you say we should do?"

They had arrived at the elevator bank. Shem had stopped the cart, but he made no move to get out. Instead his eyes searched Asa's, and he gripped his arm, shaking him slightly. "What?"

Asa tried to imagine himself having to make such a decision, and he could not. "I—I don't know," he said.

"*Neither do I!*"

"But surely the Old Ones, the first Yggdrasilians, saw that such a thing could happen."

"Oh yes." Shem had begun to climb wearily out of the cart.

"And what?..."

"I could never condone what they recommended. But there are others who could. With no qualms whatsoever." His lowering brow overshadowed his eyes, and the strange flickering lights around them glimmered on the creases that arced down from his eyes and into the top of his beard. "That is why Alva must not fail! It is why *you* must not!"

"But—what must I do?"

"Undo what you and the others have done. Somehow. *Keep Alcheringia pure.*"

"But I can't stop—"

"Thinking. I know. And asking questions. And being angry that the answers you find are never adequate. Being delighted that they lead to more questions. And more. I know you can't stop. And that too is why you are here, and not sitting with your friends Rusl and Kenet, with your head full of air. *You might find answers!*" Shem entered the elevator and they rode up in silence. "I shall be busy for several days," he said as they parted, "but I've arranged for others to answer all your questions, and to supply you with any information you require. They will escort you any place you wish to go on Asgard. As soon as I can I shall meet with you again, and we shall make another short journey together."

"Where?"

"To SKULD," Shem said.

That night Asa was tormented by evil dreams.

These were not the lucid dreams of Val, the cathartic dreams that left only serenity in their wake. These dreams were full of dread. In some he was trapped between massive blocks. In some he was lost in an endless labyrinth, made more horrible by casual clouds passing overhead and the singing of negligent birds. In some he was pursued by innumerable straight lines, slicing from infinity to infinity again. In all, he was vulnerable. In all, the threat was a mindless and fleshless thing. In all, the spider creatures looked on and, dying, laughed. In all, beyond the little frenzy in which he was entrapped, the sane world proceeded.

Several times that night he screamed and lashed out blindly. Several times the solicitous monitor that had emerged from the wall above him drew back rapidly and hung suspended, waiting until its sensors reported that the subject slept again before it moved close and resumed its testing.

SEVEN

THE SQUEAKING OF THE CART'S TIRES IS LOUDER THAN THE purr of its electric motor. It enters Asgard Station One, hisses across the polished concrete, and stops. The man wearing the uniform of the Biological Unit dismounts and enters the waiting elevator. He is carrying a slim briefcase.

Nidor has not returned to Asgard since his meeting with Shem, and the absence has not distressed him. He wishes he were not returning now. The intrigue and political maneuvering of the place disgusts him, dependent as they are on emotion and indefinable human chemistries. However, Nidor's feelings do not show on his face. Nothing shows on his face; it could be the mask of an automaton.

He arrives at his floor, walks a short distance down the corridor, and is shown into a room with a fireplace and aborr weapons hanging on the walls. His distaste registers involuntarily with a slight twitch of his lip; from the type of briefing requested he has expected someone purged of atavism.

Seeing the uniform, Moran laughs nervously. "I was expecting someone from Ethnology," he says.

"The responsibilities overlap. However, given the nature of your request—"

"Of course." Moran gestures to a chair near the fire, but Nidor selects a distant one.

"Your question has been treated hypothetically. So far as I know, the full elimination of an aborr population has never been considered by the Arborea."

Moran waves placating fingers. "It's not being considered now," he says. "I am interested only in facilitating matters so

187

that if measures now being taken should fail . . ."

Nidor does not look up from the brief he has laid across his knees. "You have three alternatives. The first is a simple strike from Yggdrasil. This would entail—"

"No, no, no. Out of the question." Moran is poking at his fire, shaking his head. "The Arborea would never sanction it, and we'd run the risk of insurrection among the militia. Too public. Too overt. Too obviously in violation of the Principle of Diversity."

Nidor lets the room fill with the sounds of the fire and of time wasting. Then he says, "You requested a briefing on all possibilities. It is my job to present those possibilities, not to discuss their merits."

"Quite so," Moran says. "My apologies."

"The steps necessary for such an alternative to succeed are given in detail on the disc I shall leave with you. They include the reeducation of the militia."

"Umm." Moran shakes his head doubtfully. "Distasteful. Would require repression on a scale—"

"Please do not waste my time," Nidor says. His voice is like a ski in soft snow. He is very pale.

Moran nods. "Go ahead."

"The second alternative is also projected in full on the disc, complete with all necessary steps for each of the subchoices. This is the disease alternative. You have available the traditional options, of course—anthrax, bubonic plague, cholera, smallpox, typhus, and so on—as well as a range of fresh hybrid strains. We have recommended two alternatives should you select this approach. We have provided full rationale and detailed plans."

"And you guarantee success?"

"Of course." Nidor stares curiously at the large man, as if a halibut or a bullfrog has burst into song. "Provided our instructions are followed precisely. It is merely a technological exercise. Of course, if you compromise or deviate, nothing is predictable."

"Carriers? Wind drift? Residual bacteria dormant in site?"

"As I said, all eventualities, *all*, are accounted for. You will find detailed methods of containment."

"The safety of other tribes and of the land—"

Nidor's back stiffens. He inhales with a hiss. "Sir, have you brought me here to brief you or to have a fireside chat? If you have questions when you have studied and assimilated our projections, then I shall answer them. Until then, I do not have time for idle speculation. Nor do I have further patience with your persistent questioning of my foresight and competence!"

"I assure you I am not—"

"Yes you are! And without reason. If I may say so, it is precisely such witless maundering that imperils the Project!"

The slack skin at Moran's throat tightens as his jaw thrusts forward. His eyes narrow. "Don't spit in the well, my young friend. You'll be thirsty by and by." It is his turn now to let the silences speak. "I believe you have a third option for me to consider."

The tenor of Nidor's voice does not change. "The third option is sociological. Or, if you prefer, primitive-political. It would require two things: a temporary escalation of the raiding patterns of neighboring tribes, and a unifying force capable of synchronizing an attack. We have worked out several variations for your consideration. We have also made recommendations. If, for example, the object of this hypothetical study were the Alcheringians, the natural catalyst for the antagonism of all neighboring tribes would likely be found among the Kaniks. Of course, adjustments to the various codices would be necessary. All that is projected for you." Nidor folds his file and lays the computer disc on Moran's desk. "Will there be anything else?"

"No. Thank you."

The door hisses shut behind Nidor. He descends through the levels of the Asgard Central Complex to the vehicle and the tunnel which will take him back to Neffelheim, passing within a few yards of the room where Asa lies asleep.

Alone, Moran dismisses Nidor's impertinence. For the moment. Later, perhaps he will mention it to the Director of Neffelheim, or perhaps he will say nothing. Dealing with the technocrats is always notoriously difficult. They have a heretical lack of respect for chance and mystery and, consequently, for any creative vagueness. They yearn for radical simplicities.

For the moment, Moran has other matters to attend to. All night he ponders the information on Nidor's disc, leaving his terminal only occasionally, to feed the fire and to gaze into his flames.

By dawn he has made his decision.

He issues two orders. The first is to his Kanik peregrinus, Aleaha: CONTINGENCY PLANNING URGENT. COME ASAP.

The second order is to SKULD.

EIGHT

"SKULD," SHEM SAID TO ASA AS THEY DESCENDED AGAIN into the labyrinthine underworld of Yggdrasil, "is our way of knowing the future."

This time they entered an area utterly different from the others they had visited. Elsewhere there had been human bustle and the scent of human anxiety and error. Here was none of that. Instead of voices, there was only the discreet hum of machines talking with each other, interrupted occasionally by subdued clicking or rattling as wheels spun and printers activated. Elsewhere the light had been pale and sometimes flickering, as if the source of power were unreliable. Here there was a bright and absolutely steady glare of fluorescents. Elsewhere signs of deterioration had been everywhere—bulkheads and furniture chipped and worn, equipment waiting for repairs that did not get made, niggling shortages that hampered work. Here everything gleamed in its perfection. In the other areas workers had seemed harassed, but here the few attendants, dressed in immaculate white uniforms, moved serenely in their duties. They smiled when they saw Shem.

A door opened ahead of them. It bore a small brass plaque engraved with the ubiquitous tree-symbol. Beneath the symbol the sign read: SYSTEMS-KINETICS UNIVERSAL LOGISTIC DATABASE.

Inside, they passed walls of screens and dials, gauges, spinning spools and gleaming lights. "SKULD," Shem explained as they walked, "is a huge machine. Rather, it is a network of machines. We call them computers. In fact, SKULD is a giant memory. Into it is fed constantly all the information classified by the Programers. This information is vital for making what are called projections—shadows of the future. These are very like the shadows of the past, but they lack the experience of having been lived. Come."

He led the way into another small room like the one that had been presided over by Urtha. At the front of it was a screen. At the rear was a projector mounted on a large console glittering with dials, knobs, switches, and tiny monitoring screens. At this console sat an attendant, who stood up as Shem entered.

"This woman," he said, "will offer SKULD various possibilities. Based on what it receives, the machine will give you scenarios, visions of a future that may or may not happen. First, let's suppose that the Alcheringians do not change their present course. They turn the summer camp into a permanent settlement, level the forests for agriculture, and begin the taming of animals for domestic use. What then?" Shem nodded to the operator. The room darkened, and images began to appear on the screen.

They were similar to those that Asa had seen before. Time was compressed in them. Years and decades became moments. Centuries passed in minutes. Alcheringia, the airy encampment of space and light, congealed on the earth, and spread. Fields broadened around it. In no time it evolved into the concrete horror that Asa had seen in the earlier films, a scab cracked and suppurating, nibbled at by metallic flies, drained by a pustulant river. Segmented worms wriggled through its flesh.

Shem spoke a word to the projectionist, and the images vanished. "There's no point in following through to the end," he said. "The result is precisely the same as what you have already seen. I should tell you, however, that this thing is a contagion which will spread to the other tribes. They will all 'develop,' as they call it. The result will be a radical simplification of Earth and a speeding toward the Entropies. According to SKULD, the progression is inevitable.

"Suppose, however, that the old injunctions continue to be observed. What then?"

Again the projector hummed, but this time, over the centuries projected, very little change occurred in Alcheringia. Sometimes the community shrank fractionally, sometimes it grew; but essentially it stayed the same, vanishing every autumn when the two clans dispersed into their winter hunting grounds inland.

"Even if the Project fails," Shem said, "even if Yggdrasil exhausts itself and ceases to exist, the tribes are so ordered that life in them could proceed indefinitely, provided, of course, that their codes are observed."

Asa shook his head. "I think they never will be. They must always be changed, broken by a few."

"The task of the peregrini is to see that that doesn't happen."

"But if the peregrini were not there..."

Shem opened his hands as if releasing a captive bird. "That is why the Project must succeed, and why there is such urgency."

"You will not stop men from thinking."

"Thinking, no; acting, yes. In fact, we shall need *all* our intellect if *Homo sapiens*"—Shem said the words with a fleeting ironic smile—"if man the wise is to survive. We must ensure that we do not violate the limits of life itself. Biological life. If we can do that, then we shall be truly wise."

"So," said Asa, "you are saying that we should know the results of any action before we act?"

"Yes."

"But that is not *what living is*! Who could live purely reasonably? Life is chance, and—and passion!"

"Perhaps for some people, at some times, in some places. Not here. Not now. What we must do, here in Yggdrasil, is to know the future *at least* as well as we know the past. We must know the ramifications of the slightest alterations in our plans and systems. And we can. The life expectancy of these islands, this community, this Project, is known to the day and the minute. SKULD has given us that, and SKULD can change the calculation in the blink of an eye if the circumstances change. Suppose, for example, that we discover some part of the complex deteriorating faster than anticipated. Say, some metal component in our tidal generating system. We have ways of measuring that rate and SKULD can tell us the significance at once. Will it mean that the scholars have a year less to work on the Project? Six months less?"

"Time," Asa said after a moment, "is a monster. I am glad that we live our lives free of it."

Shem smiled sadly. "The Alcheringians are free of it, but not you, Asa. Not entirely. You see, *you know*. You have been infected. And someday you will have to make a choice."

The projectionist had been sitting patiently at her console, waiting further instructions, glancing occasionally at the blank screen, or at the green-lit digital clock flinging tenths of seconds into eternity. Now she said, "Will you need me any longer, sir? If not . . ."

"Only a moment," Shem replied. "The Memoir Function, please."

"Which file, sir?"

"Mammals."

"Actually, I'm not familiar with the Memoirs. It's usually Ruth who—"

"I know. Do your best. You have the call codes there?"

"Yes sir."

"No hurry." Shem turned back to Asa. "When we know that something is about to die, some species, we begin a file into which is fed everything on that creature that is known. Every last detail. I won't bore you with those that became extinct during the time of the Old Ones and before; that list is too sad and too long. But here are some that have gone in just the last few years, victims of the Old Ones' poisons that still lurk in the Waysts and in other places we don't yet know about. Ah!"

After two false starts during which irrelevant material spun across the screen, the operator found the right call codes. Images of various animals began a ghastly parade of the doomed and the forever gone. "Cougar," Shem said, naming each as they passed into oblivion. "Mountain sheep. Kit fox. Moose. Flying squirrel . . ." Each image was accompanied by names, index numbers, and brief cross-references for retrieval purposes. Of course, Asa could not read these, but several of the animals he recognized. He laughed at the idea that they should pass forever from the face of the earth, but Shem grimly insisted it was true. "Only a matter of time," he said. "In some cases, years; in some, months . . . Of course, the more that go, the greater is the probability that human beings will follow after them, leaving the world to insects. I wanted to show you these because—"

He gasped. His eyes had suddenly narrowed and fixed on the screen. The operator had erred with her call codes and inadvertently presented a new name on the screen, the name of a thing which, according to SKULD, was as surely doomed as any of the creatures they had been looking at.

"What is this?" His face ashen, Shem twisted toward the frightened operator. *"What does this mean?"*

"I—I'm not sure, sir. But I think . . . I think it must mean that someone has ordered a file begun."

The name on the screen, which Asa could not read, was *Alcheringia*.

When he summoned Asa to his office later that evening, Shem was still white and his voice trembled. He spoke quickly and urgently. "You must go back at once. Things have changed rapidly in Alcheringia. Getting worse. Much worse. I wish I had time to show you more, tell you more, but you know why you must persuade your people to keep their Tabuly. You know what will happen if you fail."

Asa nodded. "Alva—"

"The thing has grown beyond her. She can't control it alone."

"Kurc? Romoke?"

Shem shook his head. "Gone," he said. "The young men have been swayed by your arguments, and the elders that are left are too feeble to stand against them. It's changing, Asa. Very fast. And . . . and I must tell you that there are people here who will stop it if you don't."

"What? . . ."

"They'll destroy Alcheringia," Shem said.

Slowly Asa raised his hand in the Alcheringian gesture of farewell to a friend. "Will we meet again?"

Shem cleared his throat. "That depends on you. The time will come when you must make a choice. You will decide for your own reasons. I shall never send for you unless you ask." He hobbled forward with his lips shut tight against the pain, and took Asa's face for a moment between his two huge hands.

Then he embraced him.

NINE

KURC AND REMOKE DIED TOGETHER.

They were hunting with the last of their Nine, two other elders, in the hills behind Alcheringia. All day they had been on the track of a fine buck, and with the lengthening of the shadows they split up into two groups to approach the deer, which had begun to feed in an upland meadow.

Kurc and Romoke loped easily through scattered undergrowth. They were full of the joy of deep moss under their moccasins, and were young again with the drifting scent of pine and the imminence of a splendid kill.

The twang of Kanik bowstrings and the thumping of Kanik arrows into their throats seemed, in the last moments of both their lives, to be very small annoyances in the midst of wondrous vitality.

The Kanik marksmanship was flawless. Heavy war points severed spinal cords, and both men fell. With the last of his life, Kurc saw for the first time the pitiless eyes of Garm.

Across the clearing, other Kaniks shot from ambush, and other Alcheringians died, although less efficiently.

Undisturbed, the buck browsed in the clearing, where, in the last of the light, he was joined by a skittish doe.

TEN

Asa woke cold. He opened his eyes to gray moonlight through slits in the clouds.

Wet boulders pushed into his hip and ribs. He was hunched in a fetal position, wrapped in his own skins. Rain sifted out of the darkness onto his face and bare legs. He was so cold that when he first attempted to move, his joints would not respond. A mean wind gnawed at him. Somewhere the sea crashed.

After a moment he managed to straighten his legs and sit. He was shaking violently, and he knew that he must move or perish. He struggled stiff-legged to his feet.

At first, the beach below him seemed no different from many others, gleaming darkly in the drizzle and reflected moonlight. The embankment on which he stood could have been anywhere. But when he peered closely around him he recognized the little clearing where Jared had come to die. He hobbled over to the base of the cliff and found the grave of his old friend.

For a time he remembered nothing. He stood hunched against the cold rain staring at the grave and knowing only that a portion of his life had passed without his presence. He didn't know how long. The grave told him only that he had not buried Jared yesterday, because a season's grasses and flowers had seeded it over.

Then he began to remember, his banishment first, and then everything in a rush—the journey with Alva, Yggdrasil, Shem.
Shem.

He remembered his departure, and the strange way that Shem had suddenly taken his face into his hands.

Then he remembered what he must do.

Slowly at first, then more swiftly, he followed the path along the cliff tops, and by mid morning had arrived at a narrow defile about two miles from Alcheringia. He was startled here by the sudden appearance of two sentries, young warriors from this year's Nine.

"What's wrong?"

"Kaniks," they told him. "They stole women three days ago, and they killed Kurc and Romoke and two others on their way back."

"Persis? . . ."

"She's there," one of them said, gesturing toward the camp. "They didn't take her, but you have a Kanik arrow in front of the door of your lodge."

"Who posted you here?"

"Rani."

"Let me pass."

"The banishment . . ." one of them began, but the other shrugged.

"Go ahead. It doesn't matter. Everything's changing anyway."

Fear and foreboding lowered above the settlement in the aftermath of the raid. Friends barely acknowledged Asa's greeting as he passed. They were busy with children, or with the sorting of their winter's supplies, anxious to get away to the relative safety of the country. They glanced past him even as they spoke, to the surrounding hills.

Persis came running to meet him, crying, and they embraced on the path. "Asa. Asa. I thought you would not come back."

He pressed his face against her neck.

"Romoke came one day," she whispered, "and told me that he had had a vision, and that you had gone to the Islands of the Gods, and that you would be changed there. He said the man I knew would never come back. Never."

He smoothed her black hair, and kissed it, and held her face on his breast. "Romoke is dead," he said. "I am alive. And here. I love you. I shall always love you and come back to you, no matter what happens."

"Garm came."

"But you are still here. With me."

"That is his way of insulting you. Or challenging you. It is his way of showing that he wants you more. He wants *ven-*

geance more. That is the way Garm is."

Later, lying in her arms and watching the shadows of the fire play on the sloping walls of the lodge, he began to tell her all about Yggdrasil and what had happened to him there, but she drew back and looked at him with such wonder that he stopped.

"A spell," she said.

"Yes."

"Another journey among the gods of your spells."

"Yes," he said to her. "That's all it was."

The next morning Asa went to Rani's lodge. More families had left at first light, and the encampment looked desolated. It was still raining, and a cold wind brushed the sea and rustled in the sere beach grasses.

"Rani!" Asa called. "We must talk."

In a few minutes Rani emerged, smiling slyly, guardedly, and another young man came out behind him. His name was Moros. Asa knew him to be a laugher and a dreamer of exotic dreams, one who did not hunt but who lived on pieces others gave him; one who did not speak candidly at councils but who secretly mimicked and ridiculed those who did.

"Let us be quick, Asa." Rani pulled his robe around him against the wind. "There can be little to say now, and we have preparations to make for winter."

Asa smiled wryly at his old friend. "You were not always so quick to know what must be done, Rani. Tell me, what has changed you?"

"Death," Rani said levelly. "And knowledge. The deaths of elders in the time that you have been gone, and the knowledge that the gods are indifferent or impotent."

"No, Rani."

"The knowledge that you were right. We can break the Tabuly with impunity."

"That's not true. We must talk. I must—"

"Whaaat? Whaaat?" Moros edged forward grinning, and Asa saw that he was not speaking to him but to the crowd that had gathered behind him. "Is this from *Asa*? Asa, who argued for im*prove*ments, for ex*peri*ments? Asa, who was *ban*ished for speaking as we are?" Moros leaned close and mockingly searched Asa's face. "What has changed *you*, Asa? Have you been traveling among your gods again? Hm? Learning all their secrets?"

He snickered, and several in the crowd laughed with him. Asa heard the guttural snorts of Thorel.

But before Asa could reply, a deep, calm female voice said, "Yes, he has," and Alva was standing beside him.

For a moment there was silence, and Moros drew back, glancing quickly at Rani. Rani blinked once. "And did you ask your gods, Asa, where they were when the Kaniks killed Kurc and Romoke? Where were they when the Kaniks rode their horses in here, *although it is forbidden*, and killed children and stole women? Did you ask your gods why they burdened us with this helpless Gerumbian freak?"

Alva tensed. The paw slid fractionally from behind her cloak. "The Kaniks will be dealt with," she said.

"Oh yes!" Rani nodded wide-eyed. "Indeed they will! By us! You see, Asa, we have made certain decisions while you were gone, and we have made them despite Alva, not because of her. We have learned how to act against a Wanderer. *You helped us do that, Asa.* One of those decisions is that we shall winter *here*. Moros and I and whoever will stay with us. Despite the cold and *despite the gods*. And in the spring, when the others return, we shall be here, and there will be more changes made in Alcheringia!"

Clearly, Rani was no longer the frightened boy who had cowered whimpering beneath the god. He was a man who had somehow found courage to take his fate into his own hands, and with it the fate of a people.

"Rani," Asa said softly. "I beg you. Don't do this thing. Let us talk."

But Rani had made the cut-off sign and was already turning away. He and Moros returned to their lodge, and although Alva tried to speak to the little crowd, they drifted off one by one until only Asa was left.

"I've failed," she said as the two of them trudged back to Asa's lodge. "I could kill him, of course, but even that would do no good, now. Things have gone too far."

"By spring," Asa said, speaking like a weary man postponing a task until the morning, "by spring something will happen. It will be better then, in the spring. You'll see."

But Alva was shaking her head heavily. "Leave. The two of you. Get out. Never come back."

Sickened by the place, they took her advice. Late that afternoon, laden with packs, Asa and Persis paused on the crest of the trail and turned back for a last look at Alcheringia. Their view was obscured by shifting gusts of drizzle, but they glimpsed nevertheless a cluster of defiant lodges near the shore, and a forlorn figure hunched where their own lodge had stood, staring westward toward islands invisible in the fog and the encroaching night.

ELEVEN

FROM: DREAM MASTER, EAST NORRIYA.
TO: Peregrinus, Kaniks.
RE: Recent contingency plans, subject WHITEBELLY.
STATUS: Final decision imminent.
MESSAGE: Initiate Plan Three ASAP. Acknowledge.

TWELVE

Heavy snow fell early. Before the end of November it had shrouded the walls of their lodge waist-high, and in another month it had enclosed them almost completely. Only the smoke hole showed where the lodge lay beneath the drifts. In the still nights, they listened to the crackling of frost-stressed trees, and to hoot owls along the borders of the marsh, and to the mournful searching of the wolves. In blizzards, they stoked their fire.

During the few hours of daylight at the short end of the year, they performed the necessary chores—the hunting, and the butchering and cleaning—and they returned to the lodge to talk, to eat, to make love.

That winter, everything was intimate. Only a few things troubled them: the prospects of the spring and what should be done then; Asa's memories of Yggdrasil and the meaning of what had happened there; Garm.

Garm. Once Persis said, "He will not rest until . . ." and left the sentence incomplete.

She was right. Garm's humiliation was a sore festering long after the wounds of battle healed. It would fester until he was avenged.

Restless, nomadic, the Kaniks shifted constantly. Groups lived together for a few weeks and then went separate ways. Young braves moved from one group to the other in search of adventure and of women, and sometimes, alone, they retreated to the wilderness for days or weeks.

Aloneness was less worrisome to the Kaniks than to the

gregarious Alcheringians. Entering the long silences was accepted as the way to heal bruised spirits, or to invite mystery and wisdom, or to plan to avenge a rankling wrong.

So it was no surprise that for several weeks after the Alcheringian raid and his failure to find Asa, Garm lived alone in the remote western foothills of the Kanik Mountains. He had chosen the spot for its seclusion, because he did not want to be found; however, Aleaha found him.

She was a crone, Aleaha. Sometimes her name was used to frighten children into obedience, and sometimes she was the butt of scurrilous jokes. She was so old that no one could recall her history. She was so ugly that it was impossible to believe that she had ever been loved by a man, and yet it was said that she had borne children—children half beast. When she spoke her voice was like two dried trees rubbing in a wind. Her hands moved incessantly, like small crustaceans, separate from her will.

"The gods are kind!" she called to Garm.

He did not reply. He had known she was coming for several minutes. He had seen a pair of jays explode squawking from a copse of alders, heard his hobbled horse whinny softly, watched Aleaha emerge from the woods, and, pushing laboriously with her staff, begin to climb the slope.

"The gods are *very* kind," she wheezed when she reached him. "They have forgotten who led a horse raid through Alcheringia. Against the Regulae."

Garm smiled. "I want no mercy from the gods."

"An agreement, then, since your intentions are the same, perhaps." Aleaha drew a fish symbol in the dust. She drew a spear through it.

Garm laughed. "It would take a cruel man to bring the tribes into league for that. *All* Alcheringians?"

Aleaha nodded. "In return, the gods will grant *your* request." Her black eyes hardened, glittered. Her crabbed fingers searched in her garments for her otter-skin medicine bag. "And there are ways, my son, to be crueler than the world. There are ways to be harder than even you can imagine. I can help . . ."

That winter, everything delighted Persis—the high, clear days when nothing moved, the unexpected bustle of snowbirds, even the wallowing track of a wolverine through the drifts. "I wish," she said, "that this could go on forever."

*   *   *

All winter Gram traveled.

He went west first to the Abibones. He sought them out in their lodges beyond the blue mountains, and went unarmed into the tents of their leaders. He took with him no power or authority beyond his own, beyond the gaze of his gray eyes and the venom with which he hissed the name *Alcheringia* into their faces. From them he won promises to take a plan to the first council fires of the spring and to lay it at the feet of their young warriors, restive and hungry after the confinements of the winter.

Once during that winter, they saw another hunter passing in the distance, too far to be recognized. Once they heard people calling, but they saw no one. "Spirits," she said. Once Asa came upon the tracks of five men, less than two miles from his lodge, but who they were or where they were going he never learned. "I wish," she said, "that they would never find us again, and that we could spend the rest of our lives together like this, alone..."

Garm went south to the Yuloks, to the people of the sea, and found them camped in bands along the Coast, rich with their sea catch, waiting for spring. They too listened to him, their sometime enemy, and they too agreed: In the spring, at the first of their councils, they would discuss this thing that he proposed, and then they would send word to him of what they had decided. They smiled at what he proposed, imagining their strand of coast stretching north to the very limits of what was known, with no more threat of Alcheringian raiders from the sea. They were a stolid and unimaginative people in whom the fires of combat and ambition had died. They disgusted Garm with their obscene obesity and wealth, yet he smiled at them, and agreed, and offered the hand of friendship. *First the Alcheringians*, he thought. *Then you, my friends!*

She leaned over Asa so that her black hair, falling forward, shrouded both their faces. Her eyes widened with pleasure and surprise. Her breath was sweet with urgency. "I hope there is a child! Oh Asa, I want there to be a child, in spite of everything!"

*   *   *

He went north, then, swiftly and silently, straight into the
Alcheringian lands. He skirted the shore like a wraith in the
swirling snow, and his snowshoes hissed through the drifts.
He smelled smoke, and at night when he came to the camp at
Alcheringia he saw a single forlorn lodge beside the sea. He
waited until he was satisfied that the occupants were asleep,
then he went to the river and stood for a time looking at the
great falls and the ice-shrouded trees surrounding it, and at the
frozen pools, and listening to the thrust and gurgling of water
beneath the ice. From his medicine bag he took the powder
that Aleaha had prepared for this purpose. He scattered it into
the water and into the wind, which bore it in a drifting fan
across the encampment; and then, so low that his words were
lost almost to himself in the crashing of the sea, he uttered the
curse that Aleaha had taught him:

"May the soil of this place fester with corruption. May it
be an opened wound in the flesh of earth, and may the stink
of it rise to heaven. Cursed be this soil! Barren be it from this
day forward forever! May the waters of this place turn loathsome with their putrefaction, foul beyond all nature. May the
fish of the sea shun them forever, and the birds of the air, and
may the beasts flee from this place in terror and loathing. May
the very gods here sicken and die in agony, and may all those
who have lived on this soil, and their children, and their children's children carry pain in their bones forever. May they
wander forever in blighted lands, and may all their lives be
such misery that they will plead with the gods for death."

When he had finished, Garm shivered. Then he spat, and
turned northward into the wind, and in a few moments the
squalls and the darkness had absorbed him.

Asa lurched awake screaming, lunging into the wall in his
panic. He had had a dream indescribably horrible, so horrible
that he fled from the reality of it, and from its suffocating
darkness, directly into a spell. For the first time in many months
he was comforted more by phantoms than by the real woman
who held him in her arms.

Garm came at last to Gerumbia.
This place he had dreaded more than any, for the Gerumbians were creatures scarcely human. They were less a tribe
than a benighted collection of freaks, hulks, and cretins, victims

of foul genetic jokes, bound together by shared misery and grotesque malformation. Theirs was the bleakest of regions between the forest and the Wayst, sifted over with blighted dust, spotted with bent and stunted vegetation.

He knew when he had reached the borders of their land. He saw the bear heads posted as warning totems, and he heard the moaning of Gerumbian wind harps in the warped trees. He went on, cautiously, and soon saw the tracks of Gerumbians themselves, tracks sometimes scarcely recognizable as mammalian, except for the signs of toes emerging from shapeless masses that were, perhaps, feet.

Garm knew that there was little point in seeking them. He knew that their lairs were now deep beneath the snow, and that even if he were invited into them he would not want to go.

When he began to smell smoke and to see furtive shapes on the horizon, he stopped. He made his own fire in the open where he was completely exposed, and began to roast the rabbit he had shot that morning.

He saw everything, although he seemed intent only on the preparation of the meal. He saw the flurry of activity that his arrival caused as word spread among the Gerumbian lairs. He saw the appearance and disappearance of lumpish heads in the entrances. He saw a small group gather at last and, after some discussion, begin to move warily toward him.

The rabbit was cooked. Garm slid it off the spit, drawing his bow close to his side and freeing four arrows from his quiver as he did so.

He ate.

Many Gerumbians had emerged, but only four approached him. They walked almost like men, but there was something apish in the gaits of all, stooped, arms dangling in front of them. They looked like men. They wore the clothes of men and their eyes harbored the wariness of men, but their bodies were maimed and grotesque, and their faces—all but one— were so repellent that even Garm's gaze faltered when he looked at them.

They looked like lizards, crafty-eyed. One, with a mangled shoulder and a useless twig of an arm, owned a face that was beyond description, a face that might have emerged from the floor of the sea a million years before. Only one was manlike in his bearing and appearance. He was smiling.

Something turned in Garm's memory—a boy bound with

rawhide in a clearing, in pain, and a laughing band of raiders, and one of them tall and blond, like this. Garm's knuckles whitened suddenly on the rabbit bone, but he continued to eat. The fair one continued to smile blissfully, and Garm knew that whatever mutilation he had undergone was inward. He had known others like this, others with memories scrambled like gruel.

"My name is Runch," said the one with the monstrous face.

"I am Garm."

"You see that we are unarmed."

"I see. I see also that others of your kind are circling behind me, and I see that they *are* armed." Garm bit into the rabbit meat and chewed.

Runch looked up in surprise. His brow furrowed. "They are hungry," he said.

"If they feed on me," Garm replied, "they will feed on us both." His left hand dropped on his bow. He continued to eat. Runch waved the skulking Germubians back, and when Garm looked behind he saw that they had obeyed. "I have come to talk," he said.

"In my lodge."

"Here."

"As you wish."

Runch sat, and the others sat, a pace behind him.

Garm continued to eat until he had finished, watching steadily and waiting for the last restless movements to subside on the slopes around them. Then he wiped his hands on the front of his jacket. "It is a lean land you live in."

There was no response. The gaze of the Gerumbians shifted from the tiny pile of rabbit bones at his feet to his face and back again. Garm jerked his head.

"To the south, beyond the forest, the land is fatter. I have come to tell you that it could be yours."

"There are people in that place," said Runch, shaking his head as if to rid himself of troublesome flies. "There are people and they are strong."

"I have come to tell you," Garm said, "that they are less strong than you think. I want to tell you how they could be defeated and destroyed, and how that rich land could be yours."

"Speak," said Runch, smiling.

THIRTEEN

"Speak, damn you!" Fury had lifted the gnawing pain in Shem's foot into undulant waves of agony. "Tell me *why!*"

Across the table Moran turned pale. His lips moved for a moment before sound issued from them. "We have to be prepared," he said. "We must establish the alternatives."

"Prepared? Alternatives? You call ordering SKULD to assemble a memoir on Alcheringia *preparation*? You call waiving the Kanik law an *alternative*? These are *policy* decisions, Moran. You made them unilaterally. I want to know why. Now!"

"Not quite unilaterally," Horvath said. "Moran has consulted with me and I have kept the Arborea informed of these and other alternatives. It is a simple matter of contingency planning."

"So," Shem said. "I see."

"In fact, if I may say so, Shem, Moran has been more perceptive about developments in Alcheringia than you. You believed that your Gerumbian peregrinus could bring matters under control. She failed."

"She needs time," Shem said. "We all need time."

"You've had six months. No more." Horvath was immobile except for his tongue wetting his lips. "Kanik warriors have broken their codex and ridden horses through the center of Alcheringia. The Alcheringiàn Tabuly has become a farce. The situation is out of control, Shem. You know it. I know it. The Arborea knows it. At their next meeting they will give assent to the plan that Moran has prepared, fortunately, through his peregrinus."

Shem struggled to keep his pain and his horror in check.

He struggled to be reasonable. "Horvath, you're dealing with a *people*. With a unique culture. If you simplify—"

Horvath's head turned and his gaze settled slowly on Shem. It was no longer the cold stare that Shem knew well. To his astonishment, Shem saw that Horvath's eyes were clouded with pain, and for a moment he glimpsed a depth of grief and suffering he never knew existed. "Man," Horvath said softly, "do you think I don't know that? Do you think that I haven't tried everything possible? I tell you, *time has run out!*"

The clock hummed against its wall.

Horvath rose. His hand was trembling. He stood for a moment with his back to them, looking through the opened window.

"When?" Shem asked.

"When the Arborea has given approval. When the tribes can gather." Horvath moved toward the door.

"And who will survive?"

"Survive?" The master turned, his face once again a smooth mask, his eyebrows lifting in surprise. "Perhaps some women."

FOURTEEN

THEY LINGERED LATE IN THE WINTER CAMP.

They stayed until the snow had gone and the new ferns had begun to uncoil on April riverbanks. Then, at last, Asa said, "We must go back. There is something I must try to do."

"I know," Persis said.

Along forest paths lined with the fragile green of spring, the journey took three days.

They could smell Alcheringia long before they came to it. Alcheringia stank.

Sea breeze sifted the odor through the trees on the last ridge,

and down the western slope. It was the stench of death and
decay, of accumulated excreta, heaped and festering, unable
to crumble to dust in the drying sun.

When at last they stood on the crest of the hill and looked
down over the camp, they were appalled at how radically the
place had changed in the short time they had been absent.
Instead of random lodges clustering around the mouth of a
river, Alcheringia had stretched like an infection up the banks,
and some dwellings stood now even above the first falls. Dogs
had found their way among them and had been allowed to stay.
To his astonishment, Asa saw a few deer already clustered
forlornly in a pen near the center of the village, and others in
smaller pens attached to lodges. Foul with dung, these pens
were brown blotches on the green of the sea meadow. Rectangles of various sizes and shades stretched on the land beyond
the pens. Around the whole village rose a partially completed
earthen bulwark, and even as they watched they could see men
laboring to complete the unfinished ends of it, extending its
semicircle to the sea.

Neither would have recognized the place. In a few weeks
it had changed from a seasonal encampment to a rooted village.
To his shock, Asa realized that the Alcheringians *had claimed
the land*.

He cursed. Again the sea breeze shifted and wafted up to
them the stench of dung and middens.

Persis clutched his arm. "Oh Asa," she said. "Let's not go
down!"

"I must," he said.

"Please!" She spoke quietly, but her voice was trembling.
"I—I'm afraid. It's not Alcheringia anymore. It's not. The
people must have changed too much, to make it this kind of
place. Please. I'm afraid . . . here." She laid both hands on her
belly.

Asa squatted, hesitating.

"This is their madness, not yours," Persis pleaded. "Please,
let us go. *Quickly!*"

He stood and shook his head. "I am part of it," he said. He
began to walk down the path toward the village.

Twice she called after him, and when there came no response
she followed. She was weeping. "There is death here," she
said, so softly that the breath of the wind scattered her words.
"We are going down into a death."

They passed through the smoke of many fires. On both sides of the river men were felling trees and burning out the stumps. At the edges of the green rectangles, people were scratching at the bared earth with stone and wooden hoes, preparing to plant maize and other grains. The work was hard and dirty. Men and women sweated, and the soil rose in the breeze and settled on them, blackening their bodies. And yet, despite the labor and the grime, there was a cheerfulness among them. Many called out to Asa as he passed, inviting him to inspect and admire their work. "Look, Asa. We've done what you told us to do! We've swept away the old ways! We've started fresh!"

Fences were rising everywhere, some made of boulders hauled laboriously from the beach, some of spindly sticks lashed together or intertwined. Some were less spindly, and stood on solid posts with tightly laced cross members. Inside each enclosure, the earth had already been used and abused. In some, horses stolen that spring stood in the sun, morose tails switching flies. In others, caribou trotted ceaselessly, ribs protruding, beside the barrier that kept them from the freedom of the hills. Dust sifted among the lodges.

And the lodges, too, had changed, grown larger, more substantial, hunkering down more firmly on the land. Some had sprouted appendages—porches and other rooms—and from the doorways smiling women and children waved as Asa and Persis passed.

The place was noisier. The air was full of shouts, and the beating of restless hoofs, and the thudding of implements into the ground or into trees at the edge of the forest. The children, however, were quieter. Where once they had run freely through the encampment, now they were confined to the hard paths between the fences. They grinned at Asa and Persis, but shared the urgency of their elders. When Asa asked where they were going, why they were hurrying, they had answers. Purposeful and intent, they seemed to Asa to have lost the carefreeness of childhood.

The path penetrated the new bulwark through a gateway large enough for only a single cart. Inside was a wheeled apparatus of heavy, sharpened stakes, which could be quickly swung across to block the entrance. Atop the bulwark stood a small group of laborers. Asa knew them all and called out greetings to them, and they replied exuberantly, some of them leaning jovially over the wall to show Asa the length and height of the new defenses. "Kanik-proof!" they shouted. "We're here to stay!" they shouted.

Asa's heart sank. He reached for Persis' hand and held tight.

When they had passed through the gate, Rani came forward. He had been working on the rampart closer to the sea. He was laughing a kind of welcome, but there was no humor in his laughter, but watchfulness. "Asa," he said, his arms outstretched yet not coming close enough for an embrace. "Asa! We were beginning to think you were dead."

Asa raised his hand. A knot of warriors had gathered behind Rani, smiling, waiting. Asa saw Moros coming in the distance. "Things have changed in Alcheringia, Rani."

"As I told you they would. We are making progress," Rani said, his eyes shifting, smiling.

Asa nodded. "Progress. It is a word I don't know."

"It means," Rani said, "that we have begun to make things better. We are improving life, as you have always argued we should."

Asa looked slowly around the circlet of the camp, at the disconsolate livestock in their pens, at the heaps of manure, at the men toiling on the defenses and the women toiling in the little fields. He said nothing.

Rani followed his gaze. "There will be a period of adjustment," he said, smiling in a way that exposed his teeth. "Perhaps a generation. The next to come will benefit. We have a plan. We have a long-range plan."

Asa nodded again. He pointed to the largest of the lodges, the one with the biggest corral and the most spacious of the fenced fields. "Whose is that?"

"Mine."

"Yours."

"Mine. And Moros'."

"Last year it was a common, that land. Skins were dressed there sometimes. Fish were dried there."

"Things change, Asa." Rani shifted and the warriors behind him shifted also, smiling. Beside him, Asa felt Persis' yearning to be gone.

"Indeed things do change. Tell me, Rani, who are you now? Are you the chief?"

"I am."

"Are you the chief because you own the largest land? Or do you own the largest land because you are the chief?"

Rani flushed. His clutch tightened on the sharp wooden spade with which he had been working. "I am the chief *because I took the chance*! I stayed the winter. I showed that it could be done, that we could ignore the Tabuly and make our lives better!"

Asa pursed his lips and nodded. "You must be wise, Rani, to make such improvements in so short a time when so many others have considered them and not permitted them. You must have knowledge that they did not have."

"That is so," said Rani. His lips were pressed tight, and white.

"So. And may one know what this knowledge is?"

Rani hesitated, then blurted, "It is the knowledge that we *can* do it!"

"Can. And therefore should?"

"Yes. *Yes!*" Rani hissed, and the others around him began to shuffle uneasily. "How you have changed, Asa! Why are you splitting these hairs, paralyzing us with these questions, these doubts?"

"Sometimes there is good reason for doubt."

"Good reason, yes, if you would keep people hobbled, keep them in darkness and superstition. But we have passed out of that, Asa. We have passed beyond that, beyond the old beliefs forever."

Asa smiled. "Beyond all?"

"Yes. Beyond all that is constrictive, that prevents us from having our *will*."

Asa looked slowly around the circle and saw that the men were Rani's; their faces all showed the same hard purpose. "And what of the old custom of hospitality, my friend? Does that constrict you?"

Rani flushed. "Of course not."

"So we may stay with you for a while? Perhaps in the old place where our lodge stood?"

"It is your right."

"Thank you, Rani." Asa took Persis' reluctant arm and they moved together toward the sea, the little ring of men parting to let them pass. "Oh." Asa stopped and turned, raising his staff, a man who has suddenly recalled something. "And is it still my right, an Alcheringian who has been absent from the council when such important decisions were made, to hear the reasons summarized, and to speak what is in my mind?"

"Of course. It is the custom."

"The custom, still. Good. I will use that custom, Rani. Soon. Not tonight, but perhaps tomorrow." Asa raised his staff again, in a small, polite salute. Then he and Persis walked up the beach. They did not look back.

By the time they reached the site, Persis was trembling violently, and retching. She dropped her pack and walked out to the edge of the clearing, turning her face into the fresh sea wind. Despite the heat she kept her arms folded tightly across her chest inside her cape, and when Asa came up behind her and put his hands on her shoulders, she made no effort to turn to him or to embrace him.

"It is our home," he said.

"My home is where you are."

He looked down over the blighted landscape. "They are my people."

She said nothing.

"I will speak in the council one last time."

Still she said nothing.

"Persis, it is only for a little time."

She turned to him, then. "No," she said. "It will not be for just a little time. What will soon happen here will be forever." She was not trembling any longer. Her voice was steady, but there was such certainty and resignation in her eyes that Asa could not bear to look into them, for it was like looking into dark pools of time.

In silence he turned away and began doggedly to raise the lodge.

FIFTEEN

THE SCOUTS DISPATCHED BY THE CHIEF AT GARM'S URGING returned to report that what he had said was true: Garm had won the support of the Yuloks, the Abibones, the Montayners, and even the Gerumbians. They reported furthermore that Alcheringia had changed dramatically, and that the fabled mobility of the Alcheringians had yielded to earthwork defenses.

There was a moment of shocked silence when the Kanik elders at their council heard this news, silence that was soon filled with excited conversation and incredulous laughter. Kaniks had encountered such defenses before, to the west. They knew how such things dulled a people and made them vulnerable.

Behind the elders, at the edge of the firelight, Garm watched, and listened, and was content. It was no surprise to him to see the chief consult, Aleaha, in the shadows. It was no surprise when the chief stood and raised his arms for silence, and then made the raiding sign and pointed at Alcheringia.

The Kanik warriors burst into a jubilant dance.

It was no surprise to Garm when the chief pointed again, to him, and made the sign of the raiding leader.

For the first time in many months, Garm smiled.

SIXTEEN

When everyone had arrived, Rani spoke. There was wariness in his voice. "Asa has called this council," he said. "Asa has questions he wants to ask."

Asa stood and took the speaker's staff. He looked out over their heads to the sea. "You know me," he began. "You know that I have fought for this place and for my right to speak. You know too that I argued for the breaking of the Tabuly and for doing just what you have done, and for that I was banished, as Kenet and others were banished before me. Now I find that you have changed your minds. Before I say what I must say, tell me, someone, what has happened to make you do that?"

He sat. He expected Rani would reply, but was not surprised when Moros rose to speak. He saw that Moros now wore a necklace of bear claws— the shaman's symbol of authority.

"What has happened," Moros said, "is that in your absence we have left the old ways behind and found new ones. We have learned much. Knowledge has come like a bright light in our darkness. We have seen many things in this new light. The laws you spoke of, what were they but myth and superstition? We have put them behind us. We are"—Moros spread his hands and laughed—"free men! We say what our grandparents and parents dared not say for fear of retribution from the gods. What they dared not even think about, *we do*! We have taken our lives into our own hands. We are building a new society, a better way of living."

"Better. Better," said the circle of listeners, nodding at each other and at Moros.

"Better," Moros said again. "Asa, you are welcome to stay

with us. You are welcome to help us build, to help us plant, cultivate, harvest. You are welcome to take the land where your lodge stands for your livestock, yes, and more land if you need it. You are—"

Asa rose. "Hear me, now," he said, struggling to speak quietly against the dread swelling in his breast. "I was wrong to urge you to break the Tabuly. The laws are there for good reason. I have learned that from the gods themselves. Believe me." He was aware of Rusl sitting at the back of the crowd with his arms covering his head. He was aware of the elders glancing knowingly at one another: *All his life Asa has heard gods.*

"Look around you. Can you not remember what this place once was? It was rich and beautiful. You had all you needed, and more. All you desired, and more. Look at it now! See what you have made of it! Can you not see the blight you have laid on the land? Can you not smell your own filth? What kind of people have you become, and what kind of 'betterment' is this that fouls the very beds you sleep in, that cages you, that forces the earth itself to your will and makes it barren?"

"This is temporary, Asa," Moros began. "It is only for a little time, and then—"

"No. The gods can see ahead as well as behind. They know, and they have shown me. I tell you, if you persist in this madness, there is such a retribution coming that you will wish you had not been born, and your descendants will long to forget your names!"

Fear passed like a soft breeze around the circle.

"Gods? Where *are* these gods, Asa?" Rani spread his hands, looking heavenward. He was smiling, but then his gaze met Asa's and the smile vanished. In both their memories a boy lay screaming in the dirt, his arms covering his head. Rani flushed and looked away.

Moros spoke quickly. "We have defied the gods, Asa, and nothing has happened. Oh, at one time, perhaps, there was some purpose in the injunctions, but no longer. Not for us. As for this retribution you speak of, where is it? We used to hear of such things in the old days of the Wanderers, but clearly it does not exist. You say it will come in the future. Well, many things will come in the future, no doubt, some good, some bad. But for now, we think that the gods look with favor on our endeavors, Asa, and that you are wrong to admonish us for decisions that we have made when you were not present."

The hope in Asa's breast soured into despair. He felt sick. One by one he sought out the few men older than himself— Tanis and Urc, Marshal, Leec and Quiner and Paj—and one after the other as his gaze settled on them they avoided it. They looked at the ground, at their hands, at the distant sea. "You were not here, Asa," Urc said. "Moros is right. You do not know how the arguments went."

"It was perfectly reasonable," Leec said petulantly. "All legal and—and *reasonable*."

"It is not your right to come back now, when all is done, and admonish us, Asa," said old Quiner, looking restively back and forth from Asa to the sea. "We did what was required. We offered the proper arguments, and in the end we were outvoted. So be it. The thing is done. Nothing is to be gained now by opening the wound again. Let it be. Perhaps all is for the best, after all."

"Come," said Rani, crossing the council space and putting his hand on Asa's shoulder. "Help us with the harvest, later. Join the festivities this week. Share our food. Stay with us this winter. Here."

But Asa shrugged his hand away. "No, Rani, don't do it! I know what will happen. I've *seen* what will happen."

"Asa the Mad," Moros said quietly, glancing around the circle. "Asa of the visions."

"I have seen it," Asa said into the silence. "I have seen where it ends, this sitting still, this clustering together, this digging at the hide of the earth, this—this *breeding* . . ."

"This safety?" Rani gestured proudly at the circlet of earthen defenses and at the stockade.

Asa laughed bitterly. "*This* is your new safety? How long could you hold those little walls, Rani, against a serious attack? Why, you haven't warriors enough to place one every twenty paces. Will you be on guard forever? And what is your barricade against an enemy prepared to wait, to forage, to poison your water supply?"

The color drained from Rani's face. Others around the circle exchanged glances. Asa saw that, as he had suspected, they had not contemplated such a thing.

"Suppose they leave a dead horse in the Alcher. Will you drink seawater, then? And how safe are your defenses against disease, against the plagues that spread like fire where people mass together? No, this is not safety, this little fence walling is what you say you *own*. Your safety lies in dispersing through the land, as we have always done. It lies in distances. In scattering. In *movement*. See that, before it is too late. Leave this place, this autumn, and go back to the land again."

"We have gardens," Moros said. "We have homes."

"They are new words to me. I know what a plant is, and a lodge."

"Journeys are hard," said old Quiner. "The old die in the winter, in lonely camps, and the young also."

"So it has always been. There are safeties, too, in the deaths of some."

"Asa," Leec said, fixing him with the gaze of his one good eye, the eye that shone an incongruous bright blue out of the scarred, livid, and smashed face, "the way that you describe is not the way of all the tribes. You know that."

"But it is *our* way. It is the way we have lived, the way we have survived. It *works*. Why will you change it now?"

"Because," Leec said, "we are men. We must try the new things that we can imagine."

"And we must use our imagination to see why some things should *not* be tried!"

Rani grunted with impatience and made the cut-off sign. "We have been over this ground. There is nothing more to be decided, no reason to squabble like children. Asa, stay with us if you wish, leave if you wish, but let us hear no more on this matter. What was right once, for our ancestors, is not right for us now. This council is dismissed!"

They went hastily, avoiding Asa's gaze, and he was left alone in the meeting place.

For three days after that he did not eat. He sat in the sun beside his lodge, staring down into the dust and smoke of Alcheringia and ignoring the food Persis placed beside him. He drifted into and out of spells. Sometimes he went down to the river and thrust his head into it, like an animal, to drink.

Persis urged him to leave for good, and to go back with her into the wilderness where they had been most happy; but he would not, or could not.

He began to walk alone, neither scouting nor hunting, but simply walking, his gaze on the horizon. Sometimes, seized by some great urgency, he would begin to run, and he would run until he was exhausted, until his feet were cut and bleeding and he could run no more.

Hunters saw him far from Alcheringia.

Children said that they had called to him and he had not responded.

"Asa the Mad," the elders said, shaking their heads. "Always the seeds have been there, and they have grown now . . . He will not come back to you," they said to Persis. "He has gone into a country that is farther than any you can imagine."

"His mind is full of poisons, full of nightmares," said Moros, smiling. "It may be that he will die soon."

At night—those nights when he was with her—she held him close beside the fire and talked constantly, talked even when he did not respond, talked softly and earnestly, as if by talking she could bring him back from that far place where he had gone. She spoke of her love for him and kissed him. She rocked him gently, like a child. Sometimes she spoke of children and of her longing for a child, and at such times, although he did not see it, her gaze turned inward and secretive, and only then, for a little time, she lapsed into silence.

She talked of the time he had first brought her to the camp, and of the fights they had had once. She talked of their journeys, and of the winters. She talked to him of his gallantry, and of his foresight and strength. She spoke of good times that they would have in future when he was well and they would have gone far from Alcheringia.

She kissed him. Again and again she told him that she loved him and would love him forever . . .

Early in August Asa left and did not return. A week passed, then another. No one reported seeing him in the country; hunters shrugged when she inquired.

Another week passed.

Another.

Alone in the nights, Persis trembled.

SEVENTEEN

Almost dawn.

They had been waiting at the rendezvous since dusk. The Gerumbians had not come.

Garm feared that in their benighted enthusiasm the Gerumbians had gone ahead. The other warriors were restless. Twice he had had to quell fights between rivals, and still they postured and exchanged insults. Few had slept. Garm feared that his plans might end here, in a melee, and that the swift and sublime attack might never happen.

At dawn, he grew aware of movements on the edge of the forest. At first they were indistinct shadows, perhaps animals, groping on all fours. Then they coalesced into shaggy human shapes.

"Runch."

"Hello, Garm."

"We said evening, Runch. We agreed."

"It is a long way."

"Evening. Between sunset and dark."

"My people do not move swiftly. They have other talents, but they do not move swiftly. Some tire easily." As he spoke, Gerumbians edged closer to him, into the light of the fires. Other warriors fell silent. Even whispers ceased. They gazed on these allies with horror and incredulity. No one laughed.

"Let's go," Garm said.

"We need rest," Runch replied.

"It is a day's journey. It will be slow—"

"We will not slow you, but we need rest. Till sunset. Then we go."

Garm nodded, glancing eastward. "Sunset," he said.

Men ate, but not heavily. Men sang, but not loudly. They sang the low, thrusting chants of the Kaniks, the Abibones, the Montayners, and the Yuloks—the triumph chants, the prayer chants, the funeral chants. Men talked, but little, for they did not wish to say too much lest fear surface under the bravado. Men painted on friends' faces the livid shades of war—red, blue, yellow, and white. By midday the encampment was alive with ferocious masks, and the men who had sung, the men who had thought sometimes of mothers and of children, were hidden under those masks. Men checked their weapons, knocking off the last blunt surfaces of chalcedony and chert, testing the keen new edges with their thumbs.

At dusk they moved.

Rani and the elders toured the ramparts and declared them finished. The circlet was not large enough to include Asa's lodge or others on the outskirts of the village. The thinking of the elders had been that since the forest had been cleared far back, there would be adequate time to sound warning in the event of an attack, time enough for those outside to find their way into the battlements. For this purpose a large drum had been made ready in the center, together with a horn big enough to be heard over all but the wildest winds.

Shem touches buttons:

HUGIN PATROL 15 REPORTS SECTORS AD-4 AND AF-9 BELLIGERENT ACTIVITY SCALE 5. PER REQUEST: REPORT OVERDUE FROM ALCHERINGIAN PEREGRINUS.

Shem stands white and rigid with no cane, half his weight on his devastated foot.

HUGIN PATROL 39 REPORTS SIMILAR ACTIVITY SECTORS CE-3 AND CG-3. CONVERGENCE: ALCHERINGIA.

Shem stabs another button. *Where is Alva?*

"We don't know, sir. We've been unable to reach her." In the communication complex the overweight District Operations Manager sweats lightly, as a melon sweats when it is taken from refrigeration into a humid day. "We've been trying since four hundred hours. There's no response to paging."

"What's the problem, your damned hardware again?"

"Negative, sir. We have feedback on test signals. The subject is simply not responding."

"Keep trying. Please. Call me."

"Very good, sir."

The intercom light blinks off.

Shem moves to the western windows and looks over wind-blown meadows to the sea. The day is gusty but clear, and across the strait he can dimly discern the gray line that is Alcheringia.

Behind him, unseen, the monitor presents this message:

> EYES ONLY. RE INQUIRY: SKULD CONFIRMS ALCHERIN-
> GIAN MEMOIR CLOSED.

The monitor waits for a discreet ninety seconds, and when no acknowledgment is received, it prints the message with a sound like the death hiss of a lizard.

Shem does not look at the message. Standing at the window, ghastly pale, he considers ordering a helicopter into action but does not do so. He thinks of Horvath. He thinks of Horvath saying, "For reasons that we both know, this will be a difficult time for you. You will be tempted to break regulations. I advise you to remember your oath."

The day was gusty but clear.

Preparations for the festival had been going on for a week. Laughing young people had decorated Alcheringia with sprays of leaves and late-blooming flowers, a frivolity over which the old people shook their heads. Their blood remembered that it was time to move back into the country. The old people looked at the sky.

Wood was gathered for a huge fire. An altar was built at one side of it, and a huge spit erected directly over the fire.

A few paces away, woven rush mats were laid to receive a feast.

Persis did not know exactly when the preparations melded into the festival itself. Singly, in pairs, and in small groups people arrived, and when the drummers began to beat a soft and compelling rhythm, some danced.

At sunset, she watched a strange procession form and begin

to wend its way toward the council ring. Rani led, and he was surrounded by carriers of gaily decorated staffs and banners, some brightly dyed, their tips catching the last sun. Behind came a body of young warriors; Persis could not tell at first what was disturbing about them, and then she realized that they were *together*, close together, and in step. Among them there was no longer the smooth grace of the Alcheringian hunter-warriors, comfortable on their land; in this phalanx, stiffness had replaced it, and awkwardness. Behind them marched three men with council drums suspended from their shoulders, sounding a beat each time their left feet struck the ground.

Moros followed. He wore a pure white buckskin robe, so soft that it flowed around his ankles. In his left hand he held a long staff wound with vines and topped by a long, curved knife inset with tiny obsidian blades. From his right hand, a tether led back to a young stag. Its horns were wrapped in vines and scarlet leaves.

There were no women in the procession, and as it approached, the women who had been working in the council circle drew back, leaving space for the men to fill. The Alcheringians converged, the gates of the defenses swung shut, and everyone gathered, except for the guards on the parapet.

Rani waited for silence. He waited for the fire to be lit, and for the flames to gather and spread, swarming upward in the dry kindling. Then he spoke.

"We have become a proud people, afraid of no one. Afraid of nothing."

The wind moved on the sea, moved on the borders of the darkening beach, and along the foot of the parapet. "Afraid of nothing, no one," a few repeated after him, voices querulous, scarcely audible over the fire, which now roared voraciously, lunging among the piled logs. The tethered stag snorted and pulled back, wide-eyed.

"Once we feared to break even the smallest law, and when we did by accident we pleaded for forgiveness from the gods, begging them to withhold their retribution. We know now that there *is* no retribution, and that the gods smile on those who help themselves, and who take their destinies into their own hands.

"So tonight we celebrate a new beginning, for the storehouses are full, the stock is fat, the houses well sheltered against winter. And Moros has planned celebrations for our success."

He sat.

Moros still held the young stag's tether in his right hand, but a glittering obsidian dagger had replaced the staff in his left. No one else owned such a dagger, for obsidian came only from the sea traders, far to the south. It had a baleful and cruel magnificence, this dagger; it gathered into itself the hot light of the fire and gave it back in a cold gleam, such a light as winks from remote and indifferent stars.

"Tonight," Moros said, "we shall feast, for why should we not? Have we not earned that right with our labor?"

"Yes," they answered. "Yes, yes. We have earned the right. We are entitled."

Moros' gaze shifted. The wind whipped at his cassock. "Feast. And drink. And consecrate the ground so that it may forever be fertile for us and our children."

He raised the knife. The stag reared back, eyes rolling, emitting a high squeal. With a two-handed upward stroke, Moros slit its throat.

The animal tried again to scream, but air rushed whistling from its throat, together with the blood that drenched Moros and his assistants. The stag yanked convulsively against its tether. Its shoulder popped from its socket, its rear legs splayed out, and the beast ended in a pathetic squat, jowls lowered on the ruined throat.

It died slowly, and while it died, no Alcheringian, hunter or woman, did not recall the old injunction from the Tabuly: YOU SHALL NOT FEED ANY ANIMAL, OR USE ANY FOR BURDEN, OR KEEP ANY ENCAGED. One old woman began to recite the entire Tabuly in a high, keening wail, until she was silenced by her daughter.

"Come," Moros said. "We are together in this, as in all things. Come. Show now that you are a free and defiant people." He gestured to his assistants, and quickly they dipped right hands into the runnels of blood and circulated amid the crowd, offering those hands. No one refused; not even Persis.

It was dark. The darkness had grown ominous with the fretting wind. She raised her hand to her face, inhaled the fierce and fleeting pungency of drying blood, and tasted it on the end of her tongue. She said softly to herself, "Be kind to me, O gods, for I am an infant again, newborn into darkness . . ."

Dripping quarters of meat sizzled above the fire. The drummers struck a dancing beat. Someone began to chant one of the tunes of celebration, and soon a space had been cleared for dancers.

Again the smiling young men circulated, bearing bowls of fermented berries. The potion was warm, and after one had drunk it the world seemed less dark, the wind less cold curling off the sea and around the dunes.

Persis drank, beginning to move to the rhythm of the drums, and when one of the young men returned carrying a pitcher with a spout, she held out her empty cup to him.

At the place where they took separate paths, Garm gave final instructions. The Kaniks and the Abibones would strike from the front, the Yuloks from the north along the bluffs, and the Gerumbians from the south. The Gerumbians, as promised, would be the first over the parapet, and they would open the gate for the others.

Soon Alcheringian sentries on the outposts began to die. They had been lax, all of them. All knew, or thought they knew, that enemies would not come that late in the year. All wished that they were dancing in Alcheringia, drinking the berry wine, laughing with the women.

They died in various ways, depending on who was killing them. All died. Most died silently, but if they did not, it didn't matter, because nobody heard their screams.

The intercom beeps and Shem answers.

"D.O.M. West Norriya, sir. We have made the peregrinus contact you requested."

"And gave the message."

"Yes sir."

"Acknowledged."

"Yes sir."

Shem sags into his chair, then asks, an afterthought: "Any reply?"

"Well, as a matter of fact, sir, yes, there was."

"Go ahead."

"Sir, I'm not sure if—"

"Play it, man!"

There is static on the tape, or the sound of the wind. Then Alva's voice says: *"What you are doing is unforgivable, Shem. In any time, in any place, for any reason, it is unforgivable.*

Oath or no oath I will not be part of it. Good-bye. I will never come back again. Not ever."

In the moonlight, Asa saw Abibones pass. There were twenty, in full war regalia. Their pace was cautious, steady. They were sleek as wolves. They did not speak. The only sound of their passing was the scuff of deerskin leggings against undergrowth.

Asa had barely had time to leap off the path and flatten himself in the bushes. Then, just as he was about to stand, the Kaniks passed. They were at least thirty, with Garm at their head.

Asa ran.

He left his packsack and the deer he had shot that afternoon. He left everything except his weapons, and he turned and ran for Alcheringia. He went by a short route through the forest, and three miles later, when he returned to the path on the Alcheringian side of the pass, he was several minutes in front of the nearest attackers. He would have time to sound the alarm. The Alcheringians would have time to scramble in defense of their new battlements.

But the path was blocked.

Staggering, Asa almost ran into the squat person barring his way, and when he tried desperately to shove past, a misshapen paw restrained him.

"Alva!"

She had grown older. The laugh lines around her eyes had deepened into tragic creases, and the corners of her mouth sagged with fatigue and the bitterness of failure. In the moonlight she was gray. "Hello," she said.

"Alva—Kaniks! Abibones!" He tried again to push past her and again she restrained him. She was not looking at him; she was looking at the ground, and her mouth was contorted.

"Must warn—must go—"

She shook her head.

"Alva! Alcheringia! They'll kill—"

"I know!" She hissed at him. The paw descended.

There was no pain. The black and green world simply rose and rotated, trailing spectacular ribbons of light. He was no longer a functioning mind; he was wholly an eye beguiled by the softly swirling world, and when that world began to fade he whimpered like a child.

Grayness gathered. He was cold. A place on the inside of his forearm was colder than the rest, and something long and cold slid briefly along it, or into it.

He was aware that he was being cradled in strong arms, and carried.

He was aware of drops falling on his cheek, drops warmer than rain.

Against the darkness he spoke the name of the woman he loved.

Persis danced.

With the other women, she was urged on by the warm wine, and by the drums and the exuberance.

More and larger logs had been heaped upon the fire, until it had become a holocaust with a life of its own, defying the rising wind. Backing away from it, teeth bared against it, the drummers played tirelessly, and around them the dancers leaped.

Never had Persis appeared so carefree. Never had she laughed so gaily or danced so freely. As the music crested, she swirled faster and faster around the fire until she was dizzy and hysterical, until there was neither blackness nor loss beyond that moment, until she neither knew nor cared where she was or with whom she was dancing.

She did not hear, above the fire, above her own laughter and the shrieks of celebrants, the single, frail, falling cry of warning from the parapets.

Scaling the Alcheringian defenses was child's play to the Gerumbians Runch had chosen. Smiling in the darkness, never taking his gaze off the silhouettes of the guards on the parapet, he summoned them forward—men with elongated arms and legs, men with prehensile fingers and toes, men who would unthinkingly scale a hundred feet of cliff for a single gull's egg. Runch pointed where he wanted them to go—there, there, there—and they faded into the darkness as if they had never been.

The first of the guards died with his throat slit so cleanly that he never saw his attacker, died on his knees with his life spurting bright red a foot in front of him, died unable to draw breath to utter a scream, died gurgling.

The second heard above the wind the swift rustling of moccasined feet and turned to take a thick Gerumbian spear in the

diaphragm. He fell grunting, but opened his mouth to scream.
A second blow snapped his neck.

The third, sensing something in the wind, something in the
changed rhythms of the night, turned from watching the dance
and had a split second to confirm that the dark figures he saw
slipping lithe as apes down the inside of the parapet were not
mere tricks, mere shadows cast by the blaze. He shouted once
before he was cut down.

The gate swung open. Kanik and Abibone warriors fanned
into Alcheringia.

Reality was the rhythmic resonance of the drums that continued in her blood long after the actual beats had ceased.
Reality was the warmth of the fire and the memory of the
bodies that had left their touch on hers. Reality was the certain
knowledge that tomorrow Asa would return and the world would
be green again.

Reality was not that anguish beyond the fire.

Persis danced through slaughter.

Even when Garm caught her in his arms she did not stop
dancing, but carried him for a few reeling steps to the edge of
the firelight.

She did not look at his face. She stared straight ahead, at
the bloodied vest of a Kanik warrior. She did not look out into
the darkness, where the sounds of merriment had been replaced
by other sounds.

She asked, "Is it finished?"

"Except for Asa," Garm said.

She shook her head. "I do not know where he is."

When Garm lifted her chin he saw that she was telling the
truth. "So," he said. He lost himself in the paths of the mountains, imagining that day when he would find his enemy at
last, and Asa would turn at the challenge he shouted . . .

"He will not know you," Persis said. "He does not know
me. So what use could your revenge be now?"

"That is not something for a woman to understand," Garm
said.

She looked mutely for the first time at the atrocities surrounding her. She permitted indescribable sounds to enter her
silences. She laid both hands on her belly.

At dawn they would reach the horses. Garm would swing
her up behind him on his mount, and the horses, distressed by

the scent of fresh blood, would trot briskly eastward toward the mountains.

By then the spoils would long since have been divided, and only a few Gerumbian stragglers would remain in Alcheringia, kicking the ruins, sharp-eyed for signs of life.

Something stabbed at his hand. Again the sharp pain came. And again.

Asa opened his eyes to stare directly into the bright, hopeful retina of a crow. "I'm alive," he said, and the crow uttered a guttural sound and flapped away.

Asa sat up. He was somewhere in the hills. To his right a small stream cascaded from the plateaus above. To his left stretched a panorama of slopes and valleys that ended, finally, in the sea. The little glade was sheltered, and his back was warmed by a pale sun. It was going to be a hot day.

He was very hungry.

It was not unusual for him to awaken alone in such a place, returning from the spells. But for a moment he was bewildered by the fact that he had nothing—no pack, no weapons—and that a little carefully wrapped dried meat had been left beside him.

Then he remembered. He remembered the loping file of warriors. He remembered his own race through the forest. He remembered Alva in the path.

Asa stood.

He ran.

FROM: SKULD
DIS: EYES ONLY—MASTERS, DREAM MASTERS, SCHOLARS
SUBJECT: MEMOIR OF ALCHERINGIA
STATUS: COMPLETE/CLOSED
ABSTRACT: The following file has been compiled in accordance with Arborea Memorandum # DV 3546 T, "Records of Extinct Peoples," and contains the following prescribed categories:

    I   History;
   II Sociology (including etiology of deviation);
  III Physiological assessments;

Cross-references include . . .

EIGHTEEN

By noon, when Asa reached the gates of Alcheringia,
the ravens had begun to slip down through the drifting smoke.

He went first to the meadow where his lodge stood, and
discovered that of all the lodges in Alcheringia his alone had
escaped unscathed. A Kanik arrow stood upright before the
door. Its feathers trembled. The loosened door flapped discon-
solately against the wall.

Persis was not there.

He turned back then, toward the compound, through the
splintered gate and into the carnage. He believed he had steeled
himself for what he would encounter, remembering all the kills
and butcherings of his hunts.

But he was not prepared. He had gone scarcely a hundred
yards before he fell onto his knees and fists, retching. When
he forced himself forward again he was trembling and whimpering like a child. All that he looked upon he saw as through
a tunnel, as if his vision had blessedly narrowed, limited to
one horror at a time.

He did not find Persis. He did not find several of the other
young women, either. But he found the others—men, matrons,
and children.

One by one he found them.

Those who had wandered away together from the dancing

and the fire had been the first slain. Some embraced even in death; some, even in death, had tried to shield the body of their beloved.

Three of Moros' young men had died together defending him, and their bodies lay shoulder-to-shoulder. Moros himself had died with some measure of valor, for his wounds were on the front, and his obsidian blade had been clenched so tightly in his left hand that Gerumbian looters had hacked off his fingers to twist it free. Asa knew exactly how Moros had died: He saw him crouching to face the racing Kanik warrior who easily evaded the befuddled defenders and pierced Moros' belly with his lance. The curse that Moros had screamed was still there, with the agony on his lips. His eyes were wide open.

Rani had died nobly, too. He lay on his face with his arms spread wide as if to embrace the earth—or to welcome death. Asa knelt beside him and laid a hand on his cold head. He wanted to speak, but the sound he uttered was as raucous and unintelligible as the squawk of quarreling ravens that flopped, feeding, among the bodies.

Poor Rusl had died dancing unarmed into the fray in response to a call buried so deep that it had escaped purging by the gods.

Thorel had died shouting, "Brothers! Brothers!" roaring with mad laughter even as he was ringed by enemies like a bear cordoned by dogs. He had sunk first to his knees under their blows, and then onto his back so that he could die fighting and not be struck from behind. One Kanik warrior grinned at him still, sitting in a rictus of death with his hands glazed with his own intestines, and the bodies of five more Kaniks and Abibones lay sprawled around him.

Others had died less bravely.

These elders had died in their lodges, fumbling for weapons: Tanis, Urc, Leec, and Quiner.

Some others had died in a stupor, feeling the pain through which their lives flowed away as distantly as if it had been nothing more than a smashed finger, or a bent ankle.

Some died roaring in drunken laughter, convinced to the last that friends were playing a tasteless joke.

Some died without ever knowing what had struck them.

Some died knowing and terrified, running, groveling, shrieking for mercy.

Some died with stoic dignity, unflinching and defiant even

as the shafts and lances cut them down.

When he had seen all, Asa crouched in the center of the carnage so still that a few hopeful ravens hopped close and stared wall-eyed at him. He crouched facing the sea, and he sank his fingers into the bloody earth. A vaulted emptiness opened in him.

He crouched immobile while the sun moved.

At last, at dusk, he raised his head and howled toward the sea. He howled a formless gout of sound, raising both fists toward Yggdrasil. He howled again at the top of his voice, and again, stretching all the cords and muscles of his throat.

He tried to form them, but no words came.

Later, in the darkness, he lit fires and sent them surging inward like fresh hordes of voracious warriors, consuming all that they encountered and leaving the black earth purified. They swept away the fences and turned the dung heaps to ash. They swirled through the wattled lodges that remained and transformed them into glittering cones. They raced across the crisp stubbled fields, and across the dried sedge, and embraced the bodies with the quick whispers of lovers, and changed them into wraiths of transcendent beauty. They searched, they cleansed, and they joined together at last in the great stacks of driftwood behind the beach and rose there to roar their outrage against the placid indifference of the sea.

Then they turned outward, sweeping along the seafront and up the banks of the Alcher, across the middens into the blighted thickets, and then at last, with a languorous sigh, into the copses of cedar and the stands of pine.

Asa shrank from the heat and retreated back up the slope. Later, high in the hills, watching the inferno burn itself out against the cliffs, he became aware of a dull pain, and found that his right hand was blistered under its film of ash and dirt. He laid it on his face, where it left a black mark, fingers pointing toward his eyes. He did not remember setting those fires. For a long time he would remember nothing at all of the death of Alcheringia.

When the last of the blaze had flickered down, Asa saw through drifting smoke that a black ruin stretched between him and the sea. Meandering through it, the Alcher gleamed in a meek sun.

Only then did he realize that he had plucked the Kanik arrow from the place where Garm had stabbed it into the earth before his lodge. He gripped it in his left fist—a new Kanik war arrow, its tip a jasper sliver glittering in the sun, its ash shaft polished white, its clipped feathers trembling. Gradually Asa loosened his grip until the arrow lay across his palm, and as he did so he turned toward the east.

He began to walk, then to run, despite his fatigue and hunger, despite his lacerated feet and the sharp stones in the path. A single image hung in his mind—the vision of a trotting group of Kanik horses, and from one of them, Persis looking back.

Asa ran.

The trail was fresh. It led back along the route that he and his Nine had taken on their raid against the Kaniks when he had captured Persis—through the Alcheringian mountains, across the Larl, and out into the plain that skirted the Middle Wayst. The first night he stopped at the Larl and slept near the caves of the dead where the ancestors were buried, and where they had buried Noxor. Before dawn he had scooped a sluggish trout out of a backwater beneath the bank, eaten, and started out again. At noon he passed the Wayst, and late in the afternoon he crossed the Em. By evening he had reached the Kanik encampment near which he had captured Persis. This time he did not worry about a stealthy approach. He shouted Garm's name, but his call echoed in the empty hills and returned to mock him, split like crystal into a hundred parts.

The Kaniks had gone.

Even as Asa stood in the abandoned camp, the thick rains of autumn began to obliterate the trail.

Still, he followed it for three more days, followed it far east into the Kanik Mountains, followed it sometimes on his hands and knees. He followed it until it disintegrated completely into streams whose names he did not know and on slopes so barren that not even lichen grew to be scuffed away by hoofs. Even then he did not admit he had lost her. For two days he crossed and recrossed the last vestiges of trail, backtracking, working in ever-widening circles. Finally, the rains came in earnest, obliterating the depressions in all sandbars, filling all the marshes.

On his hands and knees, Asa squinted eastward against the wind and rain, and saw nothing but swaying curtains of water. Beyond, there was another valley, and beyond that another range with yet more valleys, and somewhere in the shelter of such a valley, in a camp on a southern slope . . .

"Persis," he whispered. "Persis."

After a while, like a methodical child playing on a beach, he fixed upright between his knees the Kanik arrow he had carried with him to return to Garm, embedding it as deeply as he could in the soft ground.

He turned back then. Spells came and went, and he remembered little. He believed that he walked backward sometimes. He must have eaten; he must have rested; but he could not remember.

When he reached the coast, the rain had changed to snow.

He did not go back to Alcheringia. He went north, past the place where he had buried Jared, past the devastated city of the Old Ones, past the fringes of Gerumbia and of the Northern Wayst. He went far, far north.

For the first days, hunters frequently appeared on the horizon, but he slipped back into the forest, avoiding them and traveling on. During the second week he saw only two Gerumbians, one at a distance and one in a small clearing, startled at his meal. The man was a grotesque with a lowering forehead and drooling lip, but he fled before the specter that Asa had become, leaving his meal to him.

During the third week he saw only the sails of the sea traders returning home, so far away that they might have been part of his imagining, part of the mists and trailing clouds.

During the fourth week he saw no one. He had entered a wild and beautiful place, untouched by man since the Entropies and apparently undisturbed by the Entropies themselves. For several days he traveled through this fresh and trackless country, and at last he came to a cave whose broad mouth looked out upon the sea, and in a little niche at the back of this cave he found a place where someone long ago had built a fire.

There he stayed, and there he spent the winter.

Later, he would remember only brief intervals of that white period. Instincts preserved him. He found food. He got fuel. He somehow gathered sufficient hides and stitched them into winter clothes. He made what tools he required.

He survived.

He listened to the wind, although at times he could not have said whether it moaned beyond the entrance of his shelter or in the cavern of his mind. He gazed like a dumb child on the sunlit days. He heard the mewing of jays in the soft firs, but he did not know whether they uttered a dirge or a song of birth. He watched the smoke curl, felt the warmth, saw the chimerical flickering of the fire; but he did not know whether he saw in the flames the shadows of things gone forever or the ambivalent promises of things to come.

He lived.

He lived like a mollusk in his guts and flesh, shelled over, touched by infinitesimal sparks which were not thoughts but impulses signaling all that was necessary to survive, to keep surviving, to survive although epochs rolled overhead like waves.

Gradually edging west a little more each day, the sun warmed the north wall of the cave. The snow melted to myriad pools in the hills, and rivulets spilled out of the pools and into the streams. In the ponds and lakes, drifting lozenges tinkled against each other like delicate bells moved by the wind.

One warm day, Asa sat in the mouth of the cave and ground soft kernels of vermilion hematite into powder. To this powder he added fish oil, and he mixed it into a thick paint. He stood holding the paint in a little stone pestle, looking across the undulating miles of forest to the mountains far to the north, and down over the salt marshes to the edge of the sea, and south, where he knew the Yggdrasilian Islands lay, although he could not see them.

Then he turned his back on this world and dipped his finger into the vermilion paint, and on a smooth area of wall at the entrance he drew a defiant little man, erect, his right fist raised. *I am here*, the little figure said. *I am alive in spite of you, in spite of everything! And I remember!*

Asa smiled.

He drew another figure, and another, and soon he was engrossed in the scenes that began to take shape across the wall independently of his intention. They unfolded as he worked, and only when the light began to fade and he drew back to look at what he had done did he realize that he was painting Alcheringia—not only the place and people that had once existed, but the spirit, also.

He lit a small oil lamp, held it close to the wall, and kept painting.

For several days he worked. Occasionally he ate. Occasionally he stopped to mix more paint. Sometimes he stood for a time at the entrance of the cave, looking down over the forest and the sea, and feeling the warm wind on his face. Sometimes he laughed and sometimes he wept, but he said nothing.

He painted.

Into his paintings he poured all he could remember, and he
remembered like a child, drifting from one image to the next.
His paintings were innocent of time, free in space.

He painted the great estuary as it had appeared to him every
spring throughout his childhood, so vast that it was not flat but
bowllike, sheltering all of Alcheringia. He painted the lodges
and the space around them rising to heaven. He painted the
dances, and the councils, and the wonder of love. He painted
women scolding and laughing at their work along the banks of
the Alcher and among the scaffolds where the fish were dried.
He painted the exuberance of the catch, the joyful hauling of
nets and the lifting of spears on which fish hung transfixed.
He painted the delight of the hunt, the ecstasy of movement,
the pride in strength, stealth, confidence, companionship, success. He painted children racing among the lodges and along
the beach, and his children were always in the air, unbound to
earth.

He painted death and burial.

He painted birth.

He painted raids and the bringing back of captives. He
painted the grisly masks of disease, and of hunger, and he drew
tiny fingers hunched against the endless cold of winter. He
painted the agony of bereavement, and the pain of loneliness.

He painted the once-a-year trading with the sea merchants
who came from far to the south, bringing wondrous fabrics,
and obsidian, and sometimes metal.

He painted the sharing and the comforting, and he painted
too the annual treks into the land and back to the sea again.

He painted the myths and the legends, all of them, and
although he could devise no way of painting the injunctions of
the Tabuly, he painted the strange vehicles of the gods moving
through air and sea, moving along the fringes of the Waysts
with thunderous noise, wrapped in their dust clouds. He painted
the people's fear of them—the cowed figures with foreheads
to the ground and heads covered—and he painted three among
these who were not cowed but who stood erect and stared
defiantly, fists raised against all that was forbidden and impossible: Kenet, Rusl, and himself.

Over the days he painted everything, all the details of all
the seasons of Alcheringia, for they existed nowhere else but

in his memory, and when his memory faltered they would live only here, on the wall of this cave, until the damps of earth claimed them again, forever.

Such a people lived, his paintings said.

By the time he finished, the snow had gone. The rivers had opened and on the borders of the lakes the shorebirds had begun to build their nests. Loons cried in the night. Life had returned to the warmed land, and through the days came the plaintive calls of furred creatures for their mates.

Then Asa made the last of his paintings. He had reserved a place for this far at the back of the cave, and here, with a flickering oil lamp giving the only light, he left the record of his love for Persis. In tiny drawings, as perfect as he could make them, he told the story of her capture, and of Jared's bringing them together, and of their time in Alcheringia, and of the private joys of the winters they had spent together. At the end of the tale, which moved in a circle on the wall, their two figures were joined by a third and smaller one.

When he had finished, Asa sat unmoving. The lamp guttered in the drafts, casting strange shadows across the walls. He had not spoken since the destruction of Alcheringia. Sometimes, painting, he had uttered sounds of pleasure, and pain, and rage. Sometimes he had answered the loons from the borders of the lake, or the wolves from the hills behind, or the geese clamoring in their ragged vees along the coast. But he had not spoken.

Falteringly, like a child learning a new word, he now whispered the name of the woman he loved, and he cupped his palm over the last small figure of her, as if to shield it from all harm.

Then he rose and walked into the sunlight, leaving his paint, leaving the lamp to gutter out forgotten, leaving his sleeping-robe, and his winter furs, and all his weapons. He emerged into the full heat of a spring day. He was emaciated and his hair and beard had grown long. There were streaks of gray at his temples.

Two paths diverged in front of him. To the left, the hunting path that he had made that winter led into the hills. He knew that if he followed it farther than he had ever gone he would reach the eastern plain that he had seen from the slopes of the mountains, and if he continued he would come to the Northern Wayst and skirt its top edge. If he continued even farther, turning south, he would come at last to the Kanik Mountains.

During the winter he had dreamed of taking that path despite all the hazards of the journey: the Gerumbians and other, unknown, hostile tribes; the lurking diseases; the perils of the Waysts; the attempts of Shem and the Yggdrasilians to prevent him. He had dreamed that he would find Garm again and kill him, and that he and Persis would go together so far away that even the crafts of Yggdrasil would fail to find them. He dreamed that the memories of horror would fade, never to be forgotten, but to be wrapped gently in the folds of living, to become at last pure myths each with its enigmatic lesson, myths to be whispered to grandchildren while the fire burned low and the cool night drifted over him . . .

The other path led into a broad band of sunlight that stretched away to the southwest, to Yggdrasil. *There would come a time*, Shem had said, *when you must make a choice. I shall never send for you.* Asa had made the choice with the last of the paintings; he turned toward the sea.

—Yggdrasil Control, this is Hugin One Five. Over coast approximately two miles north of Location Three Two.

—Go ahead, Hugin One Five. This is Yggdrasil.

—We have an anomaly here. A man on a beach.

—Repeat, please.

—We have a man waiting on a beach. Have you scheduled an aborr rendezvous?

—Negative, One Five.

—Stand by for video transmit, Yggdrasil.

—We have received that, One Five. Stand by for instructions, please.

In his office, Shem responds to the discreet beep of his pager. "Yes?"

"Hugin Control here, sir. We have something odd on the extreme coast of Norriya. Patrol aircraft is standing by for orders."

"You have tape?"

"Yes sir."

"Play it."

The image swirls onto the screen, trembling with the shudder of the copter's rotors. Shem rises. He exhales suddenly, softly, as if he has taken a playful blow from a child.

A man in worn skins stands with hands on hips, squinting

against the sun. Drawn large in the beach beside him is the Yggdrasilian tree.

Despite the thinness and the beard, Shem knows him instantly. He blinks rapidly and draws breath, pressing his lips together. He gives an order.

The helicopter begins slowly to descend.

One day he would go in search of her again, following the path to the east. But not yet, not now.

Now there were questions to be asked, and answered.

Now there was knowledge to be gained, and used.

Go, she had told him once. *Do what you must do*.

So, fatally enticed, Asa entered time.

ABOUT THE AUTHOR

Wayland Drew was born in Oshawa, Ontario, and received his early education there. He began to write seriously in high school and continued while studying English Language and Literature at the University of Toronto. Since graduation he has combined high school teaching and writing. He and his wife, Gwendolyn, live in Bracebridge, Ontario, where he has taught English for nine years at Bracebridge and Muskoka Lakes Secondary School. They have four children.

The Memoirs of Alcheringia is his sixth book and his first science fiction. It is the first novel of *The Erthring Cycle*, a trilogy. The next two books will be *The Gaian Expedient* and *The Master of Norriya*.